BITTER ASHES-BOOK ONE

DEATH CURSED

SARA C ROETHLE

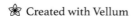 Created with Vellum

PROLOGUE

Hot breath steamed across the side of my neck, tickling the tiny hairs. At first I snuggled deeper into my pillow, thinking it was a dream. Then the bed shifted as someone climbed up beside me. Fully awake now, I froze, my thoughts racing for an explanation. I lived alone, had no pets, and didn't have the type of friends that would stay the night. Whoever was sidling up beside me had broken in.

I opened my eyes to mere slits, not wanting to alert the intruder that I was awake. The room was nearly pitch black, but the curtained window let in enough moonlight for me to see the outline of a second form standing beside the bed. Judging by the build, I was pretty sure it was a man, though I was still unsure about the person in bed beside me.

I squeezed my eyes shut as the standing intruder bent at the waist, placing his hands on either side of my pillow. He continued to lean down until his face was only inches from the large artery in my neck. The one who had climbed onto the bed shifted a little closer to my feet.

The man hovering over me took a deep breath, almost like he was scenting me, then the presence lifted away. I let out a quivering breath that turned into a scream as suddenly both figures grabbed me. The one on the bed wrapped strong hands around my ankles, as the other pulled me up by my armpits into a vice-like embrace. A large, masculine palm clamped over my mouth to stifle my screaming, overwhelming my nostrils with the scent of soap and skin. I thrashed violently, but both men held fast.

My ankles lifted as the one at the foot of the bed reached the edge and stood. The intruders began moving toward my bedroom door. I screamed against the hand covering my mouth and struggled to kick my feet, hoping to loosen their grasp. I only succeeded in straining my back and a few other muscles as the figures carried me effortlessly through the dark house. I squinted to see in the dark as we neared the back door. Unable to take full breaths with the hand pressing against my mouth and nose, my screams degraded to whimpers. The other hand pulled painfully beneath my armpit. Trying to even out my body, I flung my free arm upward, but barely managed to slap at my captor's face.

The figure carrying my feet put them both under one arm so he could fling the back door open, bathing us in a wash of chilly air. I tried to make out the features of the person holding onto my bare feet, but the clouds covering the moon stunted my vision. All I could see was the outline of broad shoulders and possibly wavy hair.

I turned my eyes skyward and began to cry, soaking the

hand that covered my mouth. Stars twinkled serenely above me as we entered the woods that bordered my house. I gave up on my thrashing and let my body go limp, but it didn't slow my attackers any more than my previous strategy.

My captors continued gracefully through the foliage. I began to shiver with the cold, but it didn't seem to bother the man carrying my upper half. He radiated warmth, even though I could feel only the fabric of a thin tee-shirt against the back of my head and neck.

It seemed like we ran on for ages, but the men carrying me never tired. I closed my eyes and told myself that I was dreaming, yet the bite of cool wind and the ache in my back did their best to shatter the illusion. Eventually, we came to a stop, deep within the darkness of the woods.

I felt dizzy from moving horizontally so quickly, and didn't immediately react as I was lowered to the damp ground.

My back sank into a raised mound of earth, soft, like it had recently been turned, with loose rocks jabbing into me here and there. Moisture soaked into the back of the tee-shirt and underwear I'd gone to sleep in, chilling me further.

I tried to sit up, but hands instantly pushed me back down. Something slithered across my arm. My panicked breathing brought in the scent of damp earth and growing things while my two captors crouched over me. My first thought as the cold, rough skinned creature made its way toward my neck was *snake*.

My heart pounded in my throat as more things slithered over me. I pushed against the restraining hands, but I couldn't budge them. I screamed, and one of the hands lifted from my shoulder to cover my mouth. It wasn't an improvement since now my head was being forced against the earth, hard enough that the soil scratched my scalp. Within seconds I was covered entirely with slithering objects. Some of the objects started reaching up toward the sky like tiny hands trying to grasp the moon.

The spindly creatures unfurled toward the dim light, casting eerie moon shadows onto my face. Something was wrong with them though. They had no heads, and instead branched off at the ends like no creature I'd ever seen. I wasn't covered in snakes. They were *vines*. I was glad the things weren't snakes, but being slowly engulfed in living vines did nothing to ease my panic. I screamed against the hand covering my mouth until my throat went raw. I fought against the vines with increased desperation, a last ditch effort to not be buried alive, but they only bound me tighter, until I could no longer move at all. They crushed my lungs, forcing out my last gasping breath. In that moment I knew I was going to die. I managed to catch one last glimpse of stars as the last of the vines covered my face, obscuring my view completely.

1

My eyes snapped open. I sat up in bed with a deep, aching breath, clutching at my chest. The last thing I remembered was vines encasing my entire body, then pulling me into the cold, moist earth. I had been buried alive while my attackers pinned me down.

I glanced around. The first thing I noticed was firelight flickering nearby, then the bed. It was *not* my own. *My* bed was back in my small house in a suburb of Spokane, Washington where I lived alone, and had lived alone for many years. It had been a long time since someone had been in that bed with me. I hadn't expected for it to finally only happen when someone decided to kidnap me.

I looked up at dimly-lit fabric above my head, realizing this unfamiliar bed was one of those four poster monstrosities with a princess canopy. I reached out and touched the nearest post, half expecting to wake up out of this nightmare at any moment. The wood was smooth to the touch, thick and obviously expensive.

My distorted reflection peered back at me from the dark, gleaming wood. What I could see of my long, dark brown hair was a snarled mess. I looked back into my blurry blue eyes numbly, and couldn't seem to think of anything beyond my messy hair.

I shook my head in an attempt to clear the fog. I had to escape. My bare feet slid to the edge of the burgundy comforter as I lowered myself to the ground. The floor and surrounding walls were made of strange gray stone that made me feel like I was in a castle.

A thud to my left caught my attention. I jumped, ready to fend off my attacker, then realized the sound was a log tumbling in the simple stone fireplace behind me. I turned to stare into the flames, wondering if they could be used as a weapon, but I had nothing to wield them with. That was just like my attackers to not leave me a torch.

"I didn't expect you to be awake yet," a male voice said from across the room.

I nearly stumbled as I tried to turn around too quickly. A man stood framed in the now open doorway, leaning against the frame casually. He wore black slacks and no shirt or shoes. It was an odd look that made it seem as if he simply hadn't finished dressing yet . . . or perhaps he just hadn't finished *un*-dressing.

I grasped at the ends of my oversized gray tee-shirt and tried to cover at least a small portion of my bare legs. I realized as I looked down that my legs were still covered in dirt from my experience in the woods, verifying that it had all been quite real. Perhaps this man was one of my kidnappers. I backed toward the fire, not wanting him near me.

He stepped into the room, casually observing me. His

straight, black hair fell well past his shoulders to frame his pale skin and dark brown eyes. My mouth went dry with fear as he took another step forward. He was tall, I placed him around 6'2", given that I'm 5'9" and still had to look up to meet his eyes as he came even closer.

I held up a hand in front of me and took another step back. "S-stop," I stammered. "Where am I?"

He cocked his head. He was attractive in an ethereal sort of way. Something about the slope of his jaw or the narrowness of his nose made him seem almost feminine, though he was clearly *all* man. "Where do you think you are, Madeline?"

"It's Maddy," I corrected reflexively, still gripping my shirt with one hand while I pushed my hair out of my face with the other, "and how do you know my name? Who are you?"

He met me step for step until my back was against the hard stone wall. When I couldn't back away anymore he stopped, not closing the final space between us. His eyes danced with amusement.

I craned my neck to look up into his deep brown eyes, feeling like a deer in the headlights.

I flinched as he reached a hand out to twirl the ends of my hair around his fingers. "Don't you want to know *my* name?" He smiled widely, and if I didn't know any better I would say I saw the points of little fangs where his canines should have been. Then again, I had just been pulled through the earth into some sort of windowless castle by vines. Maybe I didn't know any better.

"No," I gasped, side-stepping against the wall until I was

out of reach, "but directions to the nearest exit wouldn't hurt."

He smiled again, flashing his little fangs. "I like a girl who can joke when she's terrified."

I gulped, unsure whether or not he was just toying with me. "I wasn't joking," I said, voice barely above a whisper.

He grinned. "Neither was I, but I'm afraid I can't show you the exit when you've only just arrived."

"Leave her alone, Alaric," a woman's voice snapped from the doorway.

The fanged man stepped aside to reveal a woman that looked startlingly similar to him. She strode into the room confidently, trailing the ends of her gossamer-thin red dress behind her. Her black hair hung nearly to her waist, intermingling with the loose red fabric like oil on blood. There was something else about her that I recognized, though I couldn't quite place it. It tickled at the edges of my memory, letting me know I had seen her before.

Alaric left me to stand by the woman I had to assume was his sister, given their strong resemblance. He tugged on her long hair playfully like they were children, eliciting a steely glare from her dark eyes. I watched the woman's face, searching for any sign that she might recognize me as well, but she only returned her gaze to eye me coolly.

"Out," the woman ordered her brother sternly, pointing a finger behind her toward the door.

Alaric gave her a mocking salute, then winked at me. I stared back at him as he turned and glided toward the door. *Glide* was the only word I could think of to describe his walk. He moved like a cat, with light steps and limber, balanced grace.

The woman came toward me, taking my attention off Alaric's sinewy back as he left the room. She looked annoyed, yet I still instantly preferred her company to that of her brother. At least she wouldn't hit on me . . . probably.

"I'm Sophie," she introduced.

The introduction would have been nice had it been accompanied by a smile, but I decided to keep my opinion to myself. I caught a glimpse of dainty, sharp canines in her mouth as she sniffed the air around me. I gulped, suddenly glad that I'd chosen not to speak.

"You need a bath," she said with a sneer, revealing her sharp teeth more clearly.

"What am I doing here?" I asked, ignoring her statement. "I know I've seen you before."

"We've never met before, Madeline," she replied flatly. She said my name with harsh emphasis on the *e*, and something once again tickled my memory.

I saw a flash of her in my mind, sitting behind a large, wooden desk. *"This time will be different," she said with a warm smile. She wore a modest skirt suit, with her black hair pulled back into a tight braid.*

"You were my case-worker!" I blurted as realization dawned on me.

I had sat on the other side of that desk so many times growing up, and those moments were thoroughly ingrained in my memory. In fact, I was surprised I hadn't recognized her sooner.

"I don't know what you're talking about," she snapped, though her eyes shifted nervously.

I almost believed her despite the nervous twitch. She hadn't aged a day, and I'd been out of the foster system for nearly ten years. Yet, the resemblance was just too much to be a coincidence.

"Why am I here?" I repeated, beginning to panic again. "Don't lie to me, I remember you. I was in and out of your office often enough to remember."

I knew I was right. Sophie had been my case-worker as I was bounced around from home to home all those years ago. Now that I'd made the connection, I remembered distinctly how she'd said my name each time she told me that the next home would be different. A few weeks, or a few months later, I'd go back and call her a liar, but she'd never get angry.

My thoughts came to a screeching halt as my memories of childhood led to where they always led, a memory I'd done my best to block out entirely. My knees went weak.

"Wait," I said as I felt the color drain from my face, "am I here because of what happened back then? You said it would all be okay!"

Sophie's expression softened, showing just a small hint of sympathy. She knew exactly what I was talking about. I tried to shut my mind off to the memory, but I wasn't successful.

"This has *nothing* to do with what happened," she explained evenly. "I swear it. You will face no repercussions for that day."

"Um," I began weakly, my heart thudding in my throat, "then would you mind telling me why I'm actually here, and why *you're* here?"

"That is none of your concern," she snapped, leaving me to wonder if I'd only imagined the sympathy in her eyes.

"It *is* my concern," I argued. I fought them, but tears began to stream down my face. "In fact I find it very concerning that I was ripped from my bed at night, and pulled into the ground by vines! Not to mention that I'm now faced with my old social worker who hasn't aged a *day* in nearly ten years."

"Come with me," she said, then turned around, expecting me to follow her.

"I'm not going anywhere until you tell me what's going on," I replied, trying to keep my voice steady as I backed away from her.

My legs felt numb and shaky, but I managed to move my bare feet across the floor, step after step. I was sure that I was in a mild state of shock, which was probably a good thing, because it kept me from collapsing into a screaming heap on the floor.

She turned back to me with a frustrated sigh. "Do you still sense the emotions of others?"

I felt my face shutting down. She was one of the few people I'd ever told about my secret. I'd been able to sense what others were feeling since I was a child. It had made foster living absolute hell.

"Do you, Madeline?" she pressed.

I shook my head. "Is *that* why you brought me here? I was just a kid, making stuff up." *Lies.* All lies. Lies I'd learned to tell to survive. Psych evaluations are no fun.

"You made nothing up," she said matter of factly. "And that man's death? It was *your* fault, just as you've always believed. Now come with me, and I might tell you what else I know about you."

I stared at her in shock, forcing painful memories away. A fresh tear dripped down my face, then another.

"Come, Madeline," she demanded. "I promise, we mean you no harm."

I wiped the tears from my eyes, and took a deep breath. For people that meant me no harm, they sure had a funny way of showing it. "Where are we going?"

Sophie looked me up and down, a wry smile on her full lips. "You're covered in filth. We're going down the hall to the bathroom."

I stared at her a moment, looking for any sign that she might be lying. Not that it mattered. I glanced past her to the open door. She and I were about evenly matched physically, I could probably escape her . . .

"Don't," she warned. "Try anything and I'll have my brother carry you to the bathroom kicking and screaming."

I bit my lip. I could try to run now, or I could wait for a better opportunity. I didn't want her, *or* her brother, touching me.

Seeming to sense my defeat, she gestured toward the open doorway. "Run, and I will catch you."

Giving her a wide berth, I hurried toward the door, exiting into a long stone corridor. I glanced both ways, but saw nothing but gray stone one way, and a wooden door the other. Sophie walked past me, heading toward the door. Upon reaching it, I noticed that the hallway continued on to the right. So there was empty corridor behind me, and this new path. Two possible routes of escape.

Sophie opened the door and gestured for me to walk in ahead of her.

I obeyed. Against the far wall of the over-sized space

was an ornate, claw-foot bathtub made of white porcelain, standing on tarnished brass feet. To my left were the sink and toilet.

"Bathe," Sophie ordered.

"I don't-" I began, but she cut me off with a stern look that said *I know you're unhappy, but you have to listen to me regardless.* It was the same look she used to give me when I called her a liar.

She finally offered me a hint of a smile. "I will keep my brother at bay, if that is your concern. I know you are considering the best time for you to run, but I assure you, it would not be a wise choice. You will not escape this place easily."

I crossed my arms, glanced at the tub, then back to her. I was *not* going to get in that tub. "I never knew you had a brother."

It wasn't actually strange for me to not know. Most caseworkers kept their lives private from the children they worked with. It just seemed weird to me that I'd never seen him, or heard any mention of him at all.

"Well I do," she replied. "Now please, stop stalling and bathe, and I'll be back to fetch you soon."

With that, she turned and left the bathroom, shutting the door gently behind her with a soft click. As soon as I recovered from the surprise of being left alone, I ran to the door and quickly twisted the lock. I did a frantic scan of the bathroom, but didn't find anything that could aid my escape.

There was no shower, just the bathtub, a toilet, and a sink surrounded by a pale pink marble countertop. Another fire burned in a fireplace set in the wall behind the bathtub. The room, ceiling, and floor were all made of stone, with no modern ventilation that I could see. There was also no visible lighting, yet the room was somehow well-lit. I scanned the walls and ceiling, but couldn't tell where the light was coming from. Eventually, my panic took over. I collapsed to my knees and closed my eyes, willing the whole situation to be a dream. It *had* to be a dream. Vines didn't move on their own, people aged and didn't have fangs, and rooms couldn't be lit without light bulbs or candles.

I sat like that for several minutes, but when I finally opened my eyes, I was still in the strange stone bathroom. I rose shakily to my feet and looked at the bathtub again. I briefly considered just doing what Sophie told me, but couldn't bring myself to do it. Not seeing any other options, I turned toward the door.

I wasn't about to trust Sophie just because she'd been my social worker. In fact, it made me trust her even less. I had to get out of here, *now*.

Knowing Sophie was likely waiting right outside the door, I grabbed a small basket of wrapped soaps from the counter beside the sink. It wasn't much as far as weapons went, but if it could distract her long enough for me to run, I'd take it.

Not giving myself time to consider the consequences of my actions, I balanced the basket in one hand, flipped the lock with the other, flung open the door, and chucked the soap basket at Sophie where she waited outside.

I barely registered her shocked expression as I took a sharp left and fled. My bare feet pounded harshly against the hard stone, sending little jolts of pain up through my shins and into my knees. I didn't look back to see if she was chasing me. The narrow, high-ceilinged hallway seemed to stretch on forever, with no discernible landmarks to tell me where I was or how far I'd gone. I ran past several closed doors and turned another corner.

I had only taken a few more steps when I ran straight into someone who'd been walking down the hall in my direction. We'd both hit the corner at the same time, and had no time to react. I bounced off his chest and fell to the ground with a thud. The man wasn't even shaken by the impact. He looked down at me and let out a good-natured chuckle. He wore a hunter green tee-shirt and jeans that seemed out of place in our castle-like surroundings.

The man leaned down to offer me a hand, causing his chin-length, golden brown hair to fall forward.

I scuttled away from him, stumbling to my feet to run the other direction. I managed one step before he grabbed my arm and jerked me back to face him.

He lifted a golden brow, his fingers digging painfully into my arm. "Are you lost?" He had a slight southern accent, but it was faint enough that I couldn't really tell which state it came from. He looked me up and down, lingering on the fact that my bottom half was only covered by underwear.

My heart pounded in my ears. "Just looking for the front door," I growled, swinging my free arm toward his face.

He caught my fist effortlessly.

I balked, not understanding how he'd moved so fast. I opened my mouth to beg him to let me go, but my words caught in my throat as I finally looked directly into his icy blue eyes, so pale they were almost white. The rest of his face was handsome enough: a strong nose, a jaw just wide enough to be masculine . . . yet those eyes. I'd seen eyes like that before, and they hadn't belonged to the living. A flash of memory shot through me like lightning, raising the tiny hairs on my entire body. I shook away the horrifying image of a young man's eyes just as his life had left him. It had been a long time ago, and there were more pressing matters to worry about.

"Are you going to behave now?" he asked, his grips on my fist and arm unyielding.

I nodded, unable to look away from his eerie eyes.

Slowly, he released me. "Now let's get you back to Sophie—"

The moment my arms were out of his reach I dropped to the ground, narrowly avoiding him as he made another grab for me. Once I was down, I did the first thing I could think of and kicked him in the kneecap. The move would have worked better if I wasn't barefoot. As it was, all I got for my effort was a grunt of annoyance. Recovering, I tried to push away, but he grabbed me again. This time he lifted me like I weighed nothing and threw me over his shoulder.

I was so shocked by how fast he'd moved I went limp for a moment, blinking at the back of his shirt and wondering how I'd gotten there, then I started screaming, pounding my fists on his back and kicking with my bare feet.

Not seeming to mind, he carried me down the hall. "You're lucky that I like it rough," he laughed.

I pulled up the back of his shirt and raked my nails across his back. The pain I caused echoed through me.

Another little secret I'd kept as a child. If I caused others damage, I'd feel that too. He dropped me to the ground on my butt, knocking the wind from my lungs. He pulled me back up, this time pressing my back against his chest, forcing me to stumble forward. Still relearning how to breathe, I dragged my feet in vain, bruising them on the hard stone floor as we went back the way I'd come.

We rounded a corner, and Sophie came into view. She stood near the bathroom looking regal in her red dress, tapping her foot impatiently. The basket of soaps was neatly arranged under her arm. She hadn't even tried to chase me.

She approached, then grabbed my arm with her free hand, taking me from the man without a word. Moving her hand to my back, she shoved me into the bathroom. This time when she shut the door, she stayed inside with me.

"I told you not to attempt escape." She braced herself against the door and let out a shaky breath, betraying her show of confidence.

I leaned against the wall, my battered body screaming at me. "You can't really blame me for trying to escape," I wheezed back at her.

Seeming to regain her composure, she locked the door and walked over to the bathtub to start the water. I glanced at the locked door, then at Sophie's turned back, surprised that she was leaving me the opportunity to escape again.

As if reading my thoughts, she glanced back at me. "Trust me when I tell you that you are much safer in here with me, than out there with James."

James. A third kidnapping accomplice. Scariest one so

far. "Safe?" I questioned. I was feeling a lot of things, but safe wasn't one of them.

Sophie shrugged. "Relatively so. I will not hurt you unless you make me. James would very much like to hurt you." She shivered and I wondered if James had very much liked hurting her too.

I stood up straight and pushed my back firmly against the wall as she left the tub to walk toward me.

"Please tell me why I'm here," I pleaded one last time.

She pinched the bridge of her nose like I was giving her a headache. "*Please* take a bath," she countered. "It is not my place to answer your questions. You will simply have to wait on that." She breezed past me, returning to her post by the door without another word.

I looked over at the slowly filling bath. It had an old-fashioned, slender faucet that didn't let out a great deal of water at once, and the basin was filling painfully slow. Feeling awkward, but definitely not wanting to go back out in the hall with James, I undressed, wishing I'd just listened to Sophie the first time. At least that way I wouldn't have had her watching me while I bathed. I couldn't even remember the last time I'd been naked in front of *anyone*, and I really didn't like being that vulnerable in front of someone I was afraid of.

Wrapping my arms around my chest, but having nothing to cover the rest of me with, I dipped a toe into the bath. I quickly withdrew the toe, then added more cold to the water flow so that I wouldn't end up scalding my skin off. Once the temperature was bearable, I took a step in, then slowly sat, hissing through my teeth as I adjusted to the heat.

I watched the black soil swirl off my skin into the steamy water for a moment, then glanced at Sophie. Despite the circumstances, she still seemed like the same old Sophie. At one point, I'd even considered her a friend. "What did James do to you?" I asked.

She didn't answer immediately, and I was left with several moments of silence to ponder my situation. I was pretty sure I was, in fact, in shock, because all I could think about was how strange it felt to be around Sophie again, in a tub of now-dirty water no less. I'd spent so much time talking to her in my youth that it almost felt natural, even though we were now meeting under far different circumstances.

Eventually she snorted, the gesture somehow elegant, as she came out of her own private thoughts. I'd previously thought that snorting elegantly wasn't a thing, but that was exactly what Sophie did. She moved away from the door to perch on the closed toilet seat, folding her long legs underneath her in a position that didn't look at all comfortable.

"James would never dare offer me violence," she explained, "but I've seen what he likes to do to people." She turned the full power of her dark stare onto me. "The things I've seen would make a nice girl like you want to cut out her own eyes, though it wouldn't stop the nightmares."

I leaned forward to shut off the faucet, then huddled in the hot water, wincing at the bruise forming on my tailbone. I had to admit the warmth felt good, even if taking a bath was the last thing I wanted to be doing. "I've seen plenty of things to give me nightmares."

She startled as if she'd fallen deep into thought. "I

know," she answered finally. "I know much more than you'd think. The world has not been kind to you."

I swallowed past a renewed sense of panic. She knew what had happened with my last foster family, but she couldn't know about Matthew. I'd met Matthew years later, and that event was for my nightmares alone. I flashed on his dead eyes again, eyes that had looked so much like James'. I'd done it to him. I wasn't sure how, but Matthew's death was my fault. Sophie had no way of knowing anything about that.

She smiled at me like she knew exactly what I was thinking. I looked away quickly, suddenly more frightened than I'd been before, if that was even possible.

I watched her out of the corner of my eye as she reached toward the basket she'd replaced beside the sink, retrieving a new bar of yellow soap, still in the wrapper. She took off the plastic and handed the soap to me. It looked handmade, and smelled like vanilla.

"Wash," she demanded. "Once you're dressed, I'll take you to learn why we brought you here."

I began to wash myself, wishing I could wash away more that just dirt. Matthew's dead eyes were still at the forefront of my mind.

The world would be a lovely place if we could wash away fear and bad memories, but it wasn't a lovely place. I'd seen the ugliness of the world long before I'd learned to live in fear of making it worse.

2

At one point during my bath, someone delivered some clothes for me. Sophie had only opened the door a crack, so I hadn't seen who it was. I'd ended up standing in the middle of the bathroom, dressed in a slim-fitting black dress that encased my legs down to the tops of my knees. Black boots covered my calves and left just a sliver of flesh to be seen below my kneecaps.

The boots had much higher heels than I was used to. Okay, they were only three inches, but I never wore heels. I got my height early, and therefore have the tall-girl syndrome of not wanting to tower over everyone. In the boots I was 6'.

I stole a glance at myself in the bathroom mirror as Sophie leaned against the door. In addition to the uncomfortable added height, the black made my normally deep olive coloring a little washed out. Back in the real world, I never wore black without a little bit of makeup. At that moment though, my coloring was on the bottom of my list of concerns. The woman standing by the door was some-where near the top.

"Are you done primping yet?" Sophie asked impatiently. Her earlier show of camaraderie must have been a fluke, as she had already reverted back to the steely bitch persona.

I looked in the mirror again. My hair was only partially dry, and felt heavy and snarled. It was thick enough that it would be hours before it dried completely, and Sophie hadn't offered me a blow dryer.

"Where are we going?" I asked yet again, even though I knew my efforts were futile.

"I cannot tell you," she sighed, leaning more heavily against the door.

I looked back to the mirror. The dress was tight enough that it was a little hard to breathe. "Then tell me why I'm dressed like this. I feel like a lamb being led to slaughter."

Sophie crossed her arms and cocked her hip to the side. "The sooner you stop asking questions, the sooner you'll know the answers."

On that cryptic note, she opened the door and walked out, expecting me to follow her. Not wanting to risk another run-in with James, or with Alaric for that matter, I did as I was told. Sophie was the lesser evil, at least for now.

She glided down the hallway ahead of me, moving gracefully like her brother. Though I was slightly taller than her with the heels, I felt like I had to take twice the number of steps to keep up. Our heels clicked on the stone floor as we headed in the opposite direction from where I'd run.

We didn't have to go very far before the hallway expanded into a larger walkway, opening into what I could only think of as a throne room. There was no actual throne, but there was a dais against the far wall that was just begging for a gilded throne. We walked across the barren, open space and went through a doorway into a private room.

My confusion increased. Seated in front of me was a small old man. His long gray hair draped across the loose, deep blue clothing he wore, and continued on to pool on the floor in a silvery mass. With his apparent age and hair color, it seemed like he should have a beard as well, like some sort of diminutive wizard, but his face was clean shaven.

He sat at the head of a simple table made of heavy wood. There were enough seats for ten, but no one else kept him company. He turned his weighted gaze to Sophie, who still stood beside me.

"Leave us," he said simply.

With a curt nod, Sophie did just as he asked. I turned to watch her go, nervous to be left alone with the man.

"Face me, Madeline," he said softly.

I turned around slowly, somehow more nervous now than I had been since first waking up. Maybe the shock was finally wearing off, or maybe I was just losing my mind. Most likely it was the latter. Upon closer observation, I placed the man as slightly younger than I had originally thought, maybe late sixties instead of seventies. His face was dappled in only slight wrinkles that increased a bit around his pale gray eyes. His eyes seemed to radiate a *knowing* as he looked me up and down. I'd learned to read people pretty well in my younger years, and I instantly knew that this was a man that I would never try to fool.

"Forgive us for capturing you so abruptly," he began, lifting his eyes to meet my gaze. "I would have liked to leave you be, but I am afraid our need is simply too great."

I wiped my sweaty palms on my dress. I had the distinct feeling of insects crawling across my skin. "What need?" I managed to ask.

What could this man possibly need from me? A million thoughts raced through my head, none of them rational. My intuition was begging me to get far away from him.

"What do you know of the *Vaettir*?" he asked, his expression pleasant despite what my instincts were telling me.

I took a deep breath, trying to calm myself. "I don't know that term." I answered cautiously. He'd pronounced it *vay-tur*, and it sounded slightly Swedish. "Should I?"

He smiled patiently, making me feel like a child back in school. "Two more common terms for what we are would be Wiht or Wight."

"What do you mean *we*?" I asked. "Why am I here?"

"I'm attempting to explain," he replied sourly. "If you'll please answer my original question."

"I don't know anything about Wights," I answered, but that wasn't entirely true. "Aren't they similar to zombies?" I asked, still not sure what mythological creatures had to do with anything. I shifted my weight from foot to foot, glancing around the room for possibly routes of escape. He hadn't threatened me, but I had a feeling this man was the reason I'd been kidnapped. I needed to get away from him.

Not seeming to sense my unease, he continued, "In more common renditions, I suppose. Those myths began in the 1800s. Corpses would reanimate, but most were actually Vaettir. But I assure you, the Vaettir are not undead. Quite the opposite, actually. We are beings of nature, Fae, for lack of a better word. We are more alive than any others who walk this earth. In ancient Norse culture, we were revered as patrons of the land, though in later years, a less favorable picture was painted. Hence, our solitude."

I laughed, a nervous bark of sound in the quiet room. The sound seemed to startle me much more than it did the old man. In fact, his face didn't change at all. He simply waited for me to speak.

"Wait," I said finally, "you're trying to tell me that you are this Vaettir thingy?"

I was beginning to sweat profusely, and had the feeling if this conversation didn't end soon, I was going to start screaming.

The old man nodded, quite serious. "As are you," he replied simply.

The rigid smile wilted from my face. "You're kidding, right?"

His face still didn't change.

I didn't know much about Norse mythology, but I knew I wasn't part of it. "Why am I here? I don't know anything about zombies or anything else." I laughed nervously. "Next thing you'll be telling me is that I'm some sort of long-lost fairy princess."

Finally the old man smiled wickedly, turning my stomach to ice. "No my dear, you are definitely not our long-lost princess. You're our executioner."

I started laughing again, and it sounded psychotic, even to me. I couldn't help it. The old man was obviously serious, but he was talking nonsense. Feeling weak in the knees, I sat in a chair several seats down from him. "You people are insane," I breathed.

He tilted his head to the side and smiled. "What do you know of your parents?"

"That doesn't mean a thing," I replied instantly, knowing that Sophie had probably filled him in on my history. I wouldn't let them prey on the fact that I had been a foster kid. Enough people had done that already. "Not every abandoned baby ends up being a wizard, or a fairy, or ... something out of ancient myth," I finished coldly.

"No," he chuckled. "But in your case ... "

I stood, deciding that I'd rather take my chances with James or Alaric than sit around listening to crazy stories. The old man slammed his hand on the table, and my legs collapsed underneath me. I barely managed to aim my butt toward the chair to keep myself off the ground. I tried to stand again and didn't even make it halfway out of my seat before being forced back down.

"I apologize," he said serenely. "This was not how I hoped this meeting would go. This is a homecoming, not a kidnapping."

I looked around the room frantically for an explanation. My legs wouldn't work. This had to be some sort of trick. Maybe they'd drugged me.

"What's happening?" I demanded, my breath catching in my throat.

"If you would stop trying to stand," he said with a condescending smile, "I would not have to force you to sit."

My eyes widened. He was claiming that he could make me sit ... with what, his mind? Of course, I *was* sitting against my will with no other explanation to go on.

"Who are you?" I asked, panting with exertion while I clutched at the edges of my chair.

"My name is Estus," he replied. "I am Doyen of this clan."

I gritted my teeth, unable to stave off the tears that began to flow down my face once again. "I don't know what that means."

A hint of impatience flickered in Estus' eyes, cracking the kind old man act, not that I'd believed it to begin with. "We should never have left you to the humans for so long," he sighed.

"So why did you?" I asked, unable to think of anything else to say. If you can't beat 'em, then you may as well play along.

"A clan only needs one executioner," he explained. "Any others born with the specific qualities of an executioner are exiled. It would be chaos otherwise."

Each crazy thing he said made my tears flow more quickly. This had nothing to do with my years in foster care. These people were completely insane.

"Too many executioners over the centuries have ended up killing each other," he went on, ignoring my tears. "If we continued to let them live together, we'd end up without any executioners at all, and that would be very, very bad. Now, if we send the extras out into the world, we may call them back when we are in need of a replacement."

I moved my tongue around in my mouth to try and get some saliva going, but it was no use. I swallowed around the lump in my throat. "And you're in need of a replacement *now*?" I panted, still straining to stand.

"Precisely," he answered, seeming relieved that I understood. "Our clan cannot function properly without you."

If these crazy people wanted me to be their executioner, that meant they were going to try keeping me with them. It also likely meant they were going to expect me to kill people. I could never do that. Someone would have to come looking for me eventually. They had to.

I mean, people don't just disappear without the police being notified. Of course, it might take a while for them to get notified. I had no parents to report me missing, and no spouse. I had a few friends, but the scenario of them not hearing from me for a few weeks wasn't unheard of. Events in my past had led me to a life of near-solitude, keeping people at a distance for fear that history would repeat itself. My history was dark and sad, and not worth repeating.

Normal people would have at least had a boss to miss them when they didn't show up for work, but I did freelance writing for a living, so there were no coworkers or bosses to report me missing. I had a landlord . . . but seeing as it was only the 8th of October, he wouldn't be expecting a rent check for a while. He probably wouldn't sound any alarm bells until his pockets were feeling empty. Being alone was hard, but I'd never thought that being antisocial would come back to bite me in such a major way.

Estus gave me several minutes to digest everything. I still didn't believe anything he'd said, though the fact that I was quite literally glued to my seat definitely gave me pause. Regardless, it definitely wasn't the time to argue. I was better off going along with whatever Estus said until they left me alone again.

"I can see that you are having some trouble believing what I say," he stated finally.

"No," I lied quickly. "I understand."

Some of the smile slipped from Estus' face. "I will not tolerate lies, now tell me what happened with Matthew."

A searing feeling of cold shot through me at the name. My breath caught in my throat. "How do you know about that?" I croaked.

Estus eyed me steadily. "Just because we left you on your own, does not mean that we let you go. Not entirely. Now tell me."

"No," I replied. "That's private."

I gripped the edges of my chair until my hands ached as I tried to push away the memories. That specific story was one I never planned on sharing with *anybody*, let alone one of my kidnappers.

"It was not your fault," he consoled. "It is your nature."

I was beginning to shake as I held back more tears, but the memories weren't held back as easily. We'd been in a car accident. Several cars had been involved. Others had died, but we weren't overly hurt. Matthew's wrist was clearly broken, but that seemed to be the extent of it. Good Samaritans had helped us out of our car to wait on the side of the road for the paramedics.

We were sitting in the grass, and it was killing me to see Matthew gritting his teeth against the pain. I'd always been highly affected by the pain of others to an extent that made me avoid hospitals like the plague. If I saw an injury on someone else, my mind made me feel like I had it too. Even strong emotions affected me. At one point I'd gone to therapy for it, but nothing helped.

The old memory played out in my head like a movie. *I reached out and smoothed my hand across Matthew's face, hoping to soothe him just a bit, and in effect soothe myself. He looked at me, suddenly not just in pain, but frightened. His fear made my heart hammer in my throat, but I continued holding my hand to his face, not sure of what had changed.*

I felt a rush of energy as it left him, that spark of life. I watched as it left his eyes. I was so shocked as he slumped over that I didn't even scream. Later I would try telling myself that he'd damaged something internally in the accident, but I knew it was a lie. I'd stared at him as the paramedics arrived and rushed over to us, and knew for a fact that there was nothing they could do.

I still rode next to his dead body in the ambulance as they did their best to resuscitate him. I was later told that they couldn't find the exact cause of death. They wrote it off as a small brain hemorrhage, but I knew otherwise. Some tiny voice screamed in my mind that it was me. I'd killed Matthew.

"You are probably starving," Estus said sympathetically, watching the emotions play across my face. "Sophie will escort you to the kitchens. We will speak more when you are at full strength."

As if on cue, the door opened behind me, and Sophie re-entered the room. I turned wide eyes to Estus to see if I was allowed to stand.

He smiled warmly, then lifted his hands, shooing me away.

I took a deep breath and stood without any unseen force impeding me. I turned and numbly followed Sophie's slim form without another word to Estus. I felt shaky on my feet, but I kept walking. That's all we can ever really do.

We went back through the throne room and down another narrow hallway. Sophie looked back several times, but didn't say anything.

Eventually I stopped walking, feeling like I might throw up. "That man—" I began.

She stopped, then turned to face me. "Estus," she corrected.

"Did you tell him about me?" I asked. "Is he like, a mental patient?"

Sophie's eyes widened. "Do not ever let anyone hear you say such a thing," she hissed. "Estus is Doyen. All here obey him."

The urge to vomit increased. I felt like I was motion sick, but it was probably just another symptom of shock. "You're not really a social worker, are you?"

She shrugged. "I like to think I was pretty good at it."

I just stared at her, at a loss for words.

"Chin up," she said with a sudden smile.

She turned and began walking forward again, and I quickly followed, resigning myself to whatever fate might befall me. The queasiness dissipated as we walked, only to be replaced by an icy, shaky feeling that wasn't much of an improvement.

I attempted to distract myself by taking in my surroundings, and noticed with a start that I had not seen one single window in any of the thick, stone walls. The entire place was illuminated just like the bathroom, with no visible source of light. It didn't make any sense.

I trotted to catch up to Sophie and walk beside her. "Where does the light come from?"

She gave me another sympathetic look, then explained, "The Salr provides its own light."

"The sah-what?" I asked, not knowing the term.

"Salr, *Sah-lur*," she sounded out for me. "It is where we live."

"I don't understand," I replied. "How can a place provide its own light without any windows?"

Sophie stopped walking again and put a hand on her hip. "Estus explained to you what we are, yes?"

My pulse picked up again at the mention of Estus. What he'd done in that room . . . "Kind of," I answered. "But—"

"You still don't believe him," she finished for me. She suddenly gripped me by my shoulders and looked straight into my eyes. "Watch," she instructed.

Not sure what I was supposed to see, I looked into her eyes. As I watched, her dark irises flashed to golden, with large flecks of green. Her pupils narrowed until they looked like cat eyes. I tried to jerk away, but her hands held me iron-tight. A moment later, her eyes returned to normal.

"What the hell was that?" I whispered, utterly still in her unyielding grip.

She abruptly let go of my shoulders and started walking again. "My brother and I are Bastet," she explained, as if it made all the sense in the world.

I knew that Bastet was the cat-headed Egyptian goddess of warfare, but I didn't think Sophie was claiming to be a goddess.

"That man, Estus, said that you're Vaettir," I said, feeling extremely silly for discussing it so seriously. "Like zombies," I added.

Sophie smirked at me as we walked. "We are Vaettir, but we are not *zombies*. Sometimes the Vaettir reanimate after death."

"Uhh," I began, "you know that's basically the definition of zombies?"

Sophie grunted in frustration. "Perhaps, but we are not the zombies portrayed in all of those silly movies. We sometimes reanimate because a piece of our soul is left in our bodies. It gives the bodies life, but the person who inhabited that shell is gone."

I bit my lip, thinking about my reply, then tried to not sound condescending as I said, "That's still pretty much the definition of zombies."

Sophie huffed in annoyance, but didn't try to convince me further. If zombies actually existed, that would be it for me. I would lose my mind and run screaming into the dark, never to return.

We passed through a large dining area and into a kitchen the size of what a large restaurant would have. Monstrous pots brimming with boiling liquids sat on the industrial sized stove, filling the room with savory smells. Sophie retrieved a large bowl and began filling it with what looked like beef stew.

"I don't eat meat," I said quickly.

She stopped ladling and dumped the stew back into the pot. "Of course you don't," she said with a touch of sarcasm. "Because a vegetarian executioner totally makes sense."

"I'm not an executioner," I said nervously. "You've all made a mistake."

"Whatever you say," she replied. She picked up a knife and began hacking away at a large loaf of bread that had been sitting out on the counter. "Cheese?" she asked.

I nodded my head. "Yes, cheese is fine, just no meat."

"Not ever?" she asked as if she didn't quite believe me.

I shook my head.

She snorted. "Well that's irritating."

Setting down the knife, she ventured to the far side of the kitchen, opened a large, walk-in refrigerator, and disappeared inside, eventually emerging with an armful of produce. She returned to the cooking area and placed a tomato, an avocado, some lettuce, and a package of alfalfa sprouts on a cutting board. She began chopping haphazardly while I looked at the rest of the kitchen.

Large, gas station style coffee pots took up a counter to my left, and in front of me along the far wall was bar style seating, along with a few small tables and chairs set out of the way.

Within a few minutes, I was seated at the shiny counter built into the far wall with a veggie and cheese sandwich placed in front of me. Sophie had left out mayo and mustard, but the sight of her wielding the large kitchen knife had prompted me to keep my mouth shut.

My stomach was groaning painfully, arguing with my mind for not wanting to eat. When my stomach won out, I picked up the sandwich and prepared to take a bite.

"How is our little executioner doing?" Someone whispered right beside my ear, though no one had been there a moment before.

I jumped and dropped my sandwich back to its plate. It

fell apart, looking pathetic and unappetizing. I turned to find Alaric staring at me from just a few inches away.

My pulse quickened as he reached out his hand, then swept my hair away from my face to reveal my neck, turning my initial annoyance into anxiety. "You know, there's no meat on your sandwich?" he asked, looking at my neck instead of my face.

I scooted my stool a few inches away from him. He didn't seem offended. In fact, he pulled another stool up close and sat with his knee touching mine. I was glad that he'd at least found a shirt somewhere as he leaned against me.

Sophie cleared her throat behind us. She sat near the door, drinking a cup of coffee. I would have loved some coffee, but I didn't really want to ask her for anything else. I already had the feeling that she hadn't appreciated having to make a sandwich for me.

Seeing my longing gaze, Alaric rose from his seat and walked past his sister to pour two more cups from the coffee maker's spout. He returned and placed one cup beside me, then sat in his original position.

Leaning away from him, I sipped the coffee, feeling instantly more stable as the warm liquid poured down my throat, thawing the icy pit that had formed in my insides. Alaric sipped on his own coffee as he watched me.

I glanced at him, feeling increasingly awkward. "Do you have to do that?"

"Do what?" he replied as he picked up a piece of my hair to play with.

"Be creepy," I answered, gathering up my sandwich

once again. I leaned as far away as I could without falling off my chair.

He laughed and dropped my hair, but didn't scoot away. He watched me take the first bite of my sandwich like he'd memorize every movement.

"You know," he said. "A lot of women don't like being watched while they eat."

I washed the first bite down with a sip of coffee. Without any condiments on the hard bread, the sandwich was a little dry. At least the coffee was good. Definitely not the cheap stuff.

"I don't care if you watch me," I replied. "Just don't touch me."

"Well you two are obviously getting along," Sophie quipped, "so I'll just let Alaric show you back to your room."

I turned. "No!" I blurted. "Please don't leave me," I glanced at Alaric, then reluctantly added, "with him."

She smirked. "He's only teasing you, Madeline. He's not going to eat you."

I opened my mouth to argue further, but she simply turned her back and left the kitchen. I had to snap my gaping jaw shut as I turned back to Alaric.

"Eat your sandwich," he said good-naturedly, obviously not upset with the current arrangement. That made one of us.

I took another bite of the dry sandwich and had even more trouble swallowing than before. It had seemed like a good idea to eat, if only to gather my strength, but now each bite was beginning to feel like heavy lead in my stomach. I put the sandwich down on the plate, suddenly disgusted with it.

"Black isn't your color," Alaric commented. "I tried to pick your clothes, but I was over-ruled."

"Who picked them?" I asked, feeling uncomfortable that he cared what I wore.

"Sophie," he replied. "She chose them before you arrived. I take it you will be staying with us?"

I pushed my sandwich plate away. Yeah, definitely done. "Like I have a choice," I answered bitterly.

Alaric laughed as he spun down off of his stool in one liquid motion. "I suppose not."

I suddenly felt the tears welling up again. I didn't know why they chose to hit just then, a delayed reaction I guess. I looked down at my uneaten sandwich and cried, because I didn't know what else to do.

3

Alaric had waited while I cried. He didn't try to comfort me, and I was grateful. It would have been just a little too strange having one of my captors showing that type of compassion.

My tears had left me numb and thoroughly without an appetite. I left the sandwich on the counter so Alaric could walk me back to my room. He reached my door first and held it open for me, the picture of a perfect gentleman. *Yeah right.* I turned and looked at him once I was inside, wondering if he was going to leave me alone in the room. He didn't.

"I'm tired," I said, hoping to appeal to his sense of mercy.

"I know you've been through a lot-" he began.

"That's a vast understatement," I interrupted.

"And I know you probably don't have warm, fuzzy feelings toward any of us right now," he went on.

"Keep going," I sighed weakly, feeling unsteady on my feet. "You're on a roll."

He laughed. "Your ability to be sarcastic under the direst of circumstances is quite impressive."

"Would you rather I screamed and begged for my life?" I questioned.

"It might be interesting," he replied. "Though your life is in no danger."

I left him and walked further into the room to sit on the foot of the ornate bed, smoothing the thick comforter with my hands. "You don't have to die in order to lose your life," I said quietly.

He raised an eyebrow as he left the doorway and slunk toward me. "And your life was so great before?"

I glared at him. "It was nothing special, but at least I had a choice in what I did."

"And you chose to shut yourself up in your little house," he said softly. "No, I don't think we took you away from very much at all."

"How long were you people watching me?" I hissed. "I'm beginning to think that this wasn't just some random kidnapping."

"You *know* this wasn't a random kidnapping, Madeline," he replied. "Just as deep down, you know what you are."

"My name is Madeline Ville, and I'm a human being," I answered sarcastically.

Alaric kneeled in front of me, putting us at eye level. It was an oddly intimate position, but he hadn't left me room to stand, so it was either scoot back onto the bed and give him room to follow, or stay where I was. I stayed.

"Sophie told me what happened with your foster family," he admitted. "I helped cover the incident up. It must have been difficult for you to deal with at such a young age."

I shook my head in disbelief. "That's not possible. That's—" I paused, not sure what to say.

The last family I'd been placed with had been a couple in their late thirties, Ray and Nadine. They both suffered from alcohol issues, and used the foster system as an easy paycheck. It hadn't been terrible, not compared to some of the other places I'd been.

I was seventeen at the time, and they let me do what I wanted as long as I didn't rat them out for not being real parents. I was content to stay there until I was eighteen and finished with high school.

It was all fine, until one night they came home completely hammered. Nadine passed out, and Ray turned his *attentions* to me. I tried to fend him off, and things got violent. He ended up falling on the corner of the kitchen table, neck first. It sliced him open, then he hit the ground. There was a lot of blood and I panicked. I could admit to myself that I didn't care about his well being, but I knew if anything serious happened I'd be blamed for it. Plus, I could *feel* his neck wound on my own neck. It wasn't as bad as some of the other pain I'd felt, but it was still unpleasant. I'd put my hands on his neck and tried to stop the blood flow. His eyes turned up to me, frozen in terror, then suddenly, he was dead.

I had thought his death was caused by blood-loss at the time, and had dismissed the strange rush of energy I felt when he passed as adrenaline. Then Matthew died, and I had to admit that neither death had been normal. They were both *my* fault.

The night Ray died I'd called the police, and ended up in Sophie's office as the sun began to rise the next morning. I'd frantically pleaded with her to not let the cops take me, that it had all been an accident. She'd told me not to worry, that it was all taken care of. There would be no questions. I would simply wait for my eighteenth birthday in a women's shelter, rather than with another foster family.

"The police saw him," I said out loud, returning to the present. "There was no way it could be covered up. I should have at least been questioned."

"You don't need to worry about that anymore," Alaric assured.

I curled my legs up underneath me and huddled in on myself. "What really happened?" I asked in a strained voice. I didn't want to believe any of this was real, but if there was even the slightest chance I could learn the truth . . . "Why did Ray die? I've been over that memory so many times. He hadn't lost enough blood. He was conscious and cursing at me as I tried to stop the blood flow."

Alaric placed his hand on my shoulder. "It is your gift, Madeline."

I pulled away, shaking my head over and over. "I don't understand."

He stayed kneeling in front of me, but didn't try to touch me again. "You have the power to release the lives of those who are suffering."

"I don't believe you," I said petulantly, though part of me did.

I'd stayed up far too many nights wondering what had

happened with Ray and Matthew to not have considered that there was something different about me.

Alaric sighed. "You'll see in time."

"And what do you have to do with any of this?" I asked suddenly. "I still don't understand why I'm here."

"You'll understand soon enough," he explained seriously. "I promise I'll do what I can to help."

I laughed, but it turned into more of a hiccup because of my tears. "You know, I preferred you when you were flirtatious," I said, suddenly embarrassed by my breakdown.

He wiggled his eyebrows at me. "As my lady commands."

I smiled, then quickly wiped it away. A girl shouldn't smile at her kidnapper, even when he was trying to cheer her up.

"I'm tired," I said again.

He nodded. "I wouldn't go wandering," he advised. "Many things less pleasant than my sister wander these halls."

With that ominous advice ringing in the air, he stood and left the room, shutting the door gently behind him. I leaned down and took off the high-heeled boots. Apparently I'd just been dressed up to meet with Estus. He was their leader, in some way, so I supposed he merited proper attire.

I paced around the room, feeling sick and dizzy, and none too happy to be left with only the form-fitting dress to wear. There were a few dressers in the room that matched the bed, and as a last ditch effort I started going through them. Many of the drawers were empty, but eventually I came to two drawers filled with clothes. I found some silky red pajama pants with a matching shirt, but passed them over. I didn't actually want to go to sleep. I *couldn't* go to sleep. I had to find a way out.

I searched through the clothes a little bit more and came out with a pair of black jeans and an indigo blue tee-shirt. The jeans fit me like a glove. My imprisonment had obviously been well-planned. Gre-at.

I dressed quickly, nervous that someone would come calling while I was naked. I felt slightly better in normal clothing, more like myself. There was even a pair of black running shoes underneath the dresser. It was as if they actually *wanted* me to run. I was happy to oblige.

When I could find nothing else of use in the room, I sat on the bed to wait. Hopefully everyone would go to sleep and I could search for an exit unhindered. I wasn't sure how anyone could even tell that it was night-time without windows, but I felt tired enough for it to be night. That meant that it had already been a full day since I'd been taken.

I tried to just wait on the bed, but I was too nervous to sit still. Instead, I began examining the room, even though there wasn't much to it. Wood had been added to the fire before I was re-delivered to the space. The flames crackled happily as they gave off their warmth, contrasting drastically with my mood.

I stood by the fire for a while, because it beat sitting on the bed. Eventually I went through the dressers again, even though I knew I'd find the same things, and looked underneath the bed as well. There was nothing under the bed, not even dust bunnies.

Finally I'd had enough, and went for the door. I reached

for the knob and hesitated, then placed my ear against the door to listen. I couldn't hear anything on the other side, but the wood of the door was so thick that it didn't mean much. I took a deep breath and grabbed the knob, opening the door before I could think better of it. I let out my breath when it was revealed that no one was waiting on the other side.

With a steadying hand against the wall, I tip-toed out into the hallway, almost wishing I would have gone with bare feet rather than running shoes. I crept down the hall, cringing at the little tip-taps of my steps on the stone.

The lighting in the halls was more dim than it had been earlier, but still enough to see by, luckily. Not sure where to go, I finally decided to go back down the hallway where I'd had my encounter with James. I did *not* want another meeting with him, but it seemed the most likely place for an exit. From what I'd seen of the opposite direction, the other halls led deeper into the compound.

I glanced over my shoulder every few seconds, wanting to run, but afraid of the noise my feet would make. I was mid-step when I heard a low-throated growl that raised the hairs on my arms. I turned around in what felt like slow motion to see a dog the size of a grizzly bear creeping up behind me. It must have come out of one of the rooms, else I would have noticed it approaching.

I stood perfectly still as the beast took a slow step toward me, scraping its long nails across the stone floor. I swallowed the lump in my suddenly dry throat. Maybe it wasn't a dog. It had a face similar to that of a Rottweiler, but with an elongated snout. Something about its stance was wrong as well. I took a slow step back, realizing its neck was far too long, and what I could see of its tail was too thick. It had the body of a bear, the head of a dog, and the neck and stance of a giant lizard. Dark brown fur flowed over its face and body, blending the aspects of the different animals seamlessly.

The thing cocked back its head and sniffed the air, then let out another low growl. It shifted from paw to paw, preparing to pounce. Knowing that I would have no chance if it jumped on me, I turned and ran.

I was no longer concerned about my footfalls as I rounded a corner in the hallway, my heart thudding in my chest. I grabbed the knob of the first door that I saw, praying to whatever I should be praying to that it wasn't locked.

The door came open and I practically fell inside. I felt the air shift behind me as the creature went barreling by. I slammed the door shut and slid the deadbolt into place, not waiting to see if the creature came back. I was suddenly very glad that all of the doors in the place seemed to be made of heavy, sturdy wood, though it was a little strange to have a deadbolt on an interior door.

I turned to look at the room I was now trapped in as I tried to regain my breath. The room was made of stone, of course, but something dark stained the walls and floor. I couldn't tell what the substance was, as the room barely had enough light to see by, but I could tell it had been a thin liquid, spattering the walls lightly, then pooling in large puddles on the floor. I waited by the door for a moment, listening for the return of the creature, but heard nothing.

My shoulders relaxing, I walked toward the nearest wall

and touched the stains, smoothing my fingertips across the stone. My fingers came away with something thick and sticky. Older, dry stains were spread underneath the more recent ones, flowing in patterns like water. I stepped away from the wall, rubbing my fingers on my jeans as I went. I still hadn't heard a peep from the other side of the door. The creature wasn't trying to come in after me.

My sneakered feet stuck to the floor as I explored the dimly-lit room a little further. Large cages with thick steel bars came into view as I approached the far wall. The refuse inside of the cages hinted to the fact that they had once been occupied, but they were all empty now. I wondered if the cages were for other beasts like the one I'd seen. The room stank of rot and a strange burnt smell.

A scratching at the door caught my attention. My heart leapt into my throat at the thought that the creature had realized where I was, but then I noticed that the scratching was coming from somewhere beside the door, not outside of it.

I crept toward the sound, barely able to hear the scratching over the thudding of my heart. There was something small moving around where the floor met the wall, but there wasn't enough light to quite make out what it was.

I crouched down and reached out a hand to try and coax the thing into the dim light. It worked. Too fast to follow, the thing lunged for me. It was only the size of a very large rat, but it flew into my chest with such force that it knocked me to the ground.

The moist stickiness of the floor seeped into my clothing. I half sat up, frantically trying to grab at the thing that was now scratching its way up my torso. I wrapped my hands around it, but the creature was wet and slippery. It slipped right through my fingers and went for my throat, pinning me back to the ground. It wrapped tightly around my neck.

My breath wheezed in and out shallowly as I pried at the thing's fingers. Fingers? It felt like a hand around my throat. Flashes of fear and rage pulsed in my mind, just like the other emotions I could sense from people. I saw blurry scenes that I knew had nothing to do with my own memories, they were somehow coming from the creature. The scenes faded as my vision began to go black from lack of oxygen. I forced away my panic, focusing on removing the thing at my throat. I felt a small rush of energy and the thing suddenly went limp. I threw it off me and pushed myself backwards across the floor.

My vision came back in stages as I caught my breath. I could see the dark shape of the thing a few feet away, but it didn't move. I got to my feet and ran forward as steadily as I could manage in my panicked state, then stomped the creature with my heel as soon as I reached it. I jumped on it until I heard bones crunch. Sure that it was now dead, I leaned down to examine it again. It *was* a hand.

The hand was now bruised and misshapen from my stomping, but that wasn't the worst of its injuries. Right above the wrist bone, the hand had been severed from its owner. Bone gleamed in the dim light as blood continued to gush forth. There shouldn't have been that much blood in just a hand, but the thing was covered in it. That was why it had been so difficult to keep a hold of.

Yet, none of those things had been what killed it. I had killed it, just like I did Matthew. I knew it with a sickening surety. I had felt the same rush of energy when Matthew died. I had somehow stolen whatever life force had animated it.

I pushed myself away from the hand, just before I lost what little dinner I'd eaten. My vomit and tears fell to commingle with the substance on the floor that I now realized was blood. The whole room was covered in congealed blood.

I quickly got to my feet and tried to wipe my hands off on my jeans, but the blood was too sticky and I couldn't get it all off. I stumbled back toward the door, ready to take my chances with the creature in the hall if it meant I could just get out of that room. How had the hand even moved to begin with?

I glanced back at the hand in question, half-expecting it to have disappeared, but it was still just lying there. My own hands were shaking so badly that it took me several tries to undo the lock. When I finally managed to open the door, I had to jump back because someone was in the doorway. I ended up slipping and falling hard on my tailbone.

Alaric's hair fell forward over his shoulders as he looked down at me. "I thought you might try to run again. I figured I'd make sure you didn't get eaten."

"Great job," I replied shakily, on the verge of hysteria.

He crouched down and picked me up effortlessly into the cradle of his arms. He stood and carried me out of the room of horrors without a word, and I let him.

"You need another bath," he commented once we were walking down the hall.

"W-what was that room?" I stammered. I wrapped my arms around his neck to feel more secure. In that moment,

I didn't care that he was one of my captors as long as he got me the hell away from that room. "There was a hand," I added.

He chuckled. "Sometimes parts get left behind. They can be a little cross about what happened to their bodies."

For a moment I thought I might vomit again, but I managed to hold it in. "And what happened to their bodies?" I asked weakly.

"Did Estus tell you why you were brought back to us?" he asked rather than answering my question.

"He said you needed a new executioner," I answered breathlessly, as if it were a normal thing to say.

Alaric stopped to hoist me up and get a more firm grip around me. "You just met the hand of our last executioner."

"You killed him!" I exclaimed, trying to wriggle out of his grip.

"Not me personally," he replied holding on and not letting me drop. "Though I would have. He was a traitor."

The struggling was getting me nowhere, so I stopped. "What did he do?"

Alaric looked down at me with a cold expression. "He was a traitor, and we cannot afford traitors in times like these."

"Times like these?" I prompted.

"My dear executioner," he replied. "We are at war."

My next question froze on my tongue as I considered the complexities of what he was saying. Who would want to go to war with people that dismembered their victims, and let enormous, furry lizard beasts run loose in their halls? More Vaettir? Were there other places like the one we were in, with more crazy freaks populating them? I began to feel dizzy again.

"What was that creature?" I asked suddenly, remembering why I'd run into the bloody room to begin with. "It was like a dog, but not a dog. Kind of like a lizard."

"Ah," Alaric observed, "you must mean Stella. She's James' . . . pet. A lindworm, one of the few left."

Alaric let me down to my feet as we walked into the bathroom. He gave me a scrutinizing look. "I assume you can get back to your room from here?"

I looked at him as he prepared to leave me while visions of lizard dogs and bloody hands danced in my head. "Please stay," I said before I could think it through.

He looked surprised, then smiled. "You mean, *stay*?" he drew out the word as if it meant more than just staying.

My eyes widened. "Oh no," I corrected. "It's just. What if there are more body parts wandering around?"

"You handled that hand all on your own—" he began.

"Please," I interrupted.

He shrugged and entered the bathroom fully so he could shut the door behind him, then went to sit on the closed toilet seat.

"You have blood on your clothes," I observed, suddenly feeling uncomfortable.

He raised an eyebrow at me. "You have much more on yours."

I looked down. He was right. The sticky, congealed blood had soaked into the back of my jeans, and there were smears of it all over my shirt.

I knew I should ask him to leave, but I could feel bruises forming on my throat from the hand. I'd nearly died in there. "Close your eyes please," I said, making up my mind. I was more than ready to get out of the soiled clothing.

"And what if I said no?" he asked with his eyes still wide open.

"Then I would take my chances with the severed body parts," I answered bluntly, refusing to show him just how rattled I was.

He laughed at me, but still obeyed and closed his eyes. I peeled the soiled clothing off and hopped quickly into the tub. Instead of just filling it right away, I ran the water and splashed off any of the blood that was on my skin so I wouldn't have to soak in it. The pinkish water running toward the drain would have almost been pretty if I didn't know that it was from a man who had been brutally murdered. When I was clean enough, I plugged the drain to trap the hot water.

I glanced at Alaric, his eyes still closed. Really, the tub was tall enough to hide anything I'd want hidden unless he stood up and looked down, but I still felt uncomfortable.

"Can I open them yet?" he asked in a tone that implied that I was being very silly.

"Yes," I answered. "But keep your gaze forward please." If modesty was silly, then baby, call me the queen of slap-stick.

"You know it would be much more efficient if I could just hop in there with you," he joked. "At this rate I'll never get to bed."

"I'll be out soon enough," I grumbled.

The water had filled enough for me to start scrubbing myself with the vanilla soap. As I washed I realized I had blood in my hair too. I scooted forward enough to lean back and dunk my hair into the water. When I came back up, the water was pink. I quickly turned off the faucet and unplugged the drain.

"I was only kidding," he said.

"I need to refill the water," I explained, turning to look at him. "Hey, avert your eyes!"

He looked away with a laugh. "Why do you need to refill the water?" he asked, obviously trying to distract me.

"There was blood in it," I answered.

He laughed again. "It will be interesting to see how you adapt among the Vaettir."

"Why?" I asked. "Do you enjoy bathing in the blood of thine enemies?"

"Something like that," he answered soberly.

"You can't keep me here forever," I added.

He turned to look at me, but he seemed so serious that I just hunched down to cover my breasts rather than telling him to look away.

"It would have happened again," he said cryptically. "The taking of life is your gift."

"The taking of life is not a gift," I snapped, once again thinking of Matthew.

"Not always," he replied, finally averting his eyes. "Nor is it always a curse."

I shook my head. It *was* a curse. There was no way around it. I plugged the drain and renewed the water flow, then slipped down into the tub, fully prepared to sulk. *It would have happened again*, he'd said. I couldn't bear what had happened with Matthew happening with someone else.

"Tell me about this war," I said, needing to change the subject.

He sighed. "We are just one clan of many. We fight for power, land, age-old vendettas . . . " he trailed off. "Aislin, the Doyen of a clan predominantly residing in Scandinavia, and Estus have been at war for years. As far as I can tell, they're both searching for something."

I turned my shocked expression toward him, but he was still looking away. "You mean you're fighting a war without knowing what you're actually fighting for?"

He smirked at me, then quickly turned away. "You believe the wars of humans to be any different? I am simply trying to live my life in relative safety. I do as my Doyen bades, because that is the way it has always been."

I washed my hair and scrubbed my skin nearly raw in silence. These people were absolutely nuts.

"You have lovely skin," he commented, pulling me out of my thoughts. "You should probably try not to scrub it all off."

"Stop looking!" I exclaimed as I sunk down into the tub to ensure everything was covered.

"I can't protect you from severed hands if I can't *see* you," he argued, laughter in his voice.

I smiled in spite of myself. He was being a lech, but he was also trying to cheer me up again. I had to appreciate the latter, at least a little.

"If you died," I began, then cringed when I realized how inappropriate the statement sounded.

Alaric turned wide eyes to me. "Do you have plans that I'm not aware of?"

I glared and removed one of my hands from my chest to

gesture for him to look away. "If you died," I began again, "would you reanimate just like that hand?"

Alaric kept his eyes firmly forward, for once. "As would you."

I gasped. I hadn't thought about *that*. Part of me believed that Alaric actually would reanimate. I could no longer argue with all of the evidence laid before me, especially when one of the pieces of evidence had just tried to kill me. Yes, I mostly believed that Alaric and the others weren't exactly human, but me? I still couldn't wrap my mind around *that*.

"What if I had died last week? Would my corpse have walked right out of the morgue?"

Alaric laughed. "We had more than one reason for keeping an eye on you. If you had died, your body would have been brought here."

I somehow didn't find that comforting. "What if I had died in a plane crash, and my body ended up at the bottom of the ocean. What then?"

Alaric glanced at me in surprise, then looked away quickly. "Then I suppose we'd hear of sightings of zombie mermaids in the news."

He'd meant it as a joke, but the idea of my corpse walking around after I was dead gave me goosebumps. I shook my head, then dunked my hair in the water again, trying to get warm. I stayed that way for a while, but couldn't seem to wash away the cold, because it wasn't *that* kind of cold.

When I was finished, Alaric handed me two towels, one for my hair and one for my body. It was oddly considerate.

Then again, with the length of his hair he probably had to use two towels too.

He turned his back so I could step out of the tub and dry off. It only dawned on me as I finished drying myself that I didn't have any clean clothes to change into. At a loss, I wrapped the towel I'd used on my body tightly around me, then tapped Alaric on the shoulder.

Now, when someone turns around to see you, you usually expect them to take a step back to make room. Alaric turned around without the step back, and was suddenly very close to me. His pants brushed against the bottom edge of my towel, moving the fabric ever so slightly. Luckily the smaller amount of blood he'd gotten on him was already dry and didn't transfer to the clean towel.

I slowly moved my eyes upward, feeling nervous and perhaps a little bit of something else. Alaric looked down at me with a knowing smile, eliciting goosebumps up and down my arms once again. I eyed him warily, feeling small and vulnerable, but he didn't move out of my way.

"If my gift is death, like you say," I began carefully, "then shouldn't you be afraid of me?"

"You would bring a swift death to a human," he replied. "But I would only fear you if I were severely weakened." He smoothed a hand down my bare arm.

"You're really going to kidnap me, then hit on me?" I asked, pulling away from his touch.

He smiled, not in the least bit offended. "I am simply letting you know your options. The choice remains yours."

"So I have the choice of whether or not I sleep with you, but not the choice of leaving this place?" I asked, now with a hint of anger in my tone.

Alaric raised his hands in an *I give up* gesture. "That second choice is not mine to give. I would not offer you a lie."

A subtle throbbing was beginning to grow between my eyes. I pinched the bridge of my nose to ease the pain.

"I'm very tired," I said, hoping to end the conversation.

This time when I was left in my room, I really would sleep. I felt unsteady on my feet just standing there. Alaric nodded and led me out of the bathroom and back down the hallway toward the room I'd been given.

He stayed in the doorway of my bedroom, forcing me to squeeze by him in order to go inside. I half-expected him to follow me in, but he remained in the threshold. After a moment he stepped back to close the door for me, though he left it open long enough for him to peek his head back inside and leave a standing offer for him to be my "snuggle buddy".

I refused his offer. I needed a snuggle buddy like I needed hepatitis.

4

I fell asleep almost instantly, and if I dreamed, I didn't remember. I woke up confused as to where I was, until the memories of the previous day came flooding back.

Had all of that occurred in just one day? I thought about my little house, and the fact that no one would have yet noticed that I was missing from it. No one knew that I hadn't spent the last two nights safely tucked into my bed.

I was still sitting in bed dazed and confused when Sophie flung the door open without a knock. She glared down at me still snuggled in bed, annoyance clear on her face.

"Get dressed," she ordered. "Breakfast first, then you have a job to do."

The *job* they had brought me here for was the position of executioner. Did they want me to kill someone?

"I, um, I don't feel well," I stammered. "I should probably just stay in bed today." I had to get the hell out of this place.

Ignoring me, Sophie walked to the nearby dresser and started pawing through the drawers.

I watched her in apprehension, dressed in flannel pajamas I'd found underneath the red silky ones.

Straightening her back, she threw a pair of blue jeans and an olive colored tank top at me. Next came a clean bra, underwear, and a pair of socks that nearly hit me in the head. Once she was finished flinging fabric, she stood at the foot of my bed with her arms crossed.

"Well?" she prompted.

I rolled out of bed and got dressed quickly, not wanting her to throw something more substantial than socks at me.

When I was finished she looked me up and down, then said, "You know where the bathroom is. You'll find a toothbrush and whatever else you might need. I'll be waiting in the kitchen."

With that, she was gone, leaving me to fret over just what the "job" might be by myself. I peeked out into the hall to verify that the coast was clear, then hurried into the bathroom where I promptly locked the door behind me.

I debated my options. Escaping at night hadn't worked out too well for me, nor had running blind with no idea where I was going. I'd be better off going along with things until I could figure out where the exit was.

My decision made, I scanned the expansive countertop until my eyes landed on the basket where Sophie had retrieved the soap the night before. In it was a toothbrush still in its packaging, a brand new tube of toothpaste, lotion, and deodorant. I was in a B&B from hell.

I brushed my teeth and put on deodorant, then stared in the mirror. Deep bags had formed under my eyes, marring my skin. I felt vaguely unreal, like I wasn't truly there. I didn't want to leave the bathroom, to face Sophie and the others, but eventually I had to admit to myself that I couldn't just stay in there forever. I needed to plan my escape.

I sighed, knowing I needed to be honest with myself. I was grudgingly beginning to not just think about escape, but of learning everything these people might know about me. The Vaettir had verified what I had always somehow known about Matthew. That experience had kept me chaste and alone for fear of it ever happening with someone else. Maybe there was some way to control when it happened. If I could control it, I would be free to live an actual life. That was, of course, if I could not only learn control, but then escape my captors in one piece. The latter was seeming less and less likely.

Finally, I took a deep breath and went out into the hall, heading straight for the kitchen, memorizing every turn in the hall, and every shut doorway. Did more of the Vaettir live behind the doors? Or were there just more bloody rooms with dismembered body parts . . .

I picked up my pace, soon entering the kitchen. Sophie was waiting as promised, but so were Alaric and James. Sophie and Alaric were both dressed in all black again. It would have almost been cliché if it didn't look so good on their tall frames. They were also both sipping on coffee, while James had tea. I couldn't tell what kind it was, but the little green leaflet hanging from the string hinted at herbal tea first thing in the morning. I liked him less and less.

I moved to stand by Sophie, who handed me a mug of

already poured coffee. The division between the coffee drinkers and the non was highly apparent.

I eyed James nervously and he eyed me right back, sipping his tea with a secretive smile. The smile made me more uncomfortable than a thousand angry glares ever could. His golden hair was still damp enough from his shower to leave small dark stains around the collar of his charcoal gray shirt. The dark color of the shirt made the icy color of his eyes even more pronounced.

I suddenly felt nervous enough to throw up, and had to take a sip of coffee to keep it down. As the liquid was sliding down my throat I considered the possibility it was drugged since I hadn't seen it being poured. I choked on it, lowering the mug as hot coffee sloshed over my fingers.

James smiled a little wider.

A woman I hadn't met yet came walking into the kitchen. She was shorter than me, around 5'4", and had dark hair cropped closely to her head. She turned large, honey colored eyes to me, gave me a look of dismissal, then turned her eyes to James.

"Estus wants her now," she announced, as if I was no longer even there.

James winked at me. "Looks like breakfast will have to wait."

I simply stared at him in response. I wouldn't have been able to keep any food down regardless. I looked to Sophie to lead the way, but she only shrugged apologetically at me and nodded toward James.

When I still didn't move, James took hold of my arm and pulled me forward. I managed to set the coffee mug back by the industrial-sized pots before more of it could spill, though I was still craving more of it despite my fears.

Alaric watched us quietly as I was pulled away, having not said a word since I'd arrived. He seemed somewhat . . . sad?

I turned away as I was pulled out into the hall. The nameless, short-haired woman went ahead of James and I, then disappeared around the next turn. I looked over my shoulder for one final glance at Alaric and Sophie, but they had turned to speak quietly to each other, and didn't see me.

Turning forward, I tugged my arm out of James' grip and continued walking on my own. He gestured each time we were to turn down a new hall, and I went along willingly, wanting to avoid being hoisted over his shoulder again. Judging by the path we took, I began to suspect that we were going to the room where I'd been attacked by the hand. Call it intuition, but I had a feeling that was a room James frequented. My feeling of dread increased as we approached the door, but we ended up going past it and into the room immediately after it.

This new room was cleaner than the one I'd visited, but just barely. This room also had a full man, and not just a hand. The man hung limply from a set of manacles hammered into the wall. His chest was bare except for a decoration of deep cuts and bruises across his tanned skin. Blood had soaked into his blue jeans, staining the fabric.

I glanced to the side and jumped, realizing the short-haired woman was standing against the wall, just inside the door.

I turned my shocked gaze back to the manacled man as

he looked up from under sweat-matted hair. At first the look was distant as if he didn't truly *see* us, then his eyes focused on me.

"No," he breathed, his gaze filled with horror. He struggled against his manacles, clanking the chains against the stone wall. As his head thrashed back and forth, I realized he was missing an ear. All that was left in its place was a bloody hole.

"No," he pleaded more firmly, his gaze now aimed toward the other side of the room. "Please. I told you I had no choice."

It was only then that I noticed Estus standing in the corner, looking dispassionately at the man. He was still in the loose, blue outfit he'd worn during our meeting. The clothing made him look like some sort of monk, but the tortured man begging him for his life kind of ruined the picture.

I began backing out of the room, but James grabbed my arm and held it, tight enough to bruise. The short-haired woman stood silently on my other side. She didn't speak, but it was obvious by her expression that she wasn't enjoying the show any more than I was.

"Please," the man pleaded, looking at me now. "Please don't do this."

I looked away from the fear in the man's eyes. The fact that I was the source of that fear, and not the people who had tortured him, hurt my heart, even though I couldn't quite understand it. I could feel what had been done to him just as I could often feel the wounds of others, and I could taste his fear like cloying perfume on the back of my tongue.

James dragged me forward, and the fear and pain increased. By the time I stood directly in front of the man, his emotions were almost unbearable. In addition to his fear, I felt sadness and loss. He loved someone, and now knew that he would never see her again. I closed my eyes and shook my head over and over, trying to diffuse the emotions before they overcame me.

"What is she doing?" the short-haired woman asked. "Why isn't she finishing this?"

"It will come with time," Estus explained. "Her nature will take over. This is what she was born for."

I heard someone saying, "No, no, no," over and over again, and realized that it was me. His pain was too much. Something within me ached to release it, just like I'd done with Matthew. I *wanted* to reach out to him.

The man sobbed, and I could feel his defeat.

I forced my eyes open, the rest of my body frozen in fear.

"Just do it!" the man broke down and shouted, flinging spittle in my face.

His pain was palpable. I thought that if I could reach out and touch it, I could ease that pain. I *wanted* to reach out and touch it. It pulsed in front of me. I had taken several steps toward him without even realizing it. I began to reach out a hand. No. If I touched him, he would die.

James pushed me forward so that the man's face was only inches from mine. The man could have tried to kick me or head-butt me, but he didn't. I felt his bitterness. He had given up.

"Please," the man whispered right against my face. "Please just let it be over before my body gives out. I know

I'm not getting out of here alive, and I don't want to be stuck in a corpse like all the others."

"Stuck in a corpse?" I questioned distantly.

"If we kill him and you do not release him," Estus said from across the room. "A part of his spirit will remain in his body, forever."

It was just like what Sophie had said, but the gravity of it only hit me just then. His body wouldn't just be animated like a zombie. Part of his soul would be trapped for eternity. What would happen to the rest of his soul if it was missing a part? I felt sick. I wasn't even sure if I believed in souls.

I met the tortured man's pained gaze. His eyes were a light brown with flecks of green in them. He obviously believed what Estus said. His eyes pleaded with me to act.

I reached a trembling hand toward him, cradling his face. I knew what to do even though it had never been taught to me. Images flashed through my mind of a woman, and I almost pulled away. I felt his love for her, and his sorrow in knowing he would never see her again. I did my best to take that sorrow away. I held the man's gaze as the light faded from his eyes. His energy soaked into me in a warm rush as it left him.

"Thank you," he whispered with his last breath.

I lowered my hand, then turned back to the room, awestricken. I noticed a figure in the doorway. Alaric stood framed in the light of the brighter hallway, watching me calmly.

He offered me a solemn smile and said, "Not always a gift, but not always a curse either."

I wanted to run out of the room, but seemed incapable of moving my feet. I had just killed a man, and didn't even know what his crime had been. I had felt his emotions to the very end.

"What did he do?" I asked to no one in particular.

"He fought for the wrong side," Estus answered apathetically.

I glared at him, anger bubbling up inside of me. I felt giddy with the man's residual energy, and I could still taste his bitterness on the back of my tongue. It spurred my rage on. His memories clung to me, chastising me for what I'd done, even though he'd asked me to do it.

I walked toward Estus, pointing an accusatory finger. "You took him away from someone who loved him!" The dead man's loss felt like my own. I thought of the woman who'd survived him, and how I'd felt when Matthew died. "What did *she* do to deserve this?"

Estus held his ground and stared back at me, daring me to act.

"How could you possibly know that?" James asked from behind me.

I spun on him. "I felt it!" I cried. "I *saw* her. She was the last thing he thought of. His greatest concern was the idea of never seeing her again."

"Interesting," Estus commented. "An empath and an executioner. I do not envy you, my child."

I turned back to the old man. I said very slowly, emphasizing each word, "I *will not* be doing *that* again."

"This is war, Madeline," he replied. "We all do what we must."

"What war?" I spat gesturing back to the corpse on the wall. "I don't see any battles happening! All I see is torture."

Tears were running steadily down my face, and I

couldn't seem to stop them. The man's last emotion was just too much for me to digest. The images of the one he loved were already fading from my mind, but the emotion was as fresh as ever.

"Not all war is battle and bloodshed," Estus replied, finally letting a hint of his own emotion show through. "And I will not let my people be slaughtered because of one squeamish executioner."

"What do I even have to do with it!" I shouted. "I'm not part of this!" I knew I was bordering on hysteria, but I just couldn't stop myself.

Estus walked forward. "Without an executioner," he said very carefully. "We do not truly die. Would you leave us all to that fate?"

"This can't be my responsibility alone," I sobbed. "There must be another way."

Estus sneered, making me wonder if the kindly old man act had ever even existed. "We could have chopped that man up and put him in ten different boxes, and still some part of him would have lived. He would no longer have thought or spoken, but the life force would have remained."

A horrifying realization dawned on me. "Is that what you did to the last executioner?" I asked. "Is the rest of him still alive in a box somewhere."

"It is a fate befitting his crimes," James said from beside me. I hadn't noticed how close he was standing to me until just then.

I took a step away from him. "Take me to him," I demanded.

Estus smiled. "So, you would kill another?"

"You owe me for *this*," I gestured wildly to the dead man. "Now take me to him."

Estus simply nodded and walked toward the door. I followed him, but everyone else stayed put. Alaric stepped out of the doorway as we walked by to give us space. I followed Estus out into the hall, then into the room where I'd found the hand.

"I see you have already met with part of him," Estus commented as he kicked the dead hand aside.

He walked to the wall with the cages and felt across the stones. A brush of his fingertips revealed a handle I hadn't seen before. Estus gripped the handle and pulled, causing the stone to come out of the wall like a drawer.

I didn't want to look into the drawer. I knew it would be something horrific and bloody, but I also knew that the life, or soul, or whatever you wanted to call it, was still trapped inside this man's dismembered corpse. It wasn't right.

Estus stepped away from the drawer to make room for me. Before I could think better of it, I walked forward, avoiding blood puddles as I went, and looked down into the box. Inside was a human heart. It didn't beat, yet blood seeped steadily out of the severed ventricles. The box wasn't sealed at the edges, and the blood dripped through the cracks onto the floor. I felt rage and betrayal radiating from the heart, and somehow knew that it could sense my presence.

"The heart is the key," Estus informed me. "Release the heart and the soul is free."

Not thinking about what I was doing, I reached down and stroked a finger across the heart. I should have been horrified, but I was more intrigued by the heart than anything else. The muscle that composed the thing felt thick and alive. I willed the life out of the heart, but nothing happened.

"It's not working," I whispered to myself.

"Do what you did in the other room," Estus advised as if I'd been talking to him. "Do not will the life away. Take its pain."

Feeling like I was in a trance, I reached out again and felt the soul's hatred and pain. Yet the emotion that outweighed everything was betrayal. If this man was a traitor, it was not by choice. He was killed by the ones he considered kin. I took a shaky breath. This time, instead of willing the life away, I focused on taking the heart's pain, and taking away the feeling of betrayal.

The heart gave a final shudder, then collapsed in on itself. More blood leaked out as the heart deflated and then was still.

Estus shut the drawer and dismissed me with a wave of his hand like he was tired. After a mostly sleepless night and no food, I should have been exhausted, yet I was filled with energy. Electric currents ran through me to collect in my fingertips, which felt heavy like they were filled with too much blood.

I left the macabre room to find Alaric waiting for me in the hall. He looked at my expression carefully, attempting to judge my mood.

I did my best not to cry, but something must have shown in my face, because he wrapped me tightly in his arms. I didn't know him well enough to receive that sort of comfort from him, but I didn't know where else I was going to get it, so I returned the hug. A sob racked my entire body, releasing some of the emotions I'd absorbed from the dead man and the executioner's heart. I clenched my eyes shut, and did my best to slow my breathing. We stayed that way until I had gathered myself, then Alaric gave me a final squeeze and pulled away.

"Let's get you some breakfast," he said softly.

I shook my head. "I don't think I could eat. I feel . . . strange."

Alaric placed his hand gently at the base of my spine and guided me forward. "Let us at least distance ourselves from these rooms."

I could tell by the tone of his voice that he was just as appalled by the torture rooms as I was. I felt oddly relieved at the sentiment.

We had only traveled a few steps when a screeching roar sounded in the hallway, grabbing both mine and Alaric's attention. I turned wide eyes up to him for an explanation.

"Get back to your room and lock the door," he ordered.

"Wha—" I began to ask, but he had already left me to run down the hall.

Estus, James, and the short-haired woman all ran by before I could even move. They all disappeared around the next bend, and suddenly I was alone.

I glanced around. It was the perfect opportunity to search for an exit, yet something kept my feet glued in place. I was horrified by what had happened to the man in the torture room, but I was even more horrified by my part in it. I had killed him, and part of me, just a tiny *dark* part, had liked it. Could I really return to the normal world without learning more about my terrifying *gift*? Without learning how to stop it?

I stood frozen in the hallway until I heard the sounds of distant fighting as the others reached whatever the original sound had been. My mind snapping into the present, I started to run in the opposite direction that they had gone, but stopped beside the room where I'd taken the life of the first man.

His body was still hanging against the wall, limp and lifeless. How could I return to my safe little house, when I could accidentally take someone's life with a touch, just like I'd done to the poor man hanging on the wall?

I wrapped my arms tightly around my stomach, feeling ill. The people down here were monsters, but maybe, just maybe, I was a monster too.

5

I stood outside the torture room, questioning my own sanity. These people had just made me kill a man. I couldn't stay, not even to gain knowledge of my curse. With the sound of fighting in the distance, I turned and ran the other direction. I had nearly reached the end of the hall when I heard a blood-curdling scream. Goosebumps erupted across my arms. My feet slowed. Somehow I knew the scream had come from Sophie. Even through the stone walls and space between us, I could sense her pain. Sophie, who had helped me through my childhood, and who I was pretty sure was *still* trying to help me. Well *shit*.

I turned and ran the other way. I kept going toward the sound of fighting, cursing my choice even as I made it. I had no idea how I might be able to help, but I couldn't just think about myself and ignore what was happening. I knew deep down that Sophie was a good person. When I'd been in foster care, she was someone I'd actually almost considered a friend. She'd made me feel safe in a world of chaos and pain.

I went around several bends in the hallway and came to the room that I thought of as the throne room, already slick with blood and littered with corpses. I skidded to a halt, then ducked out of view, clutching at my stomach as the pain in the room hit me. Leaning against the wall, I resisted the urge to vomit, instead taking deep breaths to distance myself from the violence. Mixed emotions sang through me —fear, pain, bloodlust . . . I shivered, forcing them to the back of my mind. I'd come to find Sophie.

Releasing my stomach, I gripped the wall and peered around the corner. The intruders, at least I guessed they were the intruders as I watched James slash a throat with a long knife, were dressed in ornate leather armor. The pieces of armor reminded me of insect carapaces, and didn't fit at all with the modern day attire everyone else wore.

The dog/lizard creature I'd encountered in the hall the previous night darted across the room to crash into one of the intruders, and suddenly the shrieking roar made sense. The creature must have been the one to find them. I assumed the intruders were other Vaettir, though everyone in the room appeared human.

I stared in utter shock, unable to move. I corrected my original thought that the attackers looked *human*. Only half of the violence was done with weapons. The other half was done with what I could only refer to as magic. A woman swiped her hand in front of a man's face, and his skin erupted with blood like he'd just been sliced by invisible claws. One of the male intruders pushed another man to the ground and climbed on top of him, pinning down his arms. The man struggled to free himself, but slowly his body iced over until he could no longer fight. I looked away from the frozen man as his icy pain shot through me. Corpses fell quickly, painting those who still fought with their blood.

Finally, my gaze fell upon someone lying in a heap in the far corner. *Sophie.* I couldn't tell if she was breathing. I leaned a little more into the hall, then realized my folly. One of the intruders quickly spotted me, then started in my direction. His movements reminded me of a snake as he wove through the chaos with his eyes focused solely on me. As he got closer, a long, serpent-like tongue flicked out of his thin lips. I froze in place as the man drew near. I glanced around for help while backing toward the hall, but everyone else was engaged in the fighting.

My mind screamed at me to run, yet fear held my limbs rigid. I could hardly even breathe. The intruder came to stand in front of me, but only remained there for a moment. In the blink of an eye a black shape barreled into him and sent him flying back into the thick of the fighting.

I didn't take the time to see who had saved me, and instead hurried to hide in one of the nearby rooms. I should have closed the door, locked it, and piled every piece of furniture in front of it, but I couldn't make myself do it. I still needed to reach Sophie.

I peeked back out into the fighting, which had suddenly all but halted as the last of the intruders were put down. The furry lizard tore into the stomach of one of the dead, splitting the armor like the delicate petals of a flower. The creature found the intruder's spinal cord and tore a chunk of it free. Its dog-like mouth munched happily, flinging dribbles of blood down its face.

I forced my gaze away and found Alaric, crouched over the now-dead snake-man. Blood and thicker bits ran down Alaric's face and onto his chest. As I watched, he spat a thick glob of flesh onto the ground. He'd bitten the man's throat out. Alaric looked over at me with eyes that had turned entirely feline, and I was horrified to see the teeth to match.

He turned away from me, assessing the dead and injured. James still lived, though his arm hung limply at his side, and Estus seemed completely unharmed. Sophie was still lying in the corner.

I stepped out into the room, feeling almost as if I was floating. I didn't feel anything else, and wondered vaguely if I was going into shock again. Alaric cast one final glance at me with a face that had returned to normal, then hurried to his sister's side.

I started to step around a body, then made the mistake of looking down. It was the short-haired woman that had led James and I to the torture room, now lying completely still. The side of her head was a bloody mess, the skull damaged. Though she was dead, the pain of the blow hit me like an icepick, doubling me over.

Without a thought I reached down and smoothed a hand across her face, releasing her life force. I was instantly horrified that I'd done so without thinking. What if she could have been healed? If these people could maintain their lives when they were chopped up in little boxes, maybe her head would have healed.

I withdrew my trembling hand and straightened, then

noticed Alaric seated against the wall, rocking his sister back and forth like a child. Her body hung limp and unresponsive in his arms.

James came to stand beside me, though his gaze was all for Alaric and Sophie. "You need to release the dead," he instructed. "Do it now."

"But what if they can heal?" I asked, unable to take my eyes off Alaric and Sophie.

"They will not heal," he said darkly. "Once we are dead, we do not come back, but we do not fully die either. It is our curse." His voice shook as he said it, surprising me.

I closed my eyes. There was so much pain in the room that it was almost unbearable. The dead man nearest to me was the one that the lizard creature had half-eaten. As I looked at him, the pain in my stomach made me ill. It was only a small fraction of what he'd felt. My feet swayed beneath me, and I fell to the ground, curling up to shut out the pain. My cheek was in a pool of blood and I didn't care. I just wanted the pain to go away.

I forced my hand out toward the man and took his pain. As soon as he was truly dead, my own pain eased, but there was still plenty more to go around. I forced myself to my feet. If I released them, the pain would go away.

I went around the room and took the lives of the fallen one by one. Each life that I took seemed to stick to me, leaving a little bit of itself behind. As I went, the collective pain lessened each time, just as the remnants of life force remaining with me grew.

Finally, all that was left was Sophie. I could tell that her throat had been cut without even looking at her, since it was the only physical pain left that was strong enough to ring though me. The wound was not nearly as brutal as some of the others, but her pain hurt my heart more than anything else.

I could feel Alaric's pain too, like a heavy weight on my soul, mourning the loss of his sister. The others left living felt pain, but nothing like what was coursing through Alaric's veins at that moment.

I came to stand before him, and he looked up at me with human eyes, his tears streaming down to mingle with the blood staining his mouth. I crouched across from him and looked down at Sophie. Her blood was beginning to congeal in her loose, black hair. She looked pale and very dead.

I reached my hand out slowly, looking at Alaric rather than Sophie. His loss was almost unbearable. I touched her shoulder, meaning to soothe her pain, but instead tried to soothe his.

I focused on taking that sense of loss away while I stroked my hand down Sophie's arm. I felt the clinging remnants of the lives I'd taken leave me while I touched her. At first they slowly dripped off like water, then they leapt from me in a mighty torrent. I looked down, surprised at the sensation, to find that Sophie's eyes had opened. She took a deep, rasping breath and sat up in her brother's lap. The wound in her throat was gone.

Alaric looked stunned for a second, then laughed, hugging his sister to him. Pushing his arms away, she scooted out of his lap, seeming rather cranky, so he turned to me instead. Before I could react he pulled me against him and kissed me. I could taste the blood and salty tears on his mouth, but underneath that I could taste him. I was too shocked and overwhelmed to pull away.

After a few seconds I managed to gather my wits about me and pushed my hands against his chest. I fell back from my crouch, landing on my butt. I took a shuddering breath, then looked into Alaric's eyes, sparkling with joy. He laughed, and I found myself laughing with him, or maybe I was crying, but there was still a smile on my face. We laughed together, covered in blood, and surrounded by corpses, and I knew with a surety that my life would never be the same again. Maybe I didn't want it to be.

No one said a word as Alaric helped me to my feet, then guided me around the carnage. Those who watched looked at me with wide eyes, like they didn't quite know what I was. Alaric continued to smile, paying them no heed.

I met Estus' gaze just before we left the room, and he gave me a small nod of recognition. I didn't like the nod. I wanted as little of Estus' attention as possible, and I had a feeling that I'd just gained his undivided interest.

I shivered as we walked out of sight. "Why do I get the feeling that I did something highly out of the ordinary?" I whispered, my voice sounding distant to my own ears.

Alaric raised an eyebrow at me. "Should we not be amazed that you just brought my sister back to life?"

Hearing him say it out loud made things seem all too real. I was just coming to terms with the idea that I could kill with a touch, but people killed things all the time. Bringing someone back to life was a little more difficult to digest.

"I mean, can't you all do things like that?" I asked, knowing it sounded dumb.

"No, Madeline," he said softly as we neared my room. "I've never even seen an executioner perform such a feat."

"Maybe it was just a fluke?" I suggested. "Like some sort of miracle?"

"Miracles don't happen in our world," he stated as the smile finally slipped from his face.

I shook my head and looked down at the ground. "They don't happen in my world either."

We reached my room and kept walking, though since I really didn't want to be left in my room alone, I didn't question it.

"Why didn't you run?" he asked suddenly as we took another turn in the hall. He still huddled close to me, as if he was afraid I might run now.

"What?" I asked, startled because my mind had began to wander.

"Why didn't you run when we were attacked?" he clarified. "We were all distracted. You'd think it would have been the perfect opportunity to escape."

I shrugged, feeling suddenly uncomfortable, and maybe a little embarrassed. "I thought about it."

"But?" he prompted when I didn't elaborate further.

I sighed. "I don't know how I can go back, knowing what I know now. Knowing that I could kill someone with a touch. If there's some way to control it . . . " I trailed off.

"You would regret not staying to find out," he finished for me, "because if you could control it, you could have a normal life."

I nodded as we stopped beside a closed door that looked like all the others. Alaric opened it to reveal a bedroom more modern than mine. The bed was simple, with a deep blue bedspread and several fluffy pillows. The rest of the room was taken up by a large dresser, a desk, and a bookshelf, the contents of which had overflowed onto the floor.

As we walked inside, I crouched down and picked up one of the books, but it was in a different language. I put the book back down quickly as I noticed the blood on my hands. It was probably on my face as well. I felt sick and dizzy enough that I had to sit on the edge of the bed before I lost my feet. Alaric shut and locked the door, then came to sit beside me.

"Is this your room?" I asked numbly.

"I figured you might want some space," he explained. "If I had put you in your own room, you would have been bombarded with visitors and questions soon enough."

I took a shaky breath. "Good thinking, but don't even think about trying anything now that we're alone."

I scooted back on the bed and pulled my knees up to my chest, my thoughts a jumbled mess. I was beginning to question everything I knew, and everything I thought I was. Alaric sat beside me, watching me quietly and not complaining that I was getting blood on his bed.

I met his eyes as the gears slowly clicked in my mind. I was no longer a part of my old world, and I wasn't sure I really ever had been. I knew with a surety that I was going to remain among the Vaettir long enough to learn more about my gifts.

"I won't kill anyone," I stated. "If someone is already dead, I will—" I hesitated, "*release* them, but that's it. I won't release someone's life while they're still alive."

Alaric nodded. "I will state your terms to Estus," he hesitated. "And Madeline?"

I blinked up at him, still shocked I was actually considering staying.

"Stay away from James."

I tilted my head. "Why?"

He reached out a hand as if to touch me, then stopped, letting it fall to his lap. "You may be our clan's new executioner, but James is the *questioner*."

I didn't have to ask what that meant. I'd seen that man's battered and burned body.

I let out a shaky breath, then nodded. I would learn what I needed to learn, and find an escape route in the process for when I was ready to leave. While I was there, I would grant the Vaettir their final deaths. Anything to be able to live a normal life again, eventually.

Did that make me a monster, or did it just make me practical? Who knew.

6

"It's time," Alaric announced, way too chipper first thing in the morning. He was dressed in gray sweats and no shirt. I would have felt more comfortable if he was wearing a shirt, but I suspected if I said anything, he would only tease me. His long black hair was tied back in a low ponytail, making his dark eyes stand out.

"I don't think this is a good idea," I began.

I had been waiting in my room, already dressed in my own workout attire of black yoga pants and a matching sports bra, but now my nerves were kicking in. The previous day's events had left me reeling, and now Alaric wanted to teach me to fight. If there was another battle, I wouldn't be utterly defenseless.

"Of course it is," he replied happily. He took my hand and pulled me up off the bed.

We hesitated for a moment as he held my hand, and I almost thought that he might kiss me again, but then he simply led me out of the room. I trailed behind him with a nervous flutter in my heart, which I instinctively squashed. Alaric was part of a dark world that I didn't belong in, not really. Once I learned to control my *gifts* ...

My thoughts lingered on our kiss. The sight of him spitting out the gob of flesh that had once been a man's windpipe was a bit unsettling. More unsettling still, was the fact that I had almost enjoyed the bloody kiss afterward.

James came into view down the hall, clearly waiting for us. I found the golden-haired, handsome man way more unsettling than anything else put together, and that was really saying something.

"What are you doing here?" I asked, sincerely hoping that he wasn't planning on joining us.

James laughed. "Like I would miss the little mouse receiving her first lesson in combat."

"Just be careful that she doesn't turn her training on you," Alaric commented. "You might have all of the torture techniques, but Maddy has the follow through."

James looked down at me smugly. "I'm okay with follow through. Be sure you save some of it for this evening."

My heart stuttered to a stop. "This evening?"

"We have another traitor in our midst," he said ominously.

My stomach lurched at the news. Part of me had been hoping the man I'd killed had been a fluke, and that perhaps I wouldn't be needed again unless we were attacked. Even if the body was actually dead before I arrived, the final pain and emotions lingered. I'd felt every excruciating moment of the last man's death. His pleading eyes haunted me more deeply than anything I'd seen during the battle.

James watched as the emotions played across my face, then seemingly satisfied, turned and walked away. Alaric glared after him.

I tapped his shoulder, but he kept glaring, deep in thought. I could feel the edges of his anger dancing across my skin like tiny flames.

Remembering his warning from the previous night, I muttered, "I'm sensing some sort of rivalry there."

Alaric still didn't look at me. "No rivalry," he corrected, "just moderate hatred. I told you what he does."

I nodded as we began walking again. "Yes, but how can hatred be moderate? Hatred is the extreme."

He finally glanced over at me, his expression unreadable. "That's not true. There are many different types of hatred. I doubt you've felt most of them."

I stopped walking and put my hands on my hips. "What the hell is that supposed to mean?"

Alaric turned to me, still looking angry, then his expression softened. "I meant it in a good way. You don't seem to be the grudge-holding type. Hatred gets you nowhere, but even knowing that, it's difficult to avoid."

"That's not true," I growled. "I've felt plenty of hatred in my life."

He shook his head. "You're an empath, Madeline. While I can't begin to understand how that feels, I know you can sense the deeper emotions of others. How can you hate, when at least a part of you can understand where everyone else is coming from?"

I frowned, annoyed that he was right. I hated, sure, but I also understood. I couldn't hate blindly. I was yet to meet someone purely evil, purely deserving of hate. Evil usually sprang from long-hidden pain.

"Well I can at least hold a grudge," I grumbled. "I'm still angry about being kidnapped. *That's* a grudge."

"Yes," he replied, "but you're also still here. You could have tried to flee when we were attacked, but you came back to help instead. You're angry and confused, but you don't hate us. You don't even hate Sophie, and that's . . . uncommon."

"I appreciate Sophie," I admitted. "She doesn't try to tell me pleasant lies. She never has."

Alaric looked surprised. "And I do?"

I started walking again. "I'm not sure yet, but you do pretend like nothing is wrong when your people are in the middle of a war."

"*Our* people," he corrected, catching up to me.

Our people. I still hadn't quite processed the fact that I was one of the Vaettir myself. To sound monumentally cliché, I'd always known I was different, but I never would have guessed I was a member of an ancient race populated with people and creatures that were quite literally the stuff of fairytales. Being a little empathic was one thing. Living in a magical domicile with people that killed each other for being *traitors* was quite another.

"Our people," I agreed slowly, "but you've distracted me. Why do you hate James? It can't just be his . . . occupation. I'm sensing something else."

"It doesn't matter," he replied. He stopped next to a door and held it open for me, gesturing for me to walk inside. "Just as long as you don't trust him."

"Well I don't really trust *anyone* here." I flicked my gaze up to him. "No offense."

A hurt look passed across Alaric's face, but he didn't comment. I considered telling him that I trusted him, maybe just a little, but it would have been a lie. I might not be a very hateful person, but I'm also not stupid. At least not stupid enough to trust someone that had participated in my kidnapping and subsequent imprisonment. He might have been nice and protective since then, and he may have cheered me up when no one else could, but it didn't cancel out the original act.

I walked through the doorway ahead of him to take in the room beyond. I had hoped that my combat lessons would take place outside, but I was apparently out of luck. The room we entered was large enough to be a banquet hall, and boasted numerous racks of weaponry, but not the open blue sky I'd been craving. Humans needed sunlight. The lack of it was depressing, and a bit maddening. Maybe that was the real reason the Vaettir were killing each other.

I walked around and perused the weapon racks, wondering if I'd be able to sneak one out of there. The floor of the room was covered in thick exercise mats that squished beneath my feet. It was a nice change from the hard stone floors of the rest of the compound.

"Isn't there an outdoor area to practice in?" I asked hopefully.

Alaric retrieved a blade the length of his forearm from one of the racks. "No part of the Salr is outside," he explained, moving the weapon from hand to hand, testing its weight.

"Well can't we just walk out the front door?" I asked.

Alaric laughed. "Have you seen any front doors since you've been here?"

"Well no—" I began.

"The Salr isn't fully aligned with the human world," he explained. "Do you remember how you got here?"

"I was *kidnapped*," I said hotly. "I told you already, I haven't forgotten that."

He had the grace to look abashed. "What I'm trying to say is that we have no front door," he explained, giving his weapon an experimental swing. "The Salr is a protective enclosure. A place cannot be a sanctuary if people can just walk right through the front door."

Watching the sharp edge of the blade, I took a step back. "But those Vaettir that attacked us found a way in."

He sighed. "They found the way that you came through. It has since been sealed."

Sealed? Did that mean there was no way out at all? "Are you telling me I never get to go outside again?" I gasped.

"You will," he answered. "When it's safe."

My shoulders relaxed, just a bit. "Do *you* get to go outside?" I pressed.

He spun the blade around in his hand like he knew what he was doing. "I'm beginning to think that you're just trying to distract me from giving you your lesson." He walked toward me with the blade.

My heart thudded in my chest. "Last question, I promise," I blurted.

"Yes Madeline, I get to go outside." He swung the blade at me. I was so shocked that I almost didn't move, but at the last moment instinct kicked in and I dropped to the ground to avoid the blade's razor sharp edge.

I looked up at him wide-eyed. "You could have killed me!"

He tsked at me as he spun the blade casually in one hand. "I was only testing your reflexes. I wouldn't have hit you."

I believed him, because if he'd wanted to hit me, I'd be dead, reflexes or no, but I wasn't about to stand so he could swing at me again. "I don't think it's fair for me to have to spar with someone that outweighs me by at least fifty pounds, especially when that someone has a blade and I don't."

"Would you rather learn from Sophie?" he asked, swinging the blade aside to offer me a hand up.

I thought of Alaric's hot-tempered sister teaching me to fight. The size was the only less intimidating thing about her. If I had to choose, I'd say I'd end up with many more bruises if Sophie were my teacher.

I grabbed Alaric's hand and got to my feet. "Can we at least not start out right away with the sharp pointy objects?"

He laughed and dropped my hand, then went to put the blade back into the rack. I followed him with my eyes, and couldn't help but watch the smooth muscles work in his back as he walked away. I've always been a sucker for a nice back. I quickly averted my gaze as he turned around to face me, but his small smile let me know that I'd been caught.

He came to stand in front of me once again. I was relieved that he was empty handed this time, but my relief only lasted for a moment as he suddenly lunged for me. In the blink of an eye, I ended up on the ground for a second time that day. Alaric came down with me as I hit the mat, straddling my hips and pinning me to the floor.

He grabbed my wrists in one hand and held them against the mat above my head at an angle that was almost painful. I'd made the mistake of leaving my hair loose, and now it was pinned underneath me, making the position even more awkward.

I struggled against him, but it didn't do much good. "How is this helping me learn how to fight?" I huffed.

"The best way to learn is to do," he explained. "Now do your best to get me off of you."

"I already did," I replied hotly.

He still didn't move. "Try getting your legs underneath you," he advised.

I did as he instructed. Rather than doing it slowly and asking for approval, I got a firm planting then bucked my hips upward. When I had a little bit of room to work with, I flipped over onto my stomach. I managed to turn my wrists enough in his grip that I could somewhat comfortably bring my knees up under myself. With my new vantage point, I rolled him off me, then scuttled away out of arm's reach.

Alaric sat on the mat smiling at me. "See? Now what did you learn?"

I glared at him. "I learned that you're an ass."

He rose to a crouch then lunged for me again.

Despite my best efforts, I was on my back within a few seconds. This time he stretched his body over me, pinning me more fully.

His mouth was only inches from mine when he asked softly, "Now what would you do in this situation?"

I smirked, beginning to enjoy the game in spite of myself. "I would probably headbutt you. Or," I decided, "I could seduce my attacker into kissing me so I could bite out his tongue."

"Well I like the first part of that second option," he said, bringing his lips even closer to mine.

My pulse sped, sending shivers through my entire body.

"This isn't like any combat training I've ever seen," a woman's voice stated from the doorway.

I craned my neck to see an upside-down Sophie as she came to stand over us. I tried to wiggle out from underneath Alaric, but he wasn't budging.

"Sure it is," he argued, looking up at her. "I think any attacker coming after Maddy would definitely try to put her in just this position."

Sophie snorted. "*You* are such a lech."

Alaric finally rolled off me and helped me to my feet. "Well if you can manage to spar with her without being the least bit tempted, then be my guest."

I took a few steps back, not wanting to spar anymore with anyone. Sophie turned toward me with a mischievous grin. That grin was the only warning I had before she jumped me with much more force than her brother had used, though she only pinned me for a moment before letting me go.

Alaric side-stepped out of the way as I got to my feet and fled from Sophie, only to be knocked to the ground again.

"You can't just leave me here," I groaned, curling up on the mat so Sophie couldn't knock me down again.

"Just try the kissing maneuver!" he called out as he left the room.

With my cheek on the mat, I rolled my eyes, then stood to continue my lesson.

With Alaric gone, Sophie actually began to instruct me as she attacked me. Just as I'd guessed, she was a much more aggressive fighter than Alaric, and she was *fast*. She darted and dove around like a cat, which was an accurate description given her and her brother's . . . feline qualities.

It was nearly impossible to fend her off as she continued to tackle me over and over again, shouting out instructions on what I should be doing to avoid her. The only problem with her method was that since she was telling me what to do, she knew how to counter my movements before I made them. I eventually stopped listening to her instructions in an attempt to get one step ahead of her, but it didn't do me much good.

Finally, she knocked me down one too many times and I refused to get back up. My entire body ached like I'd been hit by a truck. I expected Sophie to try and force me back up, but instead she sat down beside me.

"You're developing feelings for my brother," she observed without warning. She didn't look like she just had an hour long workout. I probably looked like I'd been working out for a week straight.

I sat up. "No, I'm not." Sure, we had chemistry, but chemistry and *feelings* were two very different things.

"Well I'd advise against developing any," she replied bluntly. "Not for his sake, but for yours."

"What do you mean?" I pressed, suddenly very interested in the conversation.

"I like you," she said. "You're very sweet, and Alaric would only hurt you."

I crossed my legs so I could lean forward. "I can take care of myself."

These people obviously all just thought I was some mushy cream puff. I was really more of a muffin, or some other moderately firm baked good.

Sophie rolled her eyes. "I'm trying to be nice here," she chided. "Alaric's attention tends to shift quickly. I don't want to see you get all goo-goo-eyed just to have him shift his attention to someone else. Plus, the only reason he's drawn to you is because you are an entity of death."

I raised my eyebrows at her. "What the hell is that supposed to mean?"

"Really, Madeline," she sighed. "One would think you would have thought more deeply on your gifts. Yours is the power of death. Alaric and I are Bastet, we were born in her image."

"And?" I pressed, still not getting it.

"Bastet is a goddess of war," she explained. "War, and death. Alaric likes you because your energy resonates with him. It is why I feel a certain kinship with you as well. Like attracts like."

I thought about what she was saying, feeling a little sick at her explanation, but grateful for it as well. I was more drawn to Alaric than I'd ever been to a man, even though the rational side of me knew I shouldn't be. Still, it was hard to argue with the feeling of comfort I felt when I was around him. Maybe it was artificial, but I still *felt* it.

Sophie frowned, watching my thoughtful expression slump into disappointment. The feeling in my heart might have been hard to argue with, but that wouldn't stop me from trying.

"I hope I didn't burst your bubble," she apologized.

I shook my head. "I know better than to try living in a bubble."

"Good," she nodded to herself. "Very good."

Yeah, I knew better. The world was full of rusty needles just waiting to pop all of the shiny happy bubbles that came rolling along.

7

I wanted to ask Sophie more, but James entered the room. He didn't actually say anything, or even approach us, but his presence was enough to halt our conversation. He looked so harmless standing in the corner with his golden hair and country boy charm, until you got to his eyes. You could see the dark soul, or lack thereof, in those eyes.

Sophie glared at him. "You don't get her until this evening," she said coolly.

"I need her now," he said in a tone that made Sophie's iciness seem like mid-summer. "Maya isn't talking."

"That doesn't explain anything," Sophie snapped.

I could sense intense emotions from her. Something about this Maya person had her on edge.

James sighed. "I just need Madeline to *scare* her. No one is going to die . . . *yet*."

I raised my hand to join in the conversation. James and

Sophie both turned their attention to me, and I wished I'd just sat quiet.

"Um," I began, turning toward James, "no offense, but I'm guessing if *you* can't scare her, then I won't be of much help."

Sophie laughed bitterly, but James answered, "The final death is a greater threat than any damage I can do. If she sees you, she'll know we mean business." He didn't seem happy about the admission.

I glanced at my bare stomach, then back to him. "Can I at least change first?"

He scanned my attire. "Make it quick."

With a final long, somehow meaningful look at Sophie, James retreated from the room in a whirl of angry energy. That he didn't make any quips about my state of dress, or about Sophie and I "getting sweaty" together, made me think that this Maya woman had him seriously annoyed, but the look on Sophie's face told me there might be another reason.

She glared at the space where James had been, reminding me of Alaric earlier, except there were tears in her eyes.

"You both really hate him, don't you?" I asked.

"Both?" she questioned, turning her gaze to me as she quickly wiped the moisture off of her cheeks.

"You and Alaric," I amended. "Your brother wears a very similar look when James is around."

"Hate is a very complicated word. Mostly, I just don't trust him," she answered quietly.

"There seems to be a lot of that going around," I mumbled, "but I get the feeling there's something else."

She looked at me for several seconds, and for a moment I thought she might actually explain the raw pain in her eyes, then she shook her head and turned away.

"You should get dressed," she ordered curtly. "I have things to do."

With that, she stood and fled the room. I stared at the empty doorway, then stood. Whatever was eating at Sophie would have to wait. My issues were a bit more pressing.

I was supposed to go and threaten this woman with death. I'd never honestly threatened anyone before. It just didn't feel right, even though what I was threatening to do felt natural to me. Releasing pain was instinctual. Yet, growing up around humans and not knowing what I was had given me a different moral scope than what seemed common among the Vaettir.

I exited the room to find one of the Vaettir waiting to escort me. He was tall with black hair and large features. Giving him a wary glance, I headed back to my room to change, not looking forward to finding something else to wear. Almost everything Sophie had picked out for me was black, tight fitting, and expensive.

I reached my room, glanced once more at my escort, then shut the door behind me. I pawed through the dressers, searching for something appropriate to wear. The jeans I ended up with were a perfect black, not the faded gray that most black jeans turn to, and the long-sleeve shirt was a deep purple that almost managed to be as dark as the jeans.

After getting dressed I looked around for something else to delay my journey to the torture rooms, feeling ill at the remembered scent of blood, death, and burned flesh. I found myself wondering if the hand that had attacked me had been severed while the previous executioner was still alive.

Shaking my head, I tugged on a pair of low heeled boots and exited the room. My silent escort waited outside. I ignored him.

When I reached the chamber where I was expected, I paused to push my ear up against the thick wood, heedless of the man watching me. I could hear someone speaking quietly, but the door was too dense for me to make out the words.

I was leaning against the door with my ear pressed firmly to the wood when it suddenly swung inward. I stumbled into the room and nearly bit it on the stone floor.

Estus offered me a small smile that made the slight wrinkles decorating his face bunch up. His long gray hair was twisted into an intricate braid that trailed all the way to his ankles. He looked like a diminutive, jolly, Santa Claus, but I was quite sure he was the scariest thing I'd met in the Salr so far.

I steadied myself, wondering with a shiver if Estus had opened the door using the same power he'd used to glue me to my seat. There was a twinkle of laughter in his pale blue eyes that said *yes*.

James stood near his latest victim, watching me with interest. His hands were covered with fresh blood, and there were little spatters of it on his handsome face. The blood had come from the woman I'd come to intimidate, though she hardly seemed broken despite her wounds. The name Maya suited her. Her proud eyes and aura of calm made her seem like some sort of fallen goddess.

She was in plain white underwear that had been stained with sweat and blood. The fabric of her bra was also singed at the bottom corner, drawing my attention to the fact that her dark skin was covered in what looked like brands, though they had no specific shape to them. The smell of burnt flesh wafted off of her, making the room smell like an acrid campfire. I tried to breath shallowly through my mouth, but it was a mistake. Even when I returned to nose breathing, I couldn't get the taste of burnt flesh off the back of my tongue.

I looked down the length of Maya's muscled body to see that she was also missing a foot. The skin at the stump of her ankle had been cauterized. My stomach threatened to crawl out my throat. This woman had been undergoing torture for a while if James had gotten to the point of cutting her foot off, yet she still eyed me defiantly. I backed away. I couldn't be a part of this. This was *wrong*. I didn't care what this woman had done, no one deserved this.

My steps slowed as I noticed something else strange about Maya. I couldn't sense her pain. Not that I minded the lack of pain, but if she was feeling it, I should have felt it.

"I don't feel it," I said to myself, not expecting anyone to reply.

"Yes," Estus replied. "We've come to the conclusion that she does not feel it either."

I looked down at the woman's missing foot again, then to James' frustrated face. It must have really chaffed his hide to have his intimidation tactics nullified.

"Madeline is our executioner," Estus announced to Maya.

Rather than showing fear, she only laughed. "She doesn't look like an executioner," she observed. "Just look at those innocent blue eyes."

James grabbed my arm and pushed me forward.

I struggled against him, not wanting to get closer.

He yanked my arm hard enough that I thought my shoulder might dislocate and I stumbled forward, unable to tear my gaze away from Maya.

She looked down at me. Her black, curly hair had been ripped out of her scalp on one side, leaving a bald patch to slowly ooze blood as she watched me with a predatory expression. "Have they told you what they want to know from me?" she asked as if the men were no longer in the room. "Do you know what all of this is for? Why you're here?"

James squeezed my arm tightly, obviously wanting me to lie.

"No," I answered honestly.

Maya smiled. "Not an obedient pet after all. Maybe you'll be smart enough to run away before you end up like their last executioner."

"What do they want to know from you?" I asked.

James began to jerk me away, but Estus simply shook his head. James let his hand fall from my arm, though he obviously didn't like it.

"Come closer," Maya said with a smile. "I'll tell you a secret."

I obeyed hesitantly. I didn't feel her pain as I stepped closer, but she could still try and injure me once I was within reach. Yet, something in her face made me trust her. I stepped close enough for her to reach her mouth down toward my ear. The manacles she was shackled to held her slightly off the ground, but I was tall enough and she was short enough that we ended up face to face.

She leaned in a little closer until her lips touched my ear and I had to force myself to not jerk away. "Find me tonight," she whispered.

The sound was barely audible to my own hearing, so I knew James and Estus would not be able to hear. "Listen to what I have to say," she continued, "and I'll tell you every-thing that your *friends* want to know. It will be up to you whether or not they get to know it. Not everything is as it seems in this place."

I stepped away and tried to hide my shaking hands. I balled them in fists at my sides and turned toward Estus.

"She's not afraid of me," I announced. "I can't help you."

Estus nodded, as if he'd known all along, which made me suspicious. Why summon me at all, and why allow Maya to whisper in my ear?

"We will call you once she has spoken," he assured.

"But—" James began, but Estus cut him off with another look.

I backed out of the room while I still could. The woman kept her gaze focused on me as an eerie smile crept across her face. I made it out into the hallway and shut the door behind me with a thud. I almost leaned against it, but then remembered how Estus had made me fall inside the first time, and walked a few steps down the hallway to where my escort awaited.

Ignoring him, I leaned against the stone wall and tried to think. Maya's words echoed in my mind, *not everything is as it seems*. I didn't know how things seemed. I didn't know anything at all, so how could she tell me any different? After growing up in foster care, then living a life of solitude, being confused and alone was nothing new, but it was time for me to stop accepting my fate. I needed answers if I ever hoped to take back my life.

The odd thing was, for the first time in a very long time, I felt like I somewhat belonged. Alaric and Sophie were stronger than normal humans. I wouldn't accidentally kill them with a single touch. But what if this was all some scheme to use me, and then discard me when I was no longer needed? Would I end up just as alone as before, with no real answers?

I had seen a few other Vaettir within the Salr, but most gave me a wide berth. At first I thought they knew about my gifts, and it made them nervous, but maybe they didn't fear me. Maybe they just feared I'd find them out. I had to know for sure. Even if I couldn't escape, I at least would not be led like a lamb to slaughter. If this so-called traitor could give me answers, then I would be an idiot to not listen.

"Are you okay?" someone asked from behind my turned shoulder, opposite my escort.

I jumped, as I hadn't heard anyone else approach. I turned and had to look down to see the woman who had spoken. She couldn't have been more than 5'2", with wispy white-blonde hair and large lavender colored eyes. She wore a spider-silk thin dress that matched the bluish-purple of her eyes.

"I'm fine," I answered instinctively.

She offered me an innocent, closed-lip smile. The bones of her face were so delicate that I thought they might crumble with the movement. She flicked her gaze to my escort, then shooed him away.

To my surprise, he obeyed.

I turned to fully face the woman. "I'm surprised you're actually speaking to me."

"Most are afraid of you," the woman said, still smiling.

I licked my dry lips. "Why are they afraid?"

"Your gifts can be dangerous for those who are weak of will," she explained. "I am not weak of will, and so I am not afraid. My name is Sivi." She held out a dainty, bony hand to me.

I took her hand, careful to not squeeze. Her fingers seemed longer than they should have been, and wrapped around my hand with more force than I expected.

"Maddy," I replied, wondering what this tiny creature wanted from me.

"I know," she said cheerfully. "I'd actually like to bestow a favor upon you." She looked around the hallway as if someone could have snuck up on us. "But not here," she added.

She switched her grip from my hand to my wrist and pulled me down the hall toward an area of the Salr that I was yet to visit.

"Where are we going?" I asked as she rushed me along.

Instead of answering, she stopped suddenly to open a door and pull me inside. The room we entered smelled of moss and mildew, which probably had something to do with the giant pond that took up most of the floor. Vines and lichen grew out across the stones surrounding the reflective water, framing the surface in shades of green.

Sivi pulled me toward the pool, then dropped down

into a seated position, forcing me to follow suit. She curled her dainty legs demurely and smiled at me, then ran her hand across the surface of the water while her other still gripped my wrist. As the water rippled, the vines began to shiver. She swirled the water more and the vines came to life and grew outward, searching for something to grab onto.

I flashed back onto the experience of being pulled by vines into the ground, and tried to pull my wrist out of Sivi's grasp as my pulse sped. Her grip was like iron, and she didn't seem to struggle at all as I continued my attempt to pull away.

"Look," she said pointing down to the water.

I looked down automatically. Before, the reflection had been of the stone ceiling, but now I could see trees and blue sky, as if I was in a lake looking up through the water, rather than looking down.

"What is that?" I asked nervously. One of the vines crept across my jean-clad leg, then continued its blind search.

She grinned, exposing pointy little teeth. "It's a way out. For *you*."

"Alaric said the only way out was sealed," I argued, though I couldn't really argue with the scene in front of me.

"Sealed from people coming in," she countered. "Not from going out."

"Why are you showing this to me?" I asked, suddenly suspicious. "What do you want?"

A thousand thoughts competed in my mind. I could escape and go back to my little house. No one would even know that I'd been gone. I would never have to see Estus or

James again . . . until they found me and stole me away once more. Maybe I could go into hiding.

"I am only trying to offer you your freedom." She continued to smile, though now the smile seemed slightly strained. Her lavender eyes flicked to the door then back to my face.

"Why?" I pressed, more to delay making a decision than anything else.

She sighed and let the smile slip from her face with another glance at the door. "Are you always this ungrateful?"

I shook my head. "Not ungrateful. Suspicious."

"Yet you are not suspicious of Alaric and Sophie," she snapped. "Where does your suspicion draw the line?"

"I'm suspicious of everyone," I answered honestly. "It's nothing to get offended over."

"Do you not want to go home?" she asked, seeming increasingly impatient.

"I do," I answered. "But—"

"But what?" she interrupted. "Either you do or you do not."

"It's not that simple," I interjected. "It's not safe for me to be around humans. I want to know who—*what* I am. I *need* to know."

Sivi cocked her head like she didn't understand me. "You've spent your entire life in that world—"

"And it was fine at first," I finished for her. "I didn't kill anything, not until . . . " I hesitated, not wanting to say Ray or Matthew's names out loud. "Eventually I had to be alone," I finished. "If I go back, I'll have to be alone again. I can never touch anyone again."

"And you hope Alaric can help you with this, alone-ness?" she questioned. "The Vaettir can die just like humans. There is no safeguard against being alone."

"Well he's a lot less likely to die," I replied sullenly, "and I won't be the one to kill him."

Sivi laughed. "How many have died since you came to us? Will you be able to give Alaric the true death when his time comes? You would not need to do so for a human."

I shook my head. "At least if I did bring him death, it wouldn't be an accident."

"If you went home," she began anew, ignoring my argument, "you could learn to control your gift. Now that you know what you are, you can learn to interact with humans. There is no need for you to hide in the dark any longer."

I shifted uncomfortably, gazing down at the pool. I *wanted* to go, but why did Sivi want me gone so badly, and why hadn't she offered this before?

"I'll think about it," I said, hoping to escape her until I could think things through. She seemed to want me to jump in the pool right that moment, but I wanted to talk to Maya first. If she could tell me what I needed to know, I might be able to leave.

Sivi eyed me as if she didn't fully believe me. "See that you do," she answered finally. "I may not want to help you so much tomorrow, and the next day I may want to help you even less."

She stood, then crossed her arms and turned her back, dismissing me. I stood slowly and backed away from the pool, watching the vines warily. I backed all the way into the hall until I could no longer see Sivi's tiny form, then turned and ran back to my room. Panting and feeling shaken, I shut and locked the door behind me.

I was becoming increasingly unsure of who my true enemies were. It was funny how small things could change your perspective. In a few short hours I'd had cryptic warnings, I'd threatened a footless woman, and I was offered an escape through a vine-filled, magical pool. You know, small things.

8

I stayed in my room for the rest of the day. No one bothered me. Laying with my back on the bed, staring up at the stupid canopy, I began to grow anxious about finding Maya. I highly doubted the escort awaiting outside my door would let me go wandering. I'd have to figure out some way to escape him, but first, food. My stomach growled painfully.

I sat up. I knew the way to the kitchen, but really didn't want to leave the solace of my room. What if another attack occurred, or what if James wanted me to torment someone else?

My stomach growled again.

Giving in, I stood and made my way to the door. I opened it a crack to peer outside, then stifled a groan. Sure enough, the same dark-haired man from before waited for me. I opened the door the rest of the way then walked out, dutifully ignoring him as I turned toward the kitchen.

Shouts echoed down the hall as we neared. I almost

turned around and fled, but I recognized Sophie's voice. Curious, I peeked into the kitchen.

Though I didn't make a peep, Sophie froze and turned a tight-lipped frown my way. James wore a similar expression that said, *Oh great, here comes naïve little Madeline, she really has some nerve interrupting us.* I tried to back out of the kitchen, but Sophie stormed past me before I had the chance.

Well, now that I'd butted in, I might as well eat. I ended up slurping on a bowl of mushroom soup while James watched me like I was a new toy that he might purchase . . . though really he was more of the shoplifting type.

"Maya was even more smug after she saw you," he said suddenly.

"Maya?" I questioned, startled that he had finally spoken.

"The woman you met earlier," he explained.

"Oooh," I said, though I already knew who he was talking about. "The woman whose foot you cut off."

"I had to make her talk," he replied as if it justified his actions. "And I don't see that you're in any place to judge."

"I've never tortured anyone," I replied coolly, though my thoughts echoed, *Murderer.*

I could take people's lives and still be morally righteous . . . at least that's what I kept telling myself.

He laughed. "Give it time. You'll be one of us soon enough."

I laughed right back, though mine sounded tired. "So you're saying everyone else here is an egotistical sadist like you?"

"The sadist part at least," he said with a smirk. "Even Alaric."

"I'll be the judge of that," I mumbled, not meeting his eerie white-blue eyes.

He laughed again. "We all have the same nature Madeline. Some just hide it better than others."

When I didn't reply, he watched me in silence. As it became obvious that I was now ignoring him completely, he stood and left the kitchen. I let out a breath at his departure.

I stood and threw the rest of my soup into the large kitchen sink. I didn't bother washing it. Let my silent watcher wash it if it bothered him. Crossing my arms, I met his gaze. How to escape him . . . I drummed my fingers on my arm.

"I imagine you can find your way back to your room on your own?" he asked.

I raised my eyebrows at him. He was actually just going to leave me alone? Staring at him blankly, I nodded.

He turned and left the room.

Debating my options, I wiped sweaty palms on my jeans. Something was fishy. Why escort me around all day, only to leave me to my own devices now? Was it a test? Maybe Estus wanted to see if I still planned to escape. Maybe Sivi's offer had been just a ruse too.

It probably didn't matter. My priority in that moment was Maya. She seemed the most likely person to help me make sense of everything.

The hall was empty as I left the kitchen. I strode confidently forward so that if I encountered anyone, they wouldn't think I was up to anything. When in doubt, act like you know what you're doing and people usually won't question you.

I went around a corner and let out my breath as I saw that the next hall was empty as well. Despite the fact that I was lucking out, I still felt a little bit wary that I wasn't seeing anyone. While I'd interacted with few of the Salr's inhabitants, I'd seen others during the battle. I knew they were around . . . somewhere.

By the time I came to stand in front of the door to the torture room I felt queasy and cold. I took a deep breath and grabbed the knob. If someone was inside with Maya, I'd simply lie and say I was checking to see if they needed me. It was my *job* to be there, kind of, so they couldn't really question me.

I strode into the room, fighting an overwhelming sense of revulsion, to find it empty. Completely empty. The manacles that once held Maya hung loose against the wall. Panic shot through me. What if James had killed her? Would he have mentioned it? I shook my head. That wasn't right. He wouldn't kill her until he got what he wanted from her. Plus, if she was dead I would have been called to release her spirit . . . unless Estus decided to put her heart in a box.

I searched the room for any evidence as to where she might have gone, but came up empty. Other than the blood staining the floor and walls, there was nothing to see. She could have been moved anywhere within the Salr, and I hadn't even explored the entire compound to know how big it was, or how long I'd have to search.

I walked back into the hall, feeling numb and not knowing what to do next. At a loss, I crouched down and leaned against the wall of the hallway. Then I saw the blood. There wasn't a lot of it, but there was a definite trail of blood drips leading farther down the hall.

I stood and followed the trail through a few twists and turns of the hall, all the way to a gargantuan stairway leading downward. The stones composing each step were larger than my torso and had to weigh a few hundred pounds a piece. Speckles of blood decorated the large stones all the way down into the darkness. I paused to consider my options, then hurried down the huge steps awkwardly, straining my knees as I went.

The steps ended in a narrow corridor. Where the rest of the Salr was lit by means that weren't visible to me, this corridor was lit by torchlight, and the torches only went so far. Roughly twenty feet in front of me, the darkness was complete. I grabbed one of the torches off of the wall to light my way and almost dropped it, not expecting it to be as heavy as it was.

As I got a better grip on the torch, I began to tremble with anticipation and fear, but still I forced myself forward. I crept along, crouching every so often to hold the torch near the floor to make sure the occasional spot of blood could still be seen. The corridor began branching off into hallways on either side of me, but the blood drops led straight forward.

There was absolutely no light as I went deeper, and I began to fear that my torch wouldn't last long enough to lead me back out again. I almost turned back, but then I felt the pain. Not Maya's pain, as I couldn't feel anything from her, but old pain from others that had been kept down there. This place had to be where prisoners were kept when they weren't being tortured. The walls practically ached with despair. I blocked the pain out as much as possible and hurried onward, now sure that I was going in the right direction.

Just as I was thinking that I was lucky to only be going straight, as I probably wouldn't get lost, the blood drips took a turn to the right. I veered off and trotted down the new corridor, hoping desperately that I wouldn't have to make any more turns.

The corridor ended with a final turn that led to a cell. Behind the thick metal bars was Maya, who had to quickly cover her eyes at the sudden light. She looked even worse than when I'd left her. One of the hands that she held in front of her face was missing several fingers, and the left side of her face was a mass of swollen bruises.

"I'm surprised you came this far," she rasped. "You didn't happen to bring any water, did you?"

"I'm sorry," I said quickly. "I didn't think-"

She waved me off then lowered her hands as her eyes adjusted to the light. "I suppose I should just be glad that you aren't stupid enough to believe everything you're told."

"Why are you being tortured?" I asked, itching to escape the dark corridors as soon as possible.

"Estus wants a certain object," she said, "and I may or may not know where it is."

That lined up with what Alaric had said. Estus and someone named Aislin were searching for something, and they wanted it bad enough to kill. "What is it?"

"If he had this object," she went on, ignoring my question, "the war would be over, and Estus would be the sole man in charge."

"Is that the worst possible outcome?" I replied. "At least no one else would have to die."

Maya let out a laugh that ended in a hacking cough, making me wonder if James had damaged one of her lungs. "Tired of your job already?" she asked.

I frowned. "Can you blame me? I didn't ask to come here. I was *kidnapped*. The second I learn what I need to know, I'm getting out of here."

She shook her head. "Don't say that to anyone else. You'd be a fool to believe that the last executioner was actually a traitor."

My mouth went dry. "How do you know about that? Do you know why he was killed?"

She shrugged. With her injuries, the shrug should have hurt, but she didn't so much as cringe. "Word gets around, but we're getting sidetracked. You implied that letting Estus win might be a good thing, but you're not looking at the big picture. Of course having one leader cuts back on the bloodshed, but what if that leader is a tyrant?"

I shook my head. I didn't really care who led the Vaettir. "I don't know . . . " I trailed off.

"No, you don't," she replied. "The Vaettir withdrew from the human world for a reason. They called us wights, the undead, and burned many of us alive."

"So you—" I hesitated, "*We're* hiding so that they don't kill us?"

She laughed again. "Things are different now. The Vaettir have grown in number, and they've become twisted things. The humans were right to be afraid. We are not what we were meant to be."

"And what was that?" I prodded, desperately hoping

that what we were meant to be wasn't the terrible picture of the Vaettir that I was forming in my mind.

"We're nature spirits," she explained. "We're supposed to be guardians of the land, created in the image of the old gods. In all of history we've never gathered together like this. The Salr is supposed to be a sanctuary, not a home, and definitely not a fortress."

I let out a sigh of relief as some tension within me eased. Perhaps my nature wasn't what I'd been led to believe after all. The idea of some part of me being like James made me ill, but maybe James was the exception and not the rule.

"What does Estus want?" I asked, filing the information away. "Please, they could find me down here soon," I added to hurry her along.

She shook her head. "Estus wants a lot of things, and none of them should you give him."

I looked over my shoulder again. "Why shouldn't I give anything to him? How can I trust you? Everyone seems to have a different idea of who I should trust. Sivi said—"

"*Sivi?*" Maya interrupted

"She tried to get me to leave," I explained. "She showed me a way out of here." I bit my lip, feeling stupid for not taking it. "Maybe if I could get you out of this cell we could—"

Maya shook her head. "There is no getting me out of this cell, and I wouldn't trust Sivi either. If you want an example of what the Vaettir are supposed to be, she's it."

"But isn't that a good thing?" I asked. "Just a moment ago you were telling me that we've been twisted away from what we're supposed to be."

"She *is* what we're supposed to be. She has maintained her connection to the land, even down here." At my blank stare, she went on, "Let me guess, this alleged way out had something to do with water?"

"How did you know?"

My torchlight was beginning to seem dim, but I wasn't sure if the fire was actually getting lower, or if my fear was playing tricks on me.

"She can travel through water," Maya explained, "because it is the element that she's associated with. She is descended from Coventina, goddess of wells and springs. She has maintained that connection, making her less interested in power plays, and more interested in restoring the natural order. Sivi is very, very old, and hasn't changed much over the centuries."

"Centuries?" I laughed. "You're kidding right?"

Maya shook her head. "Her age isn't important. All you need to know is what Sivi would *do* if she could convince the other Vaettir to follow her."

"The natural order doesn't sound bad—"

Maya cut me off with a sharp motion of her mutilated hand. "The *natural* order would mean far fewer humans and Vaettir alike. She would try to knock the world back to medieval times."

My eyes widened as my mouth formed an "oh" of understanding.

Maya glanced around as if she could hear something that I couldn't. "You're running out of time," she said quickly. "Listen to me very carefully. Sivi is only looking out for her own well-being. The Vaettir by nature are solitary creatures, and she holds to that. Your escape would benefit her and only her. If you stay, you can work against both Estus and Sivi. Trust me, it's the right thing to do. Now get out of here."

I shook my head. "Wait, there's so much more I need to ask you."

"No waiting," Maya snapped. "The answer that Estus is looking for is right under his nose, only he can't find it. Only someone with a connection to death can find it. *You* can find it. Just like Sivi is a guardian of water, you're a guardian of death. Estus recently figured that part out, and that's why he suddenly wants you. That's the real reason you were brought here. I think that the last executioner failed, and so he was killed. Soon it's going to be your turn, and I'm going to help you do it."

"Why?" I asked, growing more confused by the second.

"This thing would grant Estus complete control. He'll make you find it eventually, even without my help. At least if you find it without him present, before he even knows that you're looking for it, you can decide what to do with it."

I could hear footsteps in one of the nearby corridors. "How do I find it?" I whispered.

"Estus believes that only someone with a connection to death can see the object he seeks, but he's not quite right. In truth, only the dead know where it is, so someone with a connection is needed to ask them."

The footsteps had stopped, but Maya looked around again as if she could hear something that I couldn't. "There is a place within the Salr where the worst of traitors are kept," she continued, barely loud enough for me to hear. "Their punishment is to have their souls trapped forever within their dead bodies. Only the dead can show you the way to this object, so you need to go and ask them."

"How am I supposed to ask them questions?" I rasped. "They're dead!"

The footsteps sounded again, closer this time. We both froze at the sound as someone came to stand in the cross-section where I'd turned to find Maya. I blocked as much of my torch with my body as I could and waited. Whoever it was paused for a moment, then walked on.

"Just go and try," Maya whispered, barely loud enough for me to hear at all. "It's the only chance we have. Now *go*."

I waited until the footsteps got far enough down the hallway that I could no longer hear them, gave a final apologetic look to Maya, then ran to the end of the corridor. I looked both ways down the hall, but my torch didn't cast enough light to see more than a few feet. Things seemed to echo more harshly down the main corridor, so despite my instinct telling me to run, I crept back slowly the way I'd come.

I knew I was almost back to the stairs, though I couldn't yet see them, when I heard the footsteps again. Whoever it was had walked farther down the corridor, and now they were walking back at a much faster pace than I was going. I paused for a moment, not sure what I should do, then decided echoes be damned, I needed to run.

I took off at full speed and could tell instantly that whoever was behind me had heard. The heavy footsteps quickened just as the stairs became visible ahead of me. I dropped my torch onto the ground as I used my hands to speed my progress up the giant steps.

I reached the top and ran at full speed down the hall,

refusing to look back. I ran that way until I reached my bedroom, unsure if whoever was down there had actually seen me.

Not wanting to be caught in the hallway huffing and puffing, I let myself quickly into my bedroom, only to be caught huffing and puffing by the two people sitting on my bed waiting for me.

"Where were you?" Sophie asked. "We looked everywhere."

She and her brother sat at the foot of my bed with matching worried looks in their dark eyes. The symmetry was continued by the fact that they both wore their long, dark hair loose, and they were both dressed up in black evening wear. They looked like the poster children for *Goths R Us*.

"I was just walking around," I lied, stepping away from the door. I did my best to keep my voice even in spite my racing pulse. "I can't just stay shut up in this room all of the time."

"If you were just walking around the halls we would have found you," Alaric countered. "We looked everywhere."

"I don't see why it's any of your business, either way," I snapped, feeling like my nerves were about to snap as well. I thought about what Maya had said. Part of me wanted to trust Alaric and Sophie, to believe they were different from James and Estus, but how could I? They might not have tortured Maya, but they hadn't tried to stop it either.

"Something has happened," Sophie said calmly, though it was an obvious effort for her to not snap back at me. "Estus called a gathering this evening to tell us."

So that's why the halls had been so empty. "And I was the only one not invited?" I asked, though in truth I didn't mind the exclusion.

"You tell her," Sophie growled at Alaric. As she stood, she turned to me and said, "You really shouldn't be so impossible when people are trying to help you." With that she left the room, slamming the door behind her.

Alaric stood as well, but it was to walk closer to me. I wrapped my arms around myself, suddenly feeling more nervous than I had been while running back to my room.

Alaric circled me. "Estus has asked us to search for something. It's very important."

I turned with Alaric, trying to keep him in my sights. "And what something is that?" Could this be the same something Maya had mentioned? The something that might get me killed?

"It's a small charm," he replied, stopping just a step away from me.

Did he know I'd gone to see Maya? I was finding it hard to breathe, but managed to glare at him regardless.

"Estus asked me to speak with you," he went on. "He believes that you of all people can find the thing he's looking for. He'd like your help."

My breath caught in my throat. *Bingo*. It was just like Maya had said. "Why me?" I pressed, curious to see if he would give me the same explanation that Maya had.

He shrugged. "Trust me, I'd like to know myself, but Estus is Doyen of this clan, and when he asks, I obey." There was a tightness around his eyes as he said the latter, making me think that he wasn't entirely happy with the arrangement.

I took a step back, effectively putting myself out of reach. "And what is so special about this charm?"

"That is not for us to know," he replied. His brow creased a little further.

I crossed my arms, the hint of a smug smile creeping across my face. "You don't like taking orders, do you?"

He smiled bitterly. "No one likes taking orders, but these are the times we live in. We are not free to choose our own paths as we once were. Estus says find this elusive thing," he waved his hand in the air, "and I must find it. He says use Madeline, and I must use you."

"Well I'm not going to help find it until I know what it is," I replied, "and I don't like the idea of being *used*. I'm not a tool."

Alaric took a step toward me. "This is how things work, Maddy. It's how they have always worked. We are all just tools in our little microcosm. To be here means safety, but it comes with a price."

How they had *always* worked? Not according to Maya.

I stared up into his dark eyes. "Don't lie to me," I said evenly.

He smiled again, but this time it was sad. "It seems you've been gathering information on your own, haven't you? It's how things work *now*," he corrected, "and how they have worked for a very long time."

I stood rigid, refusing to move. "Define *a very long time.*"

"For as long as I've been around," he answered cryptically. "I've known no other way." He grabbed a lock of my hair and began twirling it around his finger, distracting me. "And I don't see it changing any time soon."

"And how long have you been around?" I asked softly.

Maya had claimed that Sivi was several centuries old. I wouldn't have believed her, except I'd seen that magical pool. I'd sensed Sivi's power. That meant that any of the Vaettir might be older than I'd originally guessed.

He leaned in close and whispered, "Long enough."

I opened my mouth to ask more, but he delicately pushed his hand under my chin to shut my jaw. He then used that hand to guide my face up toward him. Suddenly the situation took on a whole new tone.

I blinked up at him, wondering why the hell I wasn't stepping out of reach.

He leaned down and kissed me.

I froze as too many emotions collided inside of me, then pulled away. "Is what Sophie said true?" I gasped.

Heat danced in his eyes. "What did she say?"

I licked my lips. "She said I'm drawn to you because death goes with war, and vice versa."

He shrugged. "Does it matter?"

I took a shaky breath. My hands rested on his arms, and I didn't quite remember placing them there. I needed to do what Maya had told me. I needed to figure out Estus' evil plan. I needed to—

Alaric leaned down and kissed me again.

My hands slid up under his shirt to feel the smooth skin underneath. I had so many unanswered questions, but I couldn't seem to pull myself away long enough to ask them.

Washed away on a wave of anxiety and fear, my palms smoothed over his chest nearly up to his throat. As the kiss intensified, I drew my hands down to either side to caress the bones of his ribcage. Suddenly I slid my hands back out of his shirt and pulled away from the kiss, surprised and embarrassed by my actions.

His fingers caressed my waist, pulling me closer. He kissed a gentle line down my throat, leaving a pleasant, burning sensation in the wake of his kisses.

My thoughts raced, telling me that I shouldn't trust Alaric to touch me, but my doubts were outweighed by the fact that it had been a very long time since I'd been touched. I hadn't been with a man since Matthew. *Matthew.* The sobering thought stopped me, and I was able to pull away completely.

Alaric let his hands fall from me, and I regretted the loss as soon as it happened. His dark eyes observed me curiously. In his eyes I saw the remnants of the heat from just a moment before, but also some sort of sadness that I didn't understand. The sudden loss of heat left me with only cold memories.

"I killed the last man I was with," I blurted out, as if it explained everything.

Alaric nodded and raised his hands as if to touch me again. "You will not be able to kill me in the same way."

I stepped back. "Someone told me that I could still harm the weak of will, even if they are Vaettir."

Alaric smirked, letting his hands fall back to his sides. "And you believe me weak of will?" he asked playfully.

I crossed my arms. "I don't know you well enough to judge," I answered. "Which is another reason why we shouldn't be doing this."

Alaric smiled and raised his hands in an *I give up* gesture. "In that case, I will have to leave the next move to you."

Despite his statement, he stepped close to me so that his chest touched my crossed arms.

"I'm tired," I lied, stepping away from his touch once again, and feeling instant regret just as I had before. Hadn't I been wanting him to kiss me again? I chastised myself for ever giving in to *that* fantasy. I barely knew him. He had been kind and protective, if a bit of a pain in the ass, but he was also one of the people holding me captive for reasons I couldn't fully comprehend.

Alaric's shoulders slumped with a heavy sigh. As he turned to leave, he opened his mouth like he might say something, then closed it. He left the room without another word.

I regretted everything as soon as the door was shut. I regretted the kiss, and I regretted ending it. Being alone with only memories was a terrible thing, even if it was the thing I was most used to.

If I'd known what I was sooner, Matthew wouldn't have died. If I'd been raised among the Vaettir from the start, maybe I'd have had some idea on how to live my life. Maybe I'd actually know how to have a normal romance with someone, not supernatural chemistry with my kidnapper. My *ifs* were more torturous than James or any of the other Vaettir could ever be.

Even as I half-wished that Alaric would come back, Maya's words still rung clearly in my mind. I didn't fully trust her, but she'd given me enough information that I didn't trust anyone else either.

I couldn't trust Alaric with my heart, just as I couldn't place my fate in Estus' hands. There was nothing I could do about Alaric, so I'd focus on Estus. If I could find what he was looking for without him or Alaric knowing, then I would have the upper hand. It was time to stop being such a willing prisoner.

I crawled into bed fully clothed, though I knew a nap was unlikely. The large, four-poster bed and burgundy bedspread still felt foreign to me, and I found myself missing my little house and my small bed. I'd only been gone a few days. Sadly, it wasn't likely that anyone back home had even noticed I was missing.

I sighed and thought about the kiss, trying to convince myself that I was right to end it. Yet, even with my rational thoughts laid before me, my conclusion marked me as a total idiot.

9

I awoke, surprised that I'd managed to fall asleep in the first place. I was even more surprised by the fact that someone was crouched over me in my bed. At first I thought maybe Alaric had returned, but the form was far too small to be him.

Tensing, I lunged at them, but they dove easily out of the way. My room slowly lit up of its own volition, as if noticing I was awake, and I blinked against the sudden brightness.

Sivi crouched beside me, eyeing me like a pale bird of prey. The light shining through the curtain of her hair made me realize that it wasn't actually white, it was translucent. Her strands of hair looked like impossibly thin lengths of fishing line. Her violet eyes stood out in the paleness of her skin like amethysts.

"Time is up little one," she whispered. "Will you stay or go?"

I crept backward out of bed, putting some distance between us. "I haven't decided yet."

"Well I might not want to help you later," she taunted from her perch on my bed.

"And why do you want to help me now?" I asked. "Why is it so important to have me out of the way?"

"You ungrateful little wretch," she hissed. "I've seen countless executioners die one after another over the centuries. What makes you think you're so special?"

"Well," I replied, "you sneaking into my bedroom for a private conversation was my first hint. Like you said, you've seen countless executioners die. Why would you finally choose to help one?"

She smiled ruefully. "If only you knew the creatures you've chosen to align yourself with. In time you'll wish you had taken my offer, but it will be too late."

I crossed my arms. "I haven't aligned myself with anyone."

She crawled off my bed with snake-like grace and went for the door. With her hand on the knob, she stopped to regard me one last time. "It will be interesting to see which one of them kills you, once they get what they want. I'd like to see your face in that final moment of betrayal."

The slamming of the door made me jump. I blearily wondered what time it was. Did the lighting of the room mean I'd slept half a day and an entire night? It sure felt like it. I stretched my arms, then hurried to my dresser to get a change of clothes, shaking my head at the surreal encounter. Estus expected me to look for the charm today. I'd look for it alright, though I hadn't yet decided what I'd do when I found it. Maybe it was a like a weapon of mass destruction and suddenly I'd have power over them all. Fat chance, but I still wanted to find it.

Estus obviously knew that someone of my talents was needed to find it, but he didn't know as much as Maya. If he did, he would have sent me straight to the corpses of the alleged traitors to *ask* them. No, he thought I'd somehow be able to *see* the charm where others could not. That thinking was probably what had gotten the last executioner killed.

I picked out an outfit to suit my mood: black jeans, black silk top, and low-heeled black boots that went up to my knees. That morning I was beyond caring how black looked with my coloring. Clothes in hand, I ventured out into the hallway toward the bathroom. If I was lucky, no one would get in my way. Unfortunately, I'm rarely lucky.

"I don't get it," James said, reaching an arm in front of me to block my way.

He had been waiting in the hall, still in his clothes from the previous day, letting me in on the fact that he was yet to get any sleep.

I tried to push past his arm, but didn't have much success. "Don't get what?" I huffed, giving up on forcing my way through.

"I don't get why Estus is so fixated on you, and I *really* don't get why Sivi was in your bedroom a few minutes ago. I think I might have to dedicate a bit more time to finding out what's so special about you."

I took a step back, but he instantly closed the gap. Instead of stepping back again, I met his eyes with a glare. "Is that a threat?"

He smiled, and I was reminded of the first time I'd met

him, and how he'd callously thrown me over his shoulder. Sophie had improved since that night. James had not.

"Is my attention such a frightening thing?" he asked playfully, putting an arm on either side of me, trapping me against the wall.

"Yes," I answered honestly. I dropped down out of the circle of his arms and wiggled my way to freedom.

I backed away from him toward the bathroom, even though I knew he wouldn't let me go so easily. He matched me step for step until he had me pressed against the bathroom door instead of the wall. This time he put his whole body into trapping me. He wasn't as tall as Alaric, and being tall myself, I could nearly meet his eyes directly. I tried to remain calm in front of his icy blue eyes, but it was hard to keep my panic down below the surface.

"Get away from her," a voice said from behind James.

I peeked around James' broad shoulders to see Alaric walking down the hallway toward us. He'd changed into clothes more casual than what he'd worn the night before, but the entire outfit was still black. James looked back at him, giving me enough room to maneuver. Repeating to myself, *I'm not a cream puff, I'm not a cream puff,* I took a deep breath and drove my knee up into his groin.

His pain echoed through me, but it was worth it. He grunted in surprise and backed up a step, hunching over. Giving in to the fact that I was being a bit of a masochist, I punched him with every ounce of oomph I could muster. The punch didn't rock him back much, but the satisfying crunch I felt told me that maybe I'd broken, or at least damaged, his nose. The sudden pain in my own nose verified it.

I resisted the urge to rub my sore nose. "I'm not your plaything," I said calmly as blood dribbled down his shocked face. "Don't ever touch me again."

I opened the bathroom door and went inside. Before I shut it, I noticed Alaric as he held up a hand in front of his face to hide his silent laughter. His eyes met mine for a brief moment, and then I was blissfully alone in the bathroom. I quickly turned the lock before I took a second to catch my breath.

I would have preferred a quick shower, but I only had the tub. Still, not willing to forgo bathing, I turned on the water and stripped down. I half-expected James to start pounding on the door, but the hall outside was silent.

I washed myself quickly and got dressed, the whole time nervous that someone would interrupt me. Fully clothed, I was finally able to breathe easy as I went for the door.

Alaric stood leaning against the wall directly outside of the bathroom. "About time," he said. "You're not the only one who takes baths around here."

I glared at him, suddenly embarrassed about our kiss the night before. "I'm sure there are other bathrooms."

He grinned as he walked in and I walked out. "But I like this one."

"You were protecting me," I observed, turning back to look at him. "I think I proved that I can handle James on my own."

"You proved that you're dumb enough to piss off the world's biggest bully," he countered, "and I was not protecting you. I was simply waiting to take a bath.

Speaking of, if you for some reason didn't get clean enough, you're welcome to hop back in with me."

I smiled sweetly. "Let me get my coffee, then I'll get back to you with a clever retort."

I turned to saunter away, trying very hard to keep my mind off of the idea of Alaric in the bathtub. It didn't work, and I simply had to be grateful for the fact that no one could see me blush as I walked away.

I could feel him watching me, and it took a great deal of self control to not simply scurry to the nearest hallway where I'd be out of sight. Finally, I heard the bathroom door shut. I picked up my pace, eager to get on with my search. It seemed I'd been relinquished of having a constant escort, and I didn't want to press my luck, but I really needed some food first, and I *definitely* needed coffee.

I had a well-thought idea of where I'd look first, but there were drawbacks to my plan. I stood a good chance of running into James again if I went to the room where Estus had shown me the executioner's still-beating heart, and he probably wasn't happy about his nose. Still, since there'd been one heart hidden there, there were probably more. I wasn't sure about somehow *communicating* with them, but I'd sensed the magic and pain in that first heart. I had to try.

I reached the kitchen to find it already occupied by three people I'd never seen before, sitting at the counter together drinking coffee. I gritted my teeth, hoping none of them would note the fact that I was alone. They watched me silently as I poured myself a cup from the massive coffee maker. I turned my back to them, but could feel their eyes following me as I went to the large pantry to find something to eat. I couldn't help feeling that they were just waiting for me to slip up like the last executioner, but maybe that was just my own fear speaking.

When I emerged from the pantry, bread in hand, they all averted their eyes and pretended like I wasn't even there. I put the bread into the toaster and slammed the handle down loudly, looking pointedly at their turned backs.

The oldest looking of the three cleared his throat, and they all stood to file silently out of the kitchen. I shook my head as I waited for the toast to pop up, and just took it dry when it did, wanting to get out of the kitchen before anyone else showed up. Something strange was going on beyond my comprehension. I was being allowed to wander around alone. No one wanted to talk to me except James and Alaric. It felt like a trap.

I left the kitchen, wondering what would happen if I hurried across the Salr to Sivi's magical pool. I could escape and go home . . . but it wouldn't be that simple. Even if I managed to hide, I could never touch another human again, and I'd always wonder if I could have learned enough within the Salr to lead a normal life.

I scarfed down my toast as I walked through the hall, nearly choking on the half-burnt dryness, then scalding my throat when I tried to wash it down with the too-hot, black coffee. By the time I reached the first interrogation room my toast was gone and I only had a half-cup of cooling coffee left to sooth my scratched and burned throat.

I took a deep breath, then reached for the doorknob and turned it. I had nothing but horrifying memories of the room, and wasn't looking forward to seeing the blood-stained walls once again, but I wanted to ensure no one was next door to catch me searching for more hearts.

I pushed on the heavy door and it opened slowly with a long creak, just like a door out of a horror movie.

"What are you doing?" someone asked from behind me.

I nearly jumped out of my skin, then turned to see that Sophie had come around the corner, catching me as I took my first step into the room. I'd been so intent on not getting caught by someone inside the room, that I'd completely ignored the possibility of someone walking behind me.

Cursing my hesitation at going into the bloody room in the first place, I turned to fully face her. "I think I lost . . . a bracelet," I lied.

"I picked out all of your clothing," she snapped, instantly sensing my mistruth. "You haven't had a bracelet since you came to us. Now tell me what you're doing."

I crossed my arms and stayed in the doorway. "Why do you care?" I asked sharply, irritated that she was snapping at me for no good reason.

She crossed her arms across her chest to mirror me, completely ignoring my anger. "Why has Sivi been lurking around your room?"

"I don't know what you're talking about," I lied, stepping out of the room to close the door.

I wasn't going to be able to look with Sophie around, so there was no reason to stay in the morbid room any longer than I had to.

Sophie narrowed her eyes at me for a moment, then brushed past me to walk down the hall. For a fleeting second I thought I was off the hook, but then she snapped, "Come with me," as she continued walking.

With a heavy sigh, I followed her tall, black-clad form down so many twists and turns in the hall that I wasn't sure if I'd be able to remember my way back. Finally, she went into a room and left the door open behind her for me to follow.

The room inside was done in deep grays and other neutrals, though rather than being bland, it was cozy. There was a large bed similar to the four-poster in my room, only it didn't have a canopy. I personally liked the canopy-less bed better. The canopy made me feel like a little girl playing princess.

As soon as I stepped inside, Sophie turned on me. She pointed. "Shut the door."

Sophie's fangs were peeking out, and her nervous energy elicited goosebumps on my arms. I debated trying to bolt before she unleashed her temper on me again, but so far Sophie had seemed to genuinely be on my side, and I didn't want to lose that just yet. I shut the door.

Now that we were alone, I expected Sophie to start talking, but instead she just stood with her arms crossed, shifting her weight from foot to foot. It was only then that I noticed that she was still in her clothes from the previous day, just like James.

She bit her lip as if she wanted to say something, but was holding back. "I don't know who else to talk to," she finally blurted out, her anger melting away like a poorly done disguise.

I took a few steps closer to her. My instinct was to reach out and comfort her, but I wasn't sure if Sophie and I were on that level. She solved the problem for me by sitting on her bed and patting the spot beside her with her palm. I sat next to her and waited for her to speak, shivering as her nervous energy touched me.

She turned her worried, dark eyes to me. "Swear to me that you'll keep your mouth shut. It could be very bad for me if anyone knew what I was thinking, and I could make it very bad for you as well."

I frowned. "You know, threatening people really isn't the best way to get them to help you."

She waved me off. "I know, I know. I'm sorry. I had a long night."

When she didn't say anything else, I cleared my throat.

Sophie glanced at me, then took a deep, shaky breath. "I need to help Maya escape." She instantly looked horrified that she'd said what she was thinking out loud.

I tilted my head, wondering if she was tricking me. Sensing she was genuine, I replied, "I think that's a wonderful idea."

"What!" she rasped. "You can't. We can't go against Estus. He is Doyen. He'll have us all killed. You're on thin ice as it is." Tears streaked down her face.

"Okay," I said soothingly, wondering what I'd gotten myself into now. "First start by telling me why you want to free Maya."

Sophie looked at me with red-rimmed eyes and bit her lip again. "She was my lover," she said finally, "and then she left. She no longer wanted to live in the Salr, but she's not a traitor. Estus claims that she's sided with Aislin, but I know she wouldn't. She wouldn't do anything that would hurt me."

"Who's Aislin again?" I asked, feeling like I wasn't fully comprehending what Sophie was trying to tell me.

"Aislin was once Doyen of a small clan," Sophie explained. "But now she has gathered many clans together.

They all answer to her. Estus is afraid that she'll come for us next, and if he's afraid, it means such a thing is likely to happen. They both want this object you're supposed to find. Estus claims it is the only way to protect us."

"So let me get this straight," I began. "Aislin was the one who sent those Vaettir who . . . killed you. Was Maya with them?"

"I told you she's not with them," Sophie sobbed. "She's going to die simply because she did not want to live like we do. Obeying orders and hiding from the sun."

I sighed. I really needed someone to trust, and Sophie had just put her trust in me.

"When I first met Maya she offered me information, but she would only tell me if we were alone. I waited until evening, then went to visit her in her cell. Some of the things she told me . . . " I let my words trail off, still not sure what I thought about everything Maya had told me.

"So you believe me?" Sophie asked like my answer mattered a great deal to her.

I shrugged. "I don't know who to believe, but I'm going to tell you what Maya told me, because I need someone to help me understand what's going on."

I filled Sophie in on everything Maya had said. About half-way through She seemed to calm down as she processed all that I was telling her.

When I finished, she looked worried. "Estus told us about this object, this . . . charm, but only told a select few of us know he wants *you* to find it. Now we know why."

"So you believe what Maya said?" I asked. "She doesn't know me. She might not have been telling the truth."

She gathered her long hair over her shoulder and

started stroking it like it was her favorite pet. "We need to tell my brother," she said finally.

I was both glad and worried that she wanted to tell Alaric. He'd been a lascivious tease, but he'd also been kind to me. Yet, the idea of telling him was troubling. He was loyal to Estus, but I could tell he didn't fully enjoy taking orders. If I had both Sophie and Alaric on my side . . . well, I might not only escape with my life, but I'd have two allies to help me figure out everything else.

"What if he doesn't believe us?" I asked.

She glared at me, though the effect was lessened when she had to sniffle her nose and wipe more tears away. "He may not believe us, but he will also not turn us in. He would never betray his own sister, and well you . . . he has a certain affection for you, even if I do not approve of it."

"How will we get him alone?" I pressed, ignoring what might have been a subtle insult.

Sophie rolled her eyes. "I imagine he'll solve that problem for us soon enough. He's developed a habit of lurking around your bedroom door."

The thought of Alaric hanging out around my bedroom brought a nervous flutter to my stomach, but I decided it would be best not to comment on it. "So *I* have to tell him?" I asked weakly.

Sophie smiled as if she was enjoying some secret thought. "Yes, you'll need to go back to your room and wait for him there. It will work out beautifully actually."

"Beautifully?" I questioned, not liking her tone.

"Well," she answered, "he's much less likely to take his anger out on *you*. So, you can break it to him, and your discussion will lead the way for me to discuss matters more fully with him."

I bit my lip, anxious to find some way out of being the one to tell Alaric. "I don't want his anger either," I argued weakly.

Sophie sighed. "He won't hurt you, and likely won't even get mad at you at all. He would, however, be extremely angry with me, so you telling him first gives him some time to calm down before I speak with him."

"Fine," I agreed sullenly. "I guess I should probably go wait, though I'm not as sure as you are that he'll just show up."

I stood to go, but Sophie grabbed my wrist to stop me. "How was Maya?" she asked, concern back in her voice. "What did James do to her? Estus won't let me see her."

"She's alive," I replied, not wanting to tell her the gruesome torture that Maya had endured. "Let's do our best to keep her that way."

Sophie nodded to herself. "Okay," she said distantly, "now go break the news to Alaric. If he gets angry . . . well, I'm sure it will be okay."

Great, I was off to play the sacrificial lamb, and the look in Sophie's eyes told me that despite her claims, I was about to get roasted.

I left Sophie and went back to my room to wait. I waited so long that I ended up falling asleep. When I awoke, the only indication of time I had was the lighting of the room. It had dimmed to almost darkness, evening, but not the middle of the night, else it would have been pitch black. Panic gripped me. I had slept the whole damn day away again. The stress must have been affecting me more than I'd realized. I'd wasted so much time.

I felt the bed shift and I froze, thinking that Sivi had decided to pay me another visit. I waited for more movement, but nothing happened. Finally, I sat up in bed and shifted my gaze to find Alaric sitting on the side of the bed next to me. He was slumped forward with his elbows on his knees and his hair thrown over one shoulder.

When he made no move to acknowledge me or say anything, I asked, "What's wrong?"

"Well," he began, "I was going about my evening when my sister found me, and she was very upset that I had not yet visited you. Now, I love my sister, but she is not really one to watch out for other women. I pressed her about it, and eventually she told me a very elaborate story."

He turned and leaned toward me enough to make solid eye contact in the dim lighting. "You do realize these allegations can be very dangerous?"

I clenched my fists in the bedding. "I'm not making any allegations. I just told Sophie what I'd been told."

"Sophie's judgment is clouded on this matter," he stated.

I sat up straighter and pulled my knees up to my chest as I watched him. "So you're not going to help us then?"

He laughed bitterly. "Well I can't just let you get caught now, can I? Sophie is determined to see this through, and if I don't agree, she'll just do it without me and get herself killed."

"So . . . you don't believe us, but you'll still help us?" I pressed.

He met my eyes again. "Something like that."

He continued staring into my eyes long enough that I finally looked down, feeling uncomfortable with the pressure of his gaze.

He reached out a hand and lifted my chin up so I would meet his eyes again. "Why does Estus believe that only you can find the charm? I've heard little of the thing until now, and suddenly it's in the Salr and only our new executioner can find it. It seems far too convenient to be true."

So apparently Sophie didn't tell him *everything*. "Maya thinks that I can somehow use the spirits of the dead to find it. She thinks that I might be able to communicate with them. I don't know how much Estus knows, but I don't think he's figured out that piece of the puzzle yet. He thinks if I search I'll be able to *see* it."

"And when the hell did Maya get a chance to tell you that?" he asked in surprise. "I doubt she'd say all of that with James around."

I blushed and was glad that he probably couldn't see it in the dim lighting. "I might have made a trip down to her cell," I admitted.

He placed his palm against his forehead in a sarcastic *now why didn't I think of that?* gesture. "Of course you did," he sighed, then turned back toward me. "You know, it would be easier to keep you out of trouble if you bothered to tell me your schemes beforehand."

"I hadn't planned on telling anyone my *schemes*," I explained. "I only told Sophie because she took a risk telling me about Maya. I figured it was safe."

He stood and started pacing in the dark. "And what makes you think that you're so unsafe here?" he asked as he walked.

I stood, finally feeling agitated myself. "What is there to make me think that I *am* safe? I was forcefully brought here, if you don't remember. Sophie almost died, and that was only from an outside attack. James seems to be torturing someone new every day. You people killed your old executioner. What did he even do to deserve it? If I can't find this charm for Estus, will I be next?"

"I'm here because I don't want you to be next!" Alaric hissed. He moved to stand in front of me. He seemed shocked at what he'd just said. Finally, as if coming to terms with his admission, he lowered his voice and added, "I don't want to see your heart in a box with all the others."

"So I ask you again," I began calmly, "How could I ever feel safe?"

He smiled bitterly, and I realized that he had gotten rather close for me to be able to see it. "You have a point, I suppose," he admitted.

"Darn right I do," I seconded.

He smiled mischievously, "Though you would probably feel safer if you had someone to sleep in this big, lonely room with you."

I looked up at him innocently. "Do you think Sophie would have a slumber party with me?"

"Sophie," he said as he took a step closer, "was not who I was referring to."

I placed my hand against his chest and pushed. "I don't think so, *buddy*. We may all be in this together now, but don't go getting any funny ideas." My words belied my racing heart.

He didn't step back.

I gulped. Damn it all, I was drawn to him. Maybe it was

all the mystical death and war stuff Sophie had told me, but it was hard to think straight. "There's something else," I said breathlessly.

Alaric nodded for me to go on.

"When I was first summoned to see Maya," I explained, trying to keep the quaver out of my voice, "she wasn't afraid of me at all, and it was like Estus knew that was the case. He even let her whisper in my ear. That's how I knew to go find her in the dungeon. There were no guards around her cell to keep her from speaking to anyone. Why would Estus let an alleged traitor tell me anything, when he's so intent on keeping me in the dark? And why was I allowed to walk around alone all morning?"

Alaric's eyebrows raised. "Maybe because he wanted you to do exactly what you're doing now." He paused in thought. "If Estus knew that Maya had information on how to get the charm, and knew she wouldn't tell him, he would logically turn to tricking someone else into finding out the information."

Icy fear shot through my gut, speeding my heart rate even more than Alaric's closeness. I was an idiot. I'd expected a trick, but I hadn't expected to fall for it. "So why hasn't he come to get it out of me then?"

His brow furrowed. "Because it would make much more sense to just wait for you to find it. Then he could take it from you and be done with it."

I shivered at the thought.

"I won't let anything happen to you," he assured.

I shook my head. "How can you promise that?"

He reached out his hand, rubbing it absentmindedly up and down my arm as his gaze turned distant with thought.

After a few uncomfortable seconds, a smile crossed his face. "I have a plan."

My thoughts were becoming increasingly jumbled at his touch. "Care to share it?" I breathed.

Alaric smiled even wider. "Nope."

He placed his other hand on my free arm and pulled me against him. All of my arguments slipped away. All I could think of was that the room was dark and cozy, and Alaric's body felt warm and exhilarating. I looked up into his eyes and felt like a field mouse caught by the big, predatory, barn cat.

He had managed to distract me from what we were originally discussing, and I wasn't sure if he was really going to help us, or just not tattle on us. Did he really have a plan, and if so, why wasn't he telling me? I suspected he was distracting me on purpose, and I should have pressed the subject, but the warm electric feeling in my chest made the fear I'd been feeling just a short time before irrelevant.

Alaric leaned down and kissed me, just a soft caress. That small touch drew out my years of solitude and sadness. The softness was nice, but I wanted more. If matters were really as bad as they seemed, I wasn't going to waste my time with gentle niceties.

I wrapped one hand around the back of Alaric's neck and the other around his waist, pulling him tighter against me. He let out a sound in his throat that made me pull even harder.

He put his hands underneath my butt and lifted, giving me the choice of either hopping up and wrapping my legs around him, or keeping them straight to be held off of the ground awkwardly. I hopped. He held me up and carried me toward the bed effortlessly.

Being carried like that was a new experience for me. Matthew and the few guys I'd dated before him had been my height or just an inch taller, which meant if they lifted me up, my torso would tower above them.

With Alaric's height, the once-awkward position was comfortable. Well, it was comfortable for the few moments it took to reach the bed. I was no longer thinking about comfort as he laid me gently on the bedspread and smoothed himself over me.

As he kissed down to my collarbone, he glided his hands up from my hips to the sides of my chest, then ran the barest of touches over my bra. I tried to hold still, but the anticipation was too much.

I pushed at Alaric's shoulders and rolled him off me. At first a look of confusion crossed his face, but it was soon erased with a wry smile as I slowly crawled up his body until I was straddling him.

I grabbed his arms and pinned them over his head, much like how he had pinned me during my sparring lesson. His smile turned into something dark and feral, just as I felt the same smile creep across my face.

See? I told you I'm no cream puff.

10

I had reveled in the feeling of touching and being touched. It was a relief to know that I could still feel that way at all anymore. Since Matthew, I had closed myself off, not even allowing myself the simple pleasure of a kiss for fear of harming someone again.

To go past a kiss and have everything thrown at me in one heaping punch of passion left me nearly delirious. Beyond that, was the feeling of actually drifting off in someone's arms. It was delectable, but something still itched at me. I couldn't stop thinking about Maya wasting away down in her cell, or even worse, about James taking another shot at her.

I believed what she had told me more than what anyone else had said. She stood nothing to gain in meeting with me, and even told me the very thing that she'd kept from James and Estus. She had tried to leave the Salr, and they brought her back and tortured her. Even the possibility of her choosing to work with our supposed enemies wasn't excuse enough for what had been done to her.

Alaric drifted into what seemed a deep sleep as I worried over a woman I barely knew. Of course, I was in bed with a man I barely knew, so I couldn't judge Maya based on that fact alone. I stayed in bed a moment longer, saying in my head *just do it, just do it*, until I finally sat up and gently placed my feet on the floor.

Alaric turned onto his side and reached toward my now-empty spot, but his eyes didn't open. I wanted to reach out and touch him, but I couldn't risk waking him. Instead, I crept around the room, picking up the pieces of my clothing that had been thrown haphazardly about. When I had everything, I dressed quickly in the corner as I watched Alaric for any signs that he might be waking up.

After quietly putting my tennis shoes on, I took one more moment to observe Alaric in my bed. It was strange seeing him in such a defenseless position, when normally it seemed like nothing could touch him. I left him there as the warmth of his embrace left my skin.

The halls had a little more light than my room, which I was thankful for, but it also meant that I would be easy to spot. Of course if Stella, the Lindworm, was out and about, she would sniff me out regardless.

I wasn't sure if I should try to find Sophie, or if I should just look for the charm. Maya had said that there was no way for me to get her out of her cell, but there had to be a way. If someone could put her in, then I should be able to get her out, especially with Sophie's help.

I hurried down the hallway, following the twists and

turns that led to Sophie's room. She opened the door before I even had a chance to knock and pulled me inside.

"What did he say?" she whispered as soon as the door was shut. "I didn't mean to tell him before you could, but he forced it out of me."

She'd changed clothes with the obvious intention of not getting any sleep, and was now dressed in skin-tight black leather pants and a billowy black blouse. There was one of those battery-powered touch lights illuminating the room, answering my question as to what we were supposed to do when the Salr decided that it was lights out. I felt a bit bitter that no one had given me a touch light.

"Well, he doesn't fully agree with us," I explained, "but he doesn't want us to get ourselves killed either. I'm not sure how much he'll help, but he'll do his best to make sure we don't get caught."

Sophie's eyes narrowed at me. "And what took you so long to come here?" she asked suspiciously. "I've been waiting *forever*."

My face suddenly felt hot. "I um-" I stammered.

Her eyes widened. "You slept with him! I told you not to."

I shrugged. "Sorry."

"Don't be sorry," she snapped. "Just don't come whining to me when he breaks your heart."

I didn't know how to respond to that, so instead I asked, "What do we do now?"

She turned away from me and started pacing, reminding me of Alaric. All I wanted was to crawl back in bed with him.

"Focus," Sophie ordered, glancing at me. "We need to help Maya escape, and we need to find the charm. The problem is which one first. If we help Maya escape, then everyone will be looking for the traitor that did it and it will become more difficult to find the charm in secrecy. We could try finding the charm first, but who knows how long it will take? I don't like leaving Maya down there."

"Maybe we just shouldn't find the charm at all," I offered. "If it's such a dangerous thing . . . "

Sophie shook her head. "If Estus wants it, it will be found. He's already figured out that he needs an executioner to find it. He *will* eventually discover that using the traitor's hearts is the key, even if Maya won't tell him. If he discovers what to do, then we'll have no chance of keeping the charm from him."

"So you agree with Maya then?" I asked. "She thinks that Estus would be a tyrant, but isn't he kind of one already?"

Sophie snorted. "He's only a small scale tyrant right now, and he's kept it hidden well. Most of our people love him. I've never held any love for the man, but my time spent here has been mostly comfortable. I was content, until I found out about Maya. Now I can't ignore the fact that I could end up in a cell just as easily. If what Maya says about the charm is true, then Estus would be a uniting leader amongst the clans. He wouldn't have to worry about keeping up appearances in order to keep his numbers strong. He would have *all* of the numbers, so what would a few extra deaths mean?"

The implications were making me dizzy. I shouldn't

care what happened to the Vaettir, but if all these freaks were banded together, what might that mean for the world at large? I slumped onto the bed. "But what would he do with the numbers?" I asked weakly. "World domination? Is he *that* power hungry?

Sophie's gaze went distant. She spoke like she was standing on the edge of a cliff. "I believe that Maya thinks he would have us on the outside world again, but not how we were before. I am not sure of that. As far as I'm concerned, Estus only wants power. Keeping his people underground under close supervision would give him that. The only thing we know for sure, is that whatever he plans, it isn't good. No one strives for such power for noble reasons. We need to find that charm and get rid of it."

I stood, my mind made up. "We need to help Maya first."

"It could ruin any chance we have—" Sophie began.

"We help Maya first," I said again. "We would still be in the dark if it weren't for her. We can't just take her information and let her rot."

Sophie eyed me very carefully, then suddenly pulled me into a hug. She whispered, "Thank you," then let me go abruptly.

She opened a large closet and started clanking around inside while I waited. I went to the closet door to watch her as she pawed through several large wooden crates.

"I have something in here that could help cut through the bars of Maya's cell," she explained. "If we can get down there with no one seeing us, we should be able to get her out."

"Are there no keys?" I asked, puzzled.

Sophie shook her head. "The Salr listens to the Doyen of the clan. If he wants someone to be imprisoned, the cell will not open without his say-so."

I nodded, creeped out by the idea of the Salr listening to Estus, or anyone for that matter. Buildings were not supposed to be sentient, even when they were magical underground sanctuaries.

I wondered if the Salr knew what we were doing, and would tattle on us to Estus. Of course, if that were the case, Sophie likely wouldn't be talking about things so openly, and we would have already been thrown in cells ourselves.

"So what do we do with her once she's free of the cell?" I asked. "If the only way out is Sivi's pool—"

"That's not the only way out," Sophie sighed.

I put my hands on my hips. "But Alaric—"

"He lied," she interrupted, finally turning to look at me. Her face softened at my hurt expression. "He had no choice. He was only following orders."

Confusion replaced a bit of the hurt, but only a bit. "Did Estus really get that specific? Why would he want me to believe there's no way out? It's not like my escape attempts were successful."

"Orders concerning you were very clear," she said bitterly. "He's not going to risk you getting snatched away. Executioners aren't exactly a dime a dozen, and we've already lost one."

I crossed my arms. "He already *killed* one you mean."

Sophie rolled her eyes like it made no difference. "What I'm saying is that he wants to keep you here, badly, and from what you've told me, Sivi wants you to leave just as badly. It all backs up what Maya said." She stood with a small, perfectly round stone in her hand.

I eyed it skeptically. "And that's going to get Maya out of her cell?"

"Yes," she replied. She closed her fingers around the stone and looked me up and down. "Are you ready?"

"W-what?" I stammered. "You want to go *now*?"

She nodded. "Isn't that what you came here for?"

I shook my head rapidly. "I came here to *plan*. Shouldn't we wake Alaric?"

Sophie's eyes narrowed again. "You left him sleeping in your bed, didn't you?"

I looked down at the floor, embarrassed. In an attempt to change the subject, I asked, "I thought we told him everything because we needed his help. Shouldn't we tell him what we're doing?"

Sophie sighed. "The purpose was to have him willing to help *you* should anything happen to me tonight."

It was my turn to narrow my eyes. "You planned on helping Maya tonight regardless of what I chose to do, didn't you?"

Sophie blushed, not quite meeting my accusing gaze. "I can't leave her there. I can't risk Estus storing her heart with all of the others. If you had chosen to find the charm first, I would have tried to help her on my own."

I clenched my jaw in frustration. At least she was honest. "So if something *does* happen to you, then what?"

"You flee the scene," she instructed. "If anyone sees you, you tell them I forced you to help me. Then you and Alaric can find the charm and get rid of it."

I shook my head. "If I blame you like that, you'll end up just like Maya."

Sophie's lips twisted into a wry smile. "If we get to the point of you needing to blame me, I will already be dead or on the run. Just promise me that if the former occurs, you'll find a way to release me. I don't want to be stuck in a box."

I nodded. "I promise."

Sophie hugged me again, then pulled away, blushing harder. "Are you ready?"

I took a shaky breath. Alaric probably wouldn't forgive me if I let his sister get killed, but it was a risk I was going to have to take. "As ready as I'll ever be," I sighed.

Sophie looked at me like she didn't quite believe me, and she shouldn't have. I wasn't ready at all. A silly, childish part of me thought that maybe with Alaric I could be happy. Sophie might argue that, and she might be right, but I could still try. Now I was going to risk the first man I'd been able to touch without the risk of killing him. Sophie thought I could get away without blame, but there was no guarantee. Just the thought of being under Estus' scrutinizing gaze made me shiver.

I could have tried forming a semblance of a life with Alaric, but instead I was about to risk it all for a woman I'd just met. It was stupid, but I couldn't just leave her there to rot, and I couldn't be blindly happy while people were being tortured for no good reason. Ignorance was bliss, and I already knew far too much.

Maybe at first I could have believed that what I was expected to do was just a casualty of war, but what did the other side think about that? It would have been nice to ask the last executioner what he thought about it, but he had been tortured and killed by James, all on Estus' orders.

Even if I didn't want to save Maya, I couldn't just wait idly by for the same fate to befall me. I shook my head at my own foolishness. I should have just left when Sivi gave me the opportunity. I was in way over my head, and sinking fast.

11

The dungeon was just how I remembered it: dark, scary, and filled with pain. We found Maya right where I had left her, but not *how* I had left her. At some point James had taken one of her hands to match her already missing foot.

Sophie started crying the moment she saw Maya curled up in the corner of her cell. The battered woman now reached her one hand through the bars for Sophie to hold while she knelt in front of her.

Sophie's back shook with silent tears. "I'll kill him for this," she rasped.

"It wasn't James' fault," Maya muttered. "He may be a sick bastard, but he was just following orders. Estus is the one who did this to me."

Sophie raised her head to meet Maya's gaze. "And that is who I mean to kill."

Maya's shoulders slumped with a sigh. "Sophie—"

I couldn't help the feeling that there were eyes on my

back. I felt for both of them. *Literally*, I could feel Sophie's heartache, but we needed to get out of the dungeon before someone caught us. "Umm, not to interrupt, but we really should get this show on the road."

"What show?" Maya asked sharply.

"We're busting you out," I explained. I offered a hand to Sophie. Her fingers trembled as I helped her to her feet.

"No," Maya rasped, shaking her head in disbelief. "You can't. You'll just end up down here too."

Sophie ignored her as she fished the small stone out of the pocket of her leather pants. Before Maya could protest further, Sophie placed the stone against one of the bars. At first nothing happened, then sparks began to fly out from underneath the stone. I watched in awe as Sophie withdrew her hand, leaving the stone in place. After a few seconds the sparks stopped, and she reclaimed the stone to reveal a clear cut through the bar.

"What the hell was that?" I asked.

Sophie didn't acknowledge me, and instead set to placing the stone on each bar until a perfect cut went about two feet across. Next she cut the bottoms of the bars, instructing me to hold each one so it wouldn't fall when it came loose. The bars were much heavier than they looked, and my arms felt like pudding by the time we had a hole big enough for Maya to fit through.

Once the bars were all set aside, Sophie crawled through the opening, then helped Maya up, balancing on her remaining foot.

"I wish we had something to help with the pain," I commented without thinking as they maneuvered through the opening.

"Maya doesn't feel pain," Sophie explained.

"How did you manage to keep that information from Estus until now?" I asked.

It seemed pointless to torture someone who couldn't feel pain. Of course, I suppose the threat of losing a foot could make a person talk regardless of whether or not they'd feel it.

"I knew better than to share my secrets around here," Maya said, looking pointedly at Sophie.

"I've learned that lesson too," Sophie said quietly.

Maya nodded and we all started forward. Eventually I went to Maya's other side to help speed our progress. She reeked of burned flesh and other smells, and I had to hold onto her scabbed skin more tightly than I would have liked, but it was necessary.

We were lucky that Maya was small, or we would have had trouble carrying her out. I couldn't help but wonder how she'd even survive out of the Salr with the condition she was in.

Sophie's eyes caught mine over the top of Maya's head. The look in her eyes was sad, yet determined, and told me exactly what she was thinking. She was going to go with Maya and leave me to find the charm on my own, even if we managed to get Maya out undetected. Sophie watched as the realization played across my face. She bit her lip, waiting for my reaction. Doubting that I really had much choice in the matter, I nodded that it was okay.

As we reached the stairs, the three of us looked up with concern. The tall steps were strenuous enough to climb in the best of conditions, and these were definitely not the best of conditions. Our worries about the stairs were erased as a new worry stepped into view. A tall figure came to stand at the top of the stairway, clearly intending to block our way, though it was too dark to see his face.

"I'll try to keep whoever it is busy," I said quietly. "You run with Maya."

"You'll be killed," Sophie replied harshly. "Or worse, you'll end up in Maya's cell, only *you'll* be able to feel the pain that James will cause you. Run to whoever it is for help. Tell them I forced you to do this."

The figure took a step down the stairs, then another. "We're caught now," I said through gritted teeth. "And me turning you in won't do any good. I'll try to take them down, then I'll follow you. I'll leave too."

The thought of leaving without telling Alaric sent an uncomfortable squirm through my heart, but it had to be done. I couldn't involve him any further. If Estus hunted Maya down, he would hunt anyone else that left too. I ran out of time to think as the figure drew closer. It was clearly a man, but I still couldn't see his face.

I let go of Maya and prepared to charge.

"Maddy?" a man's voice said. "Is that you?"

"You idiot," Sophie chided, relief clear in her voice. "You scared us half to death."

"You should be scared," Alaric whispered back. "What the hell are you two doing down here?" He eyes turned toward me as he stepped close enough for me to see in the near dark. "First you ask for my help, then you sneak out of bed while I'm sleeping and run off, once again not allowing me to help. What happened to letting me in on your schemes *before* you carry them out?"

I shrugged, at a loss for words.

Obviously frustrated, Alaric walked past me and effortlessly lifted Maya up into his arms. "The North Breach?" he asked.

"Yes," Sophie answered simply as she started forward, leading the way.

I wanted to ask what the North Breach was, but kept my mouth shut as I followed our party up the stairs, then started down the hallway silently. We walked unhindered for a while and I was just starting to feel a little less nervous when I heard clicking behind me, then something poked into my back. I jumped forward and bumped into Sophie. The forward jump wasn't enough to get me out of the way, as the next thing I knew I was on my back with a tremendous weight on top of me.

Stella's rottweiler face panted inches from my nose, forcing hot, steamy breath into my sinuses. I gagged, but didn't try to scoot away. She could have easily crushed me with her thick middle, but instead she hovered above me with her legs to either side, only placing enough weight on me to keep me in place.

"Stella!" Sophie hissed.

Stella looked up at Sophie and growled. I watched upside down as Alaric gently let Maya down to her foot. She leaned against the wall as if only having one foot was a perfectly normal thing for her.

Alaric glanced at Sophie. "I'll grab Stella, then you grab Maddy."

Sophie replied with a curt nod. As Alaric stepped closer, Stella lowered her belly more firmly against me, still not crushing, but making it obvious that she didn't want me to go anywhere.

Alaric stepped behind Stella so that I could no longer see him.

"Be ready to grab her quickly," he whispered. "I don't want Stella's claws to get to Maddy when I lift her."

I thought the idea of Alaric lifting Stella questionable in itself, since the beast had to weigh several hundred pounds. Even more questionable was the idea that Sophie could get me to my feet quickly enough to avoid getting skewered by Stella's large, bear-like claws.

"One," Alaric counted down.

"Two," Sophie said.

Before anyone could say three, Alaric and Sophie both lunged toward the creature. Suddenly I was on my feet, and Stella was thrashing around in Alaric's arms as he tried to hold her aloft.

"Go!" he grunted.

Sophie shoved me forward ahead of her, then picked Maya up in a less-than-graceful fireman's carry. It was either run or block Sophie's way, so I forced myself forward. I looked back over my shoulder as we took a nearby turn. The last thing I saw was Stella turning around in Alaric's grasp to slash him across the chest just as she let out a loud bellow.

"We have to go back!" I cried as Sophie used her free shoulder to shove me forward.

"He'll catch up!" she yelled back.

I cringed at her shout, but after Stella's warning shriek, we were no longer concerned with silence. Our only hope now was speed, and I was hindering us.

I tried to force my way around Sophie to go back to Alaric, causing her to nearly drop Maya. Sophie blocked me and got in my face as she repositioned Maya over her shoulder. Eyes that had gone full-feline stared me down. "He *will* catch up. Now *go*."

I went, not sure where I was running to, but trusting that Sophie would guide me. Tears streamed down my face as I thought of Alaric getting cut up by Stella. What if he didn't catch up? Would Estus blame everything on Alaric if Sophie and I left?

"Wait!" Sophie shouted.

I came to a skidding halt in front of a door to my left as Sophie stopped right beside me. She still had Maya over her shoulder, and her little stone was in her free hand. Sophie placed the stone against the lock on the door until it became a melted hunk of metal. She pushed the door open, then gestured for me to go inside.

I staggered in, then stopped, expecting a room and not a long, narrow hall. I forced myself to run again, even though my muscles and lungs were screaming at me from over-exertion. Sophie's steps echoed behind me. Clean stone walls whipped by, eventually showing signs of erosion. We hit an expanse of vines creeping up over cracked stones. I couldn't tell for sure since everything was a blur around me, but it seemed like the vines were moving.

The hallway ended suddenly in a writhing mass of vines. Sophie set Maya gently down amongst the serpentine tendrils. The smaller tendrils crept forward and instantly began to envelop her, just like they'd done to me when I was first brought to the Salr.

I watched in awe as Maya's form disappeared from view with barely a sound. I was so entranced that I only heard the footsteps a moment before someone grabbed my wrist and whirled me around. I came face to face with James. He watched my fear for a moment, then tugged my wrist again, bringing me toward him. My back thudded against his chest and his arm looped around me, tight enough to constrict my breathing.

"I've been dreaming about having you chained to a wall," he grunted as I struggled against him. "It looks like my dreams are about to come true."

Sophie watched us as she backed herself toward the vines. I realized what she was going to do as the first tear crept slowly down her face.

"I'm sorry, Maddy," she said softly before turning her sad eyes to James.

"I'd stop you," he began, "but what I'm going to do to your brother will cause you so much more pain than knives and fire ever could."

I started struggling again as Sophie lowered herself into the vines. She met my eyes until the vines reached her face and pulled her down into the swirling mass.

I continued struggling as James pulled me back away from the only route of escape. "You can't kill me," I grunted, gasping for a full breath. "Estus needs me."

James laughed. "Accidents happen," he said happily, forcing me back down the hallway. "An accident happened with the last executioner, and we found a new one just fine."

My mind raced at his admission. "So he wasn't a traitor then?" I breathed, already knowing the answer.

James laughed. "He couldn't figure out how to find the charm. I had hoped to inspire him, but I might have gone too far."

"So you knew?" I gasped. "You've known what Estus was looking for since the beginning?"

We had reached the door with its melted lock just as Alaric came into view. His bare chest and neck were a bloody mess. I squirmed in discomfort, feeling every little cut on his body.

Ignoring his blood dripping onto the floor, Alaric sneered his unnaturally elongated teeth at James. I had only seen his teeth look like that one other time, and that was right after he'd bitten a man's throat out. Even as injured as he was, he still planned on a fight.

James tossed me aside like I weighed nothing.

I staggered, thudding into the wall.

"You better not have hurt Stella," he hissed.

I turned as Alaric glared at James defiantly, then spit blood onto the ground. Whether it was his own blood, or someone else's, I wasn't sure. "You'll have to get through me to find out."

James took one step forward.

"*That*, will not be necessary," Estus said as he came into view behind Alaric.

Alaric stepped aside, repositioning himself in front of me.

Estus cocked his head to one side. His loose gray hair streamed over the shoulder of his dark colored robe like silk.

"Truly Alaric," he said calmly, "you could have at least *tried* to keep your sister here."

Alaric dropped to one knee and bowed his head. "I was preoccupied," he apologized, "but at least you still have your executioner."

I looked from Estus to Alaric's hunched back in confusion. Just a moment before he had been ready to fight James, and now that Estus was here, he was just handing me over? I stared down at Alaric, willing him to turn and look up at me, but he just knelt there as a small pool of blood formed underneath him.

"Take her to a cell," Estus ordered.

James looked just as shocked as I felt. "He was helping them," he stated, pointing at Alaric's still form. "I should be bringing *him* to a cell."

Estus looked directly at me when he said, "Alaric was working on my orders. Madeline is the only prisoner here."

James growled and grabbed me again, shoving me forward harder than he needed to. Alaric kept his head bowed as Estus approached him, then we turned a corner and I could no longer see the true traitor in my life.

12

My bones ached from the cold as I slowly lifted myself to a seated position. I had no idea how long I'd been left alone in the dark, but judging by the pain in my stomach, I'd say at least 24 hours. The side I'd been lying on slowly regained feeling as I groggily peered around in the darkness.

I reached forward blindly until my hands met with cool metal. I snaked my grip around the bars as everything came crashing back once more. Sophie and Maya, James, Estus . . . and Alaric. He had betrayed me, and now I was in the same dungeon we had rescued Maya from. Poetic justice at its best.

With nothing to comfort me in the pure darkness, I resorted to curling up in a corner with my back pressed against the wall. I squeezed my eyes tightly shut. The darkness was much worse than the hunger or cold. I laid there for what felt like hours. Every time I tried to open my eyes, I would panic from lack of bearings. Realistically I knew I was in a cell by myself, but when you can't even see an inch in front of your nose, you constantly feel like something is going to reach out and grab you.

A noise somewhere down the long hall that ended in my cell startled me back into full awareness. My eyes snapped open before I could stop them, only this time I wasn't assaulted by the oppressive darkness. The light at the end of the hall crept closer, and a sliver of hope made my heart race.

That hope sank to the pit of my stomach when I saw who was approaching. James eyed me thoughtfully with his cold, pale eyes as he came to stand in front of my cell. His eyes reminded me of the eyes of a corpse . . . cold, dead, and unfeeling. Not liking the feeling of him looking down on me while I huddled in my corner, I forced myself to my feet.

He eyed me for a few more silent moments, as if he'd memorize the pitiful sight of me, then smirked. "I just don't see it," he said, shaking his head.

"See—" I rasped, then took a moment to wet my throat. "See what?" The words felt foreign on my tongue after the prolonged silence of my imprisonment. Emotions that I'd been avoiding came flooding into reality now that I had a target for them.

"Why Estus won't let me kill you," he stated bluntly as he pushed his golden hair out of his face.

His hair was that annoying length where it's almost long enough to tuck behind the ears, but not quite, so it always just fell forward instead. His hair and faintly tan skin gave the image of someone who spent a lot of time hiking, or doing other outdoor activities, yet his favorite activities were reserved for dark rooms, behind locked doors. A dungeon cell was close enough.

I leaned back against the wall with my hips slightly jutted forward. I'd only done it because I was ready to lose my feet, but James didn't need to know that. When in doubt, try to look tough.

"What do you want?" I asked coolly, ignoring his insult.

James put his free hand on one of the bars of my cell so he could lean forward and leer at me. "Just because Estus won't let me kill you, doesn't mean I can't harm you. I wanted to see you so that I could picture clearly what I'm going to do to you."

I glared at him in response. The idea of being left to James' tender mercies made me want to scream. I'd seen what he liked to do to his victims. I doubted I would come out of the ordeal mentally or physically intact.

"It must have hurt when Alaric let me carry you off," he said suddenly.

I knew he was just trying to get a reaction out of me, but I couldn't help the hurt expression that crossed my face. It *had* hurt, but even more than that, it had been humiliating. I never should have trusted Alaric, and I was paying for that mistake ten-fold.

I corrected my expression to one of extreme distaste and grumbled, "Fuck off."

James lifted his hands in a mock expression of fear. "Oooh, the little girl has some teeth after all."

I staggered closer to where James was leaning and pushed my face against the cool steel, inches from where his hand gripped the bar. "Come closer and I'll show you my teeth," I taunted.

James laughed at me, but he pushed away from the bars instead of leaning closer. "All in due time, darlin'. All in due time."

With a final laugh he walked back down the hall, taking the light with him. I slumped back into my corner, feeling utterly defeated. Sophie had abandoned me, Alaric had betrayed me, and the only person who cared enough to visit my cell was a deranged sadist. I had heard that things start to go downhill when you neared thirty, but this was just ridiculous.

The darkness eased again sometime later as someone I didn't know came into view with a torch. The woman slid a hunk of bread and a single, small cup of water through the bars of my cell, then silently walked away.

As I devoured the bread so fast that I almost choked, I thought of what the food delivery might mean. Estus obviously wanted me alive, at least for the time being. He still needed an executioner to find his stupid charm, though I'd be damned if *I* was going to find it for him. He'd kill me as soon as I did. After I died, there would be no one to release my spirit, so some part of me would be stuck in my dismembered corpse forever.

The thought almost made the bread come back up, but I forced it back down with a gulp of water. By this point, I was pretty sure that Estus kept many hearts in the same place he'd shown me the heart of the last executioner. I would not be surprised if there was a drawer reserved in that room for me. There probably was one for Sophie too, if she ever came back. Alaric's heart was safe, if he even had one.

I tried to turn my thoughts away from Sophie and Alaric, but the bitter feeling of betrayal flooded in regardless. I had helped Sophie free Maya, and the two of them left me to rot. I should have never trusted Sophie or Alaric. I shouldn't have trusted anyone. To the Vaettir, I was a tool, and nothing more.

I couldn't help but feel like everything that had happened was punishment for being what I was. I could trash talk the other Vaettir as much as I wanted, but it was *my* curse to take life. It was *my* curse that had gotten me into this position. It seemed so much worse than having telekinesis or turning part feline from time to time.

I couldn't blame the humans who were frightened of us centuries ago, forcing the Vaettir to go into hiding, if I were to believe what I'd been told. In hiding was where we deserved to be. It was where *I* deserved to be. Still, if I had the opportunity, I would go live amongst the humans again, even if it endangered them. Call me selfish all you want. You'd be right.

I was startled as another light came into view. I had already been fed, and James had already taunted me, so there was no reason for anyone else to visit.

My heart pattered nervously, hoping in spite of myself that this new visitor would be Alaric. He would come and tell me that it had been an elaborate ruse. He had been on my side all along, but couldn't let Estus know. I would be freed at once and we would run away together.

I was overwhelmed by a sinking feeling in my gut as Sivi came into view. The pale, fairy-like creature swayed toward my cell, though her feet didn't make a sound. Her violet eyes and translucent hair were illuminated by a small, hovering light in the palm of her hand. I wasn't even surprised by the free-floating ball of light. I'd seen things more astounding ten times over.

Sivi cocked her head, observing me. "I told you not to trust them," she chided. "You could have been free."

"Lack of foresight is a real bitch," I grumbled. "What do you want?"

"I want the charm," she said simply. "I will free you in return."

"What would you do with it?" I asked, actually considering the offer. Sivi probably wasn't the best person to be granted ultimate power, but I'd take her over Estus any day of the week.

"I would put us back where we belong," she answered. "We are guardians of nature. To live in the cage of the Salr is blasphemy. It is not meant for this."

"And what of those who would resist?" I pressed. "Many of the Vaettir enjoy their current existence."

Sivi shrugged and made it clear by her expression that I was boring her. "They will die. Those who choose this life are abominations. This is not what we're meant to be."

I rose to my feet and walked toward the bars of my cell. I towered over Sivi, and I felt a little better looking down at the tiny woman rather than looking up at her.

"What about the humans?" I asked. "The world is not how it used to be."

Sivi spat on the ground in disgust. "The Vaettir are far greater in number now. We will not be hunted as we were in the past. Humans will grovel at our feet and beg forgiveness for what they have done."

"And that is our natural place?" I asked skeptically. "Nature guardians who rule over humanity?"

"The humans have destroyed the home granted to us by the gods," she said almost sadly, then her face contorted back to anger as she added, "and they will pay."

I shook my head. "I don't think I'll be helping you."

Sivi pressed her face close to mine and sneered so that I could see her tiny, pointed teeth. "You would rather rot here than be free?" she snarled. "You're a fool."

I shrugged. "At least this way, I'll be the only one to die."

Sivi let out an ugly laugh. "An executioner that values human life, how precious. You're as twisted as the rest of them."

I didn't really like being lumped in with *the rest of them*, since they had only brought me grief, but I kept quiet. I was more concerned with the fate of humans than I was with the fate of the Vaettir. Plus, I was beginning to believe that the Vaettir really were all evil. I didn't particularly want to help any of them. If I was going to die a gruesome, torturous death, I might as well do it with a bit of dignity.

Sivi glared at me for a moment longer, then turned to go. I watched as her slender form seemed to levitate down the hallway silently. She stopped half-way down and looked back over her bony shoulder at me with a malicious grin. "Remember when it comes time to choose sides, that one ruler locked you in the cell, and the other would have had you freed."

I fell back to the ground as she disappeared from view, regretting my decision, but knowing I could have done no different. I'd done enough harm already. While I'd take freedom if it was offered under other circumstances, I'd be damned if I was going to sacrifice countless human lives just for a chance to see the sun again. A few, maybe, but not the large scale bloodshed Sivi had in mind.

13

It seemed like a full day had passed before I once again saw the light of a torch. A man and a women I had never seen before removed me from my cell, and held me up by my arms as we walked down the hall, then ascended the enormous, stone stairway leading away from the dungeon. I was weak enough that I didn't argue or try to escape. I was just happy to be out of the darkness.

The man glanced at me nervously as we walked. He looked young, with dark hair cropped close to his skull, making his blue eyes seem wider. He seemed unsure of himself. I almost thought about trying to reason with him, but then I saw the woman's face. Her lovely hazel eyes looked at me with an expression that said it all. I was the scum of the earth, a traitor, and I deserved what I had coming to me. She tossed her ginger colored hair over her shoulder as she looked away, a gesture perfected by mean girls the world over.

I was beginning to see that Estus' power didn't only extend to telekinetic feats and a little mind reading. His real power was in the sway he held over his people. If he told them that jumping off a bridge would help their clan, I had little doubt that most of them would do it.

The couple brought me to a bathroom I'd never been to, though it was nearly identical to the one I'd used on a regular basis before my imprisonment. They shoved me ahead of them, then shut the door behind us. The woman gestured to the bathtub.

I glanced at the clean, white, tub, having no desire to hop in. I turned toward her and crossed my arms. "What's the point of bathing if James is just going to kill me?"

The woman wrinkled her nose at me. "You stink."

I looked at the tub again, then back to the man and woman blocking the doorway. I could try getting past them, but I doubted Estus would send only two people to guard me if they weren't fully equipped for the task.

Deciding that it wasn't my time to escape, I turned my back and began undressing. My black silk top was in surprisingly good shape for all I'd been through, as were the black jeans. I *did* stink though. Sweating during the attempted escape with Sophie, then lying in a dungeon for several days had taken its toll.

I slipped down into the bathtub before even filling the water, wanting to cover my nudity as quickly as possible. The man and woman watched me dispassionately, not interested in my state of undress either way.

I plugged the drain and turned on the faucet, then turned back to my prison guards. "So," I began casually, "what lies has Estus told you about me?"

The woman glared at me. "You are a traitor, working for Aislin. You freed a valuable prisoner, and so, have been sentenced to death."

I gulped, feeling sick. I'd known I was likely going to die, but hearing it out loud made it seem a little more real. "Is that where you're taking me once I'm clean? To be killed?"

The woman shook her head, but kept her eyes forward. "You must be questioned first."

The man beside her was beginning to sweat profusely. Either he was nervous to be around a *traitor*, or he didn't like what was happening. Perhaps Estus' sway wasn't as complete as I'd originally thought.

"To what end?" I pressed. "I know nothing of value."

When the woman didn't answer, the young man finally met my eyes. "That is not for us to know."

I smirked at him, though my insides were filled with sickly acid. "Your Doyen says jump, and you say how high?"

The woman sneered at me. "Hurry up and bathe. Your very presence taints us."

I tsked at her and began washing myself as I mumbled, "There's no need to be insulting."

She gave no sign that she heard me, and instead stared straight ahead. A good little soldier.

I finished bathing, and stepped out to dry myself off with a nearby towel. My guards both still stood directly in front of the door. The only way I might escape them was to try it after we left the bathroom, but at that point they would both have a hold on me again, and I was almost too weak to stand.

The female guard reached down to the floor toward a

pile of folded clothing I hadn't noticed until then. She straightened, unfolding the fabric to reveal a loose-fitting, black, spaghetti strap dress, and a black bra and panties to match. I didn't see any shoes among the offerings. Not bothering to ask for any, I took the clothing and got dressed. The dress fell below my knees and seemed a size or two too big.

I looked back up to my guards to see that the young man now held a length of rope in his hands. I began to back away, but there was nowhere to go. The woman lunged for me. I darted back, then slipped on a puddle of water, landing hard on my butt. The woman grabbed both my arms, then the man knelt and secured my wrists in a quick, efficient manner. Maybe he wasn't such a novice after all. All I could do was groan in pain and curse the pair's existence.

Once I was thoroughly bound, my escorts each gripped one of my arms, tugged me up off the ground, then opened the bathroom door to lead me back down the hall. As hard as I tried to stare down the young man on my right, I was given no further explanation of where I was going . . . though I didn't really need one. I knew exactly where I was going. I was about to end up where all prisoners ended up. We were going to the place I lovingly thought of as the torture room.

Though I was still stinging from my fall, this was my last moment to fight. Soon I'd be in shackles. I feebly threw myself backward, managing to free my arm from the young man, but not from the woman. He panicked, but the woman did not. She let go of my arm and punched me square in the jaw. I reeled away from her and nearly fell, then before I knew it, both of the guards had a hold of me once more, and I could feel a welt forming on my cheek.

They half dragged, half carried me the rest of the way to the blood-stained room where I'd first met Maya, chained to the wall, and covered in cuts and burns. I'd done my best to save her, but I doubted anyone planned on doing the same for me.

James was already in the room, dressed in a skin-tight, white tee-shirt and dark jeans. His eyes sparkled with excitement as my escorts chained my bound hands to the wall above my head from one of the manacles. The woman had to stand on a stool to reach, and I would have kicked it out from under her if I'd had the strength. Too weakened to fight, all I could do was glare into James' eerie, white-blue eyes while I tried not to cry.

Unlike Maya, I was tall enough that even hanging from the manacle, my feet still touched the ground, though just barely. Once I was secured, James nodded to my attendants and both left the room without a word. The sight of the door shutting behind them made the last sliver of hope drip from my body like icy water.

I narrowed my eyes in the dim light toward a small medical table at James' side. James stroked the gleaming metal instruments on the table as if they were his favorite pets. In a way, they were.

"I've been waiting for this since the moment I met you," James taunted as he left his table behind to approach me, "though it would be nice to see some of the fight you had in you yesterday."

"Now, now," I replied weakly. "I wouldn't want to go and make this enjoyable for you."

James laughed and took another step forward, rubbing a hand up my arm. "I'm going to enjoy this either way, Madeline."

I stifled a shiver as James moved his hand slowly toward my breast. He smiled as he watched my face. I tried to keep my expression blank, but I'm sure some of the horror I was feeling showed through. He stopped short with his hand on my ribcage. With a another smile, he let his hand drop and turned away from me.

He looked toward the door as it opened, seemingly of its own volition, to reveal Estus. James dropped to one knee in acknowledgment of his omnipotent leader, but Estus only had eyes for me.

The small man approached, surveying me with eyes even paler than James'. His impossibly long, silver braid slithered from the front of his shoulder to fall against his back as he came to stand directly in front of me. I would have given much in that moment to strangle him with it. He was dressed in his usual ensemble of dark colored, loose fitting shirt and pants.

I looked down at the elderly man and felt more fear than James would ever manage to cause me. While James was a sadist, I was beginning to sense that Estus was a complete sociopath. One might expect to feel pity, anger, or a myriad of other emotions from the person condemning them to torture, but I looked down at Estus' impassive face and knew that he felt nothing beyond his sick obsession with power.

"I will need her relatively whole," he said as he looked

up at me, though obviously he was speaking to James. "She still has a task to perform."

Movement in the doorway drew my attention as Alaric came into view. My heart stopped at the sight of him, looking tall and handsome, and none too concerned with my fate. His dark hair was tied back at the nape of his neck, giving it the illusion of being shorter than it actually was, and leaving the shoulders of his black dress shirt bare. His dark brown eyes flicked to me briefly, then landed firmly on Estus as the old man turned to face him.

"Ah, there you are," Estus said, sounding like a jovial grandfather who just caught sight of his favorite grandson. "I thought you might like to see Madeline one last time in her current state. It's always a pity when we have to ruin pretty things."

The muscles in Alaric's jaw and neck tensed, and for a moment I thought he might actually be against me being tortured, but then the moment was gone, and his face was apathetic once more.

James watched the whole scene carefully, and seemed disappointed by the results. His disappointment was nothing compared to mine as Alaric gave me one long, cold stare, then turned back to Estus.

"Will that be all?" he asked blandly.

Instead of answering, Estus motioned one small, bony hand toward James.

James' face erupted into a toothy grin as he turned his attention back to me. He sauntered over to his table and lifted a dainty scalpel into his meaty palm. He twirled the delicate knife in his fingers as he walked back toward me.

My eyes flicked around the room, looking for something to help me. Coming up with nothing, I settled on meeting Alaric's eyes as panic bloomed in my stomach. I stared at him, daring him to drop his gaze as James stroked the dull side of the knife gently down the side of my throat.

I couldn't help it as my breathing sped, but I kept my eyes glued on Alaric. As far as I was concerned, he'd tied me up to the wall himself. I cringed as the knife turned to bite into the flesh of my collarbone, but my eyes remained on Alaric. Other than a certain tension around his eyes, no emotion was visible.

I was so focused on Alaric's unreadable expression that I was shocked when James stabbed the knife into my side. I shrieked at the sudden pain and closed my eyes. Panting, I forced my eyes open to glare at the man who'd betrayed me.

I hoped to whatever deity might help me that he could read my thoughts, because if I escaped my imprisonment alive, I was going to make Alaric pay. In that moment I didn't care about hurting James, Estus, Sophie, or anyone else.

I looked at Alaric as pain screamed through my body, and I hoped he knew the hole he'd dug for himself. Normally I found the idea of leaving the soul in someone's dead body abhorrent, but for Alaric, I would gladly make an exception.

Not liking the lack of attention, James stabbed the knife into my side again. I screamed, my body reflexively jerking away, but I only managed to slam my head back against the hard stone wall. I opened my eyes long enough to see Estus smile, then he turned to go, with Alaric following close behind him. The door shut on its own, leaving me alone with James once again.

He stood inches from me, his knife at his side. His face was a bit lower then mine, but I could clearly see the satisfied look in his eyes. I took in one ragged breath after another, refusing to scream. When he didn't move away, I let out a sob and spat in his face.

He laughed, wiping the spit away with his free hand. "Now there's the fight I was looking for."

My vision began to go gray. "Well sorry to disappoint, but you won't be getting much more of it," I rasped.

I could feel blood trickling down my side and onto my leg, growing cooler as it went. James smoothed his hand against my leg, smearing the blood across my skin as his hand searched upward underneath my dress.

At first I thought things were about to get sexual, but his fingers continued on to poke at the wounds in my side. I let out a grunt of pain, knowing that his fingers were pressing on the damaged flesh, but unable to feel exactly where because my pain-receptors were going haywire.

James reached his other hand beneath my dress to grip the clean side of my waist. "I'd like to offer you a deal, Madeline," he said softly.

I was feeling so woozy that I almost didn't understand what he was saying. "W-what?" I questioned weakly.

James smiled. Bracing himself with my waist, he leaned against me so he could put his mouth against my ear. "I want you to find the charm," he said softly, "and give it to me."

"You want to lead?" I groaned, feeling dizzy and confused, but not really surprised.

James chuckled. "No, you're not getting it, Maddy. This whole time Estus has been looking for a traitor."

My head was spinning, but I managed to put together the pieces. "You're working for Aislin," I panted.

James had been the traitor all along. Apparently Estus was correct in his fear that Aislin would try and take his clan from him. The proof was quite literally staring me in the face.

"Bingo, kiddo," he replied, removing his hands from underneath my dress.

"Why are you telling me all of this?" I asked. "I could easily turn you in to Estus."

James shook his head. "I'm your only hope of survival, Maddy. You might be stupid, but I know you're not *that* stupid."

"Couldn't you have offered this *before* you stabbed me?" I rasped. I was actually considering his offer, though it was probably just the blood loss talking.

James pouted at me, and the pout seemed wrong since his hands were covered in my blood. "I had to put on a good show for Estus. Plus, I *really* wanted to stab you."

I took a deep, aching breath, then cringed from the pain. "Well if I die, then I won't be helping anyone."

James snickered. "You are Vaettir, Madeline. We are not so easily killed."

I swallowed the lump in my throat, feeling like I might vomit from the pain. "And what would I get in return for this deal?" I whispered, barely able to speak.

"Your life," James answered simply, as if surprised that I would ask for more.

I shook my head slightly. "Someone else has already offered me that. Keep trying."

James sighed. "I cannot speak for Aislin, but I'm sure she could find a place for you in one of her clans."

"I want a guarantee," I hissed. "I want a guarantee of protection from Estus."

James raised an eyebrow at me. "You're not exactly in a place to bargain, little mouse."

I tried to laugh but it came out as just a shaky breath. "I told you, I've had other offers. Now give me a reason to pick you."

James eyed me with a look of what might have almost been respect. "I'll be back," he replied.

He left me hanging, literally and metaphorically, in the darkness. Part of me wished I had simply taken Sivi's offer right off the bat, but I couldn't do that. James didn't know that though. Perhaps Aislin planned on being a better ruler than Estus or Sivi. If so, I'd be happy to give her the charm if it meant I wouldn't get stabbed anymore.

Beyond that, I wasn't sure how I felt about getting involved with another clan. It would have been nice to just go back to my little home in the above-ground world, but I knew Estus would only recapture me. I needed protection. Plus, I couldn't help hoping that another clan would be different. It was only in that moment that I'd realized just how close I'd been to my breaking point back home. Even after all I'd been through, I didn't want to go back.

Years of solitude out of fear of hurting someone had taken a toll on me. Even though Alaric was not the person I'd thought, my one intimate night with him had shown me just what I'd been missing. I wasn't sure if I could go back to my old life after that.

I'd accidentally killed my lover before Alaric, and now I

was seriously considering killing Alaric on purpose, but perhaps there could be another lover in yet another new life. Third time is the charm, right? Of course, I'd have to escape the Salr alive first. With the blood dripping steadily down my side, my chances seemed grim.

14

The door opened again a short time after James left me. I thought perhaps he was back with whatever offer Aislin had for me, but the silhouette in the doorway was too tall and slim to be James.

Rage washed over me as Alaric came into view. He watched me cautiously as he approached. His caution was unwarranted, as I couldn't have even lifted a leg to kick him, no matter how badly I wanted to.

When I made no attempt to attack him, he closed the distance between us. He wore a worried expression, but he didn't say anything as he lifted the side of my dress to examine my stab wounds. His fingers hovered over the damaged area, but didn't touch. I felt like I should have been offended that he lifted my dress without asking, but given everything else, it seemed a relatively petty argument.

"James wouldn't have hit any vital organs," he said softly. "You'll be okay."

My head was throbbing so loudly that I could barely see Alaric's face, but I'm pretty sure I managed to glare at him.

"That's all you have to say!" I choked out. "I'm going to rip your lying, deceitful head off!"

Alaric took a step back. I felt his shock and hurt at my sudden outburst.

"Don't you dare look hurt at me," I rasped. "You betrayed me. You left me in a cell to rot. *You* let James stab me. You better hope Estus kills me, because so help me, I will make your death *slow*."

Hot tears streamed down my face. The pain in my side was nothing compared to the stabbing sickness in my stomach.

"I had no choice," he interrupted before I could go on. "It wouldn't do much good if we both ended up in shackles. This was the only way, Maddy."

I shook my head over and over. It wasn't the only way. He had a choice, and he chose to save his own hide. I wouldn't have done the same to him.

"Estus knew," I sobbed. "He knew I was going to help Maya. You told him the entire plan."

He shook his head. "I didn't tell him anything. He had already figured it out, don't you see?" He reached his hands toward me, then let them fall away. "When I realized what you were doing that night, I did my best to get you out of here. If you only would have told me your plans, I could have protected you. Once Estus found us it was too late. I did the only thing I could that would ensure I had some chance of saving you."

"I don't believe you," I said coldly. I tried to hold in my tears, but they just kept coming.

He raised his hands as if to cradle my face, but I turned my head away the best I could, and his hands dropped.

"You will see in time that everything I've done, I've done to protect you," he replied sadly, "and you haven't made it an easy job."

I turned back to him, anger drowning out my sorrow once more. "Well I didn't feel very protected when you let James drag me off to a cell, and I'm sure I won't feel very protected when I die from infected stab wounds."

"The Vaettir do not contract infections," he answered, ignoring my actual point. "You're not going to die."

I opened my mouth to argue, but given I'd never had an infection in my life, I couldn't. I'd always just chalked it up to a healthy immune system.

"How can you be so calm about this?" I asked, exasperated. "How could you just stand there while James tortured me?"

"I had *no* choice," he replied vehemently. "I knew he wouldn't kill you."

I turned my gaze away from him, tears still dripping down my face. "There is always a choice."

Alaric stepped closer to me again. "I'm going to get you out of here, Maddy. You just need to be patient."

I looked down at Alaric's handsome, angular face. Part of me still ached to kiss him, and I hated it. "I'm going to get *myself* out of here, and you had better hope that we do not cross paths again."

"Maddy—" he began.

"No," I cut him off. "Please leave."

"Maddy, I couldn't save you if I was dead!" he rasped.

I managed to stop crying and glared at him. "I told you,

I don't *need* you to save me. I don't need you at all. Now *leave*."

Alaric opened his mouth to say more, then closed it. A tidal wave crashed into my heart as he turned and left. The water coursed through my veins, wiping away my thoughts, then all was silent.

By the time James finally returned, my hands and arms had lost feeling, and my feet felt like ice cubes. I'd stopped bleeding, and the blood that I'd lost had gelled to a sticky, cold mess on my side.

"I've spoken with Aislin," he began, then paused as he looked me up and down.

I noticed that he held a pair of hiking boots in his hands, and I sincerely hoped they were for me.

"And?" I asked quietly.

"*And*," he continued, "she says to name your terms."

"I don't understand," I replied.

James shook his head and smiled. "Neither do I, but that was her reply. I'm pretty sure that beats any other offers you have at the moment . . . if you really do have other offers."

I glared at him, but my eyelids were so heavy it probably just looked like I was about to fall asleep. "Get me down from here," I demanded.

James didn't move. "So we have a deal?"

"Yes," I sighed before I could think better of it.

It was probably a bad idea putting my trust in a woman

I'd never met, but it was an even worse idea to wait for Alaric to save me.

Instead of letting me down, James put the boots on my feet and began lacing them.

"If we have to run, I don't want you complaining about your poor, girly feet," he explained.

I didn't reply. Having shoes to run away in would be nice. I could suffer a few insults if it meant shoes on my feet.

James unshackled my hands, then had to take most of my weight to keep me standing as he untied the rope around my wrists. My limbs felt like jelly, and my torso felt hollow. When it became clear that I couldn't stand on my own, he finally just lifted me up into his arms.

"We have to find the charm before we can leave," he stated.

"Take me next door," I ordered.

James didn't move. "Next door?"

I sighed. I was starting to feel like I might throw up. "No one tells you anything, do they?"

James grunted. "I'm the hired muscle. All I need to be told is who to torture, and when, not why." He said it like it was something he had been told, but not necessarily something he agreed with.

"I'm going to use the hearts of all of the people you tortured to find the charm," I explained.

James nodded, either not picking up on my disapproval or not caring. I was betting on the latter. Regardless, my explanation got James to move, and it also confirmed my suspicions that there were more hearts.

I had to wrap my arms around his neck to brace myself

while he used one hand to open the door. The feeling was returning to my limbs, making them ache more than my side, which was beginning to go numb in contrast.

We walked through the doorway like nothing was out of the ordinary. As the resident torturer, no one would question James moving one of his victims to the adjacent torture room, unless they noticed the boots on my feet.

We made it to the next room without a hitch, and suddenly I was nervous. The wall where I'd seen Estus remove the heart of the previous executioner looked smooth and solid, but there had to be other drawers within the stone. Of course, there could have only been the one, and the other hearts might be somewhere else. If that was the case, we were screwed.

"What now?" James asked.

I turned my head to look up at him. "Do you know how to open the drawers?"

He stared at the wall. "Who do you think put the hearts in there to begin with?"

He carried me over to the wall without another word, then wrapped one arm more tightly around my legs so he could use the other to smooth a finger around one of the wall's stones. I could hear a soft click from within, then the stone popped out of the wall. James pulled on the drawer to reveal a fresh-looking human heart. It didn't exactly beat, but the smooth muscle of the heart rippled and twitched in irritation at being disturbed.

I looked down at the heart, not sure what to do. I could feel the heart's physical pain distantly, as if it was stuck in the memory of having its body destroyed. Beyond the pain I felt hatred, violence, and jealousy. If I had to venture a guess, I'd say that the heart had belonged to a terribly unpleasant person.

I unwrapped one of my arms from James' neck, forcing him to put both of his arms around me once again to keep me aloft. I hovered my free palm over the heart, searching for . . . something. At first all I could feel were mixed emotions, then I heard it. It was like a soft voice whispering in my ear, but I couldn't make out anything that it was saying.

"Open them all," I demanded.

"What?" James asked, seeming startled that I'd finally spoken.

"Open all the drawers," I replied.

I wasn't sure what I was doing, but some sick compulsion told me that I needed to see all of the hearts. I could feel them fluttering within the wall like caged birds.

James let me down to my feet and helped me to lean against the wall. It hurt to use the muscles in my side to keep myself erect, but it was a distant pain, drowned out by the whispering of the hearts as James began to open the drawers.

I could feel their pain, but it was more than that. Most of the hearts had been taken from their bodies years ago, some over one-hundred years ago. I could feel each heart's age along with its plea to be released.

As soon as James opened the final drawer he retracted, rubbing at the goosebumps on his arms. "What are you doing to them?"

"I'm not doing it," I replied softly. "They want to be released."

"Well you better do whatever you plan on doing

quickly. If this energy continues to grow, Estus is bound to feel it."

I knew the thought should have worried me, but my brain didn't seem to be working right. All I could think about were the hearts. Their whispers were becoming more clear as they begged me to set them free. My body ached to answer them, but I needed to find the charm first.

As soon as I thought it, the hisses and whispers grew together until I could hear just a few clear voices calling out to me.

A picture formed in my head of a place I had never seen before. A great tree was surrounded by what appeared to be burial mounds. The mounds throbbed in my mind like something alive. The voices of the hearts began to whisper in unison, "*The Key.*"

I nodded my head and could feel myself smiling. The charm was a type of key, and it was in this secret place, protected by the mounds of the dead.

"I can hear footsteps," James rasped. "We need to go."

"Not yet," I said distantly.

"Maddy, *now*," James ordered.

Ignoring him, I walked closer to the hearts, no longer feeling the pain in my side. I reached my hands into the drawers and started releasing the hearts one by one. Each release was a relief to me, yet at the same time, pressure began mounting in the air. I could feel energy swirling around me as each heart was set free. A part of each spirit left, while a part remained behind to swirl around me.

The door opened just as I touched the final heart. I turned to see Estus framed in the doorway, with two nameless men at his back. Their forms seemed foggy to me as I tried to look at them through the pulsing energy.

"What have you done, Madeline?" Estus asked calmly.

"I've undone your wrongs," I said simply.

With a thought, I sent a portion of the energy rushing forward. It collided with Estus and his men, hitting them like a semi-truck. The three of them flew backward into the hallway, hitting the stone wall with enough force to make it shudder.

"The charm isn't here," I said to James. "We need to go."

He rushed over to pick me up, but I stopped him with a palm on his chest. "I can run," I said simply, and it was true.

The energy from the hearts had healed the wounds in my side. In fact, I felt like I'd just woken up from a perfect night's rest.

Taking me at my word, James darted forward and I followed. We ran past the crumpled, groaning forms of Estus and his men, and further down the hall. We were going in the same direction we'd gone when Sophie and I helped Maya escape. I remembered the vine-filled room vividly. I also remembered Sophie disappearing through the vines, abandoning me to my fate.

James and I reached the door that led to the vine room to find a new, shiny padlock on it. Sophie had melted the last one, but she had taken the tool she used with her. I extended my hand toward the lock. It popped open without a hitch.

"How did you do that?" James balked.

"It won't last long," I explained. I could feel the energy from the hearts dissipating with each use. Knocking Estus down had taken a far greater deal of energy than healing my side or opening the lock.

James threw the lock to the ground and pushed open the door. This time, he pushed me to run ahead of him as more footsteps thundered down the hallway behind us.

He turned around, bracing himself against the door. "Don't wait for me," he ordered.

"I wasn't planning on it," I replied, then took off toward the vines.

I could hear someone banging on the door behind me as I ran at full speed down the hall. A few tendrils of vine became visible amongst the broken stones of the hallway, letting me know I was getting close to my destination. Adrenaline pulsed through me as I entered the room, then nearly burst into tears. The vines had been destroyed. Giant heaps of cut foliage littered the room, and the thick stumps of the vines were scorched black.

I shook my head, refusing to give up. I was getting the hell out of there. Not knowing quite what I was doing, I threw the last of my borrowed energy at the burned stumps. For a painful second, nothing happened. Then a shiver of movement pulsed through the vine stumps. Slowly, they began to writhe and grow before my eyes, healing just like my stab wounds.

James reached my side as the vines finished filling out. He grabbed my hand and flung us forward, just as more forms piled into the room. I braced myself, worried that we would go face first into the stone, but the vines reached out and caught us. Within seconds we were engulfed in the swirling mass. I held onto James' hand for dear life as a tingling sensation overcame my entire body, and then I was sitting on my butt in the middle of a forest.

James offered me a hand up. "We need to move." He was a mass of cuts and bruises from holding off our pursuers, but none of his injuries looked serious.

Reluctantly I took his hand, feeling shaky as I rose, but I knew I needed to keep moving. Forcing my feet into motion, I ran off ahead of him, not really worried about what direction I was heading, as long as I was heading away from where we'd arrived. Using the last of the heart's energy on the vines had taken a toll, and my legs and lungs began to burn with exertion. The forest was chilly. Distantly I remembered that it was October in the real world, so the cold, autumn air made sense. We ran with no signs of pursuit until we reached a large, icy-looking river.

"Get in!" James demanded as he reached my side.

"We'll freeze to death," I argued, but it did me no good as James grabbed my arm and threw me into the river.

Icy water clamped around me, driving the breath from my lungs. My head went under, and I had to fight frantically toward the surface with heavy, stiff limbs. I gasped as my head emerged, only to flinch away as James dove in right beside me.

Not bothering to ask if I was alright, he began swimming downstream with perfect swimmer's form.

Still in shock, it was all I could do to doggy-paddle after him and keep my head above water in the strong, rushing current.

We went downstream for what seemed like hours, but was probably only ten minutes, traveling swift and far, profoundly exceeding the speed of foot travel.

Relief flooded me as James finally swam over to the bank and lifted himself out of the water, but I overshot the area where he had gotten out as the current rushed me too far forward. James had to run along the side of the water and snatch me out when I finally got close enough.

I curled up into a shivering heap as soon as I was free of the river. My lungs and skin burned painfully. I shut my eyes against the tears that stung my skin like mini drops of fire.

After a minute, I opened my eyes to find James standing perfectly at ease above me, completely unaffected by the cold.

"What are you, superman?" I asked through my chattering teeth.

"I am Vaettir," he said simply, surveying our surroundings.

"Yeah well so am I, but I'm also currently an ice cube."

James looked down at me with a raised eyebrow. "We all have our gifts," he said cryptically. "Let's keep moving."

I just stared at him. My body had given all that it had to give. There would be no more moving for me for at least a few hours, and that would only be after I got warm.

When I didn't move, James sighed and crouched down to lift me into his arms. He took off at a steady jog away from the river. It was strange being carried around by someone I'd grown to thoroughly loathe. He'd taunted me since I'd first arrived at the Salr, and that was the least of his sins.

The hands that held my body aloft had tortured and killed countless people. He might have been acting on orders, but that didn't change the fact that he'd enjoyed every bit of it.

Now this sadistic murderer was my only lifeline. He was the only person I had left to trust. It was just me and the Devil, running through the woods.

15

James ran with me in his arms for hours, never seeming to tire. My black dress was finally almost dry, but the remaining dampness from the river still made me shiver. I attuned myself with the bumping up and down of James' gait, finding it surprisingly tolerable, though it would have been nice to know where we were going. I imagined at some point I would be delivered to Aislin so we could find the charm, or key, or whatever it was, but I was too weak and delirious to ask.

I felt myself slipping in and out of consciousness, and my bleary thoughts turned to Alaric. He'd claimed that his betrayal was the only way to save me, that if we both ended up in a cell, he wouldn't have been able to rescue me. I called bullshit. We could have fought our way back to those vines to follow Sophie and Maya out into the human world. I'd made the right choice in taking James' offer. He might terrify me, and he might have tortured me, but he worked for the other side. From what I'd seen of Estus' little clan, any side was better than his.

The trees above us faded in and out of view as I warred with my heavy eyelids. The October air of the forest that would have been pleasant had I been dry, chilled the damp parts of my clothing in an almost painful way. The only warm part of my body was the side pressed against James.

It seemed odd that he was carrying me like a bride on her wedding day, rather than in a fireman's carry, but the uneven weight distribution didn't seem to fatigue him, and I was more comfortable that way, so I didn't complain. My long hair was caught between our bodies, but I didn't complain about that either.

We seemed to run on for days, though the sun never fully set, and I was only partly conscious when he finally set me down on the ground. I looked at him in confusion, wanting to ask for an explanation, but I couldn't form the words.

"We'll stay here for the night," he explained as he walked around, observing our surroundings. "Once you've . . . recovered, we'll find the charm. I'm assuming you know where it is," he added with enough menace to let me know that what he actually meant was, *you better know where it is, or else.*

"The hearts showed me an image of where it is," I explained dizzily, "but we might need Aislin's help in finding the right place."

"They just showed you a *picture*?" he asked incredulously.

"Yes," I replied, my gaze partially focused on the light slowly fading from above the trees. It would have been nice to argue with James from a safe, standing position, but my legs felt like congealed pudding. "It was a very unique picture, and it gave me a feeling of *distance*. The charm is far away. With a little research we could probably find the right place, and I think if we get close enough, I'll be able to sense it. If Aislin is as old as Estus, she might even know where it is."

"We'll need to have the charm in hand *before* I take you to Aislin," James replied.

I mustered the strength to turn my head in James' direction. "I thought you said—" I began.

James shrugged like it didn't really matter. "I lied. Aislin wanted me to sneak another executioner into the Salr to search for the charm. I thought this way would be easier, though I'm beginning to reconsider my choice."

"What!" I asked again as a surge of adrenaline enabled me to sit up. "So there's no deal for me? You lied about everything?" I pulled my legs up to my chest and curled around them. I was in deep shit.

James rolled his eyes at me. "Trust me. If you and I can deliver the charm to Aislin, we'll both be given whatever we want."

"*Trust* you?" I snapped. "You just admitted to lying to me about everything. Why the hell should I trust you now?"

James laughed. "Do you have any better options?"

I was fuming, but he was right. Aislin was still my best chance. It wasn't a very good chance, but given that the other option was to just wait around for Estus to find and kill me . . . Alaric and Sivi had both probably lied about their offers of help too. Of course, Sivi's offer of *well, you'll be alive while I murder everyone*, didn't have enough sugar coating to be a lie, and Alaric, he'd betrayed me after fully gaining my trust. At least James was upfront about being a scheming, sociopathic jackass.

"The charm can be found inside a giant tree," I explained with anger still tinting my voice. "The tree is surrounded by large burial mounds that protect the charm. The place is very old, and hidden. I got the feeling that you could walk right by it and never know. It might even be underground."

James stood with a huff. "That's it?" he asked sharply. "That's all you got? You couldn't have asked for a map?"

I let myself slump back to the ground, curling up on my side in the dry leaves. "It wasn't like I was just discussing things with the hearts over a nice cup of tea. I seem to recall you urging me to get things done before Estus came to kill us. We had a bit of a time constraint."

James sighed and came to stand over me. "It's fine," he said, more to himself than to me. "Our plan is still the same."

"So you know how to find the tree?" I asked hopefully.

"No, but I know someone who might be able to help. We'll visit her in the morning." He began to walk away. "I'd tell you to wait here," he added, "but I doubt it's necessary."

"Where are you going?" I asked, suddenly nervous.

"I'm going to find us some dinner," he replied, his voice already a good distance away.

With a tired sigh, I curled up into a ball on the ground in an attempt to get warm. I sincerely hoped that dinner would come with a fire. I hadn't quite recovered from our swim in the icy river, and the increasingly chilly air was not helping matters. Not only that, but I felt like I had expended myself a little too much back in the Salr, like using the life-force from the hearts had taken a bit of my lifeforce along with it. At the time, using the energy had felt marvelous, almost as good as it had felt to release all of those long tortured souls, but I must have overdone it. I raised a shaky, pale hand in front of my face and could barely even force my eyes to focus on it. Yep, definitely over-did it.

I was still curled in a ball on the hard ground when footsteps alerted me to James' return. I peeled my eyes open to see that he carried a dead rabbit in one hand, and some kindling for a fire in the other. I had no idea how he had killed the rabbit, and I didn't want to know.

Without a word he set the rabbit down and began building a fire near me. His back was to me, but with a few motions of his hands, the dried grass he'd gathered under-neath the kindling began to smoke. Maybe he'd had some sort of flint.

"You're like a giant boy scout," I commented.

"Ha ha," he replied sarcastically. "Not all of us spend our entire existence among the comforts of the Salr."

James turned his attention back to his task at hand, and soon the dried grass and small twigs went up in flames. He began expertly stacking smaller logs over the flames before the small fire could go out.

I let out a sigh of relief as the fire roared to life and engulfed me in its warmth. My eyes slipped closed, allowing me to feel a measure of peace for a time as my numb extremities came back to life, then I smelled cooking meat and came to a horrible realization. The only thing we had to eat was rabbit.

"I don't eat meat," I commented weakly with my eyes still closed.

"Then you won't be eating," James replied, like it didn't matter to him either way.

"Good luck finding the charm after I die then," I replied just as casually.

"You already told me where it is," he replied. "Your death wouldn't be much of an inconvenience."

My heart climbed up into my throat for a moment, but I managed to force it back down.

"The charm is protected by death magic," I explained. "You'll never be able to get to it even if you find it."

"And when did you become so wise?" he asked sarcastically. "You only just found out what you were a few weeks ago."

"The hearts told me," I lied.

My theory was actually just an educated guess. The images the hearts had shown me had been muddled at best, but through them I could feel the mounds. I somehow knew that if I reached them, I would be able listen to them, just like I had with the hearts.

"If you won't eat the rabbit, then you'll just have to wait until morning," he said finally.

"Fine," I mumbled. I edged closer to the fire. If I was going to starve, at least I'd be warm.

I thought about my situation as James ate the cooked rabbit meat. An entire clan to choose from, and the person I disliked the most was the one I ended up with. I was beginning to think my whole life was just a cruel joke. I'd had an ounce of happiness with Matthew, then I took his life away. After years of solitude, I'd had about two seconds of happiness with Alaric, then he betrayed me. I'd killed the man who was good to me, while the bad one was still alive and well.

"How long did you serve Estus?" I asked suddenly, wondering why James was so willing to betray him, while Alaric was not.

James turned thoughtful eyes to me. I almost thought he wouldn't answer, but then he said, "Thirty years, give or take."

"So what?" I questioned skeptically. "You served him since you were a baby?"

James' eyes glittered with amusement. "For a know-it-all, you know very little."

I frowned. "Enlighten me."

"The Vaettir age slowly, some among us get to be very old indeed."

I rolled my eyes. "I know Estus is like, really old, and Sivi too, but you can tell that they're older."

"How could you tell that Sivi is old?" he asked, though I had a feeling he was trying to prove some sort of point to me.

Come to think of it, I wasn't sure. Maya had told me a bit of Sivi's history, but I'd sensed she was ancient upon first meeting her, even though she appeared around twenty-five.

"I could just sense it," I replied, not sure of how else to explain it.

"The more powerful Vaettir can live for centuries," James explained. "Some even longer. Sivi is nearly eight-hundred years old."

The news was shocking, yet I wasn't terribly surprised. I sat up and gathered my legs to my chest. The last hints of cold had been chased from my bones, and I was feeling better despite the lack of food and water.

"Then Estus must be over a thousand," I commented, trying to sound like I knew what I was talking about.

James shook his head. "Estus is younger than Sivi."

I scrunched my face in confusion. "But he looks so much older than her."

"It's a power thing," James explained. "Most of us have become more and more human as we become disconnected from the old gods we were once connected to. The change ages us. Some are even born with less power than the generations before. Sivi remained what she always has been, and so, has not aged."

It all made sense in a theoretical kind of way, though my mind didn't quite want to embrace what James was telling me. I'd seen too many things over the past weeks to ever believe the Vaettir were similar to humans, but the idea of someone living eight-hundred years and not aging past twenty-five was difficult to stomach.

"So why is Sivi serving Estus, and not the other way around?" I questioned. "If she's powerful enough that she looks a good fifty years younger than Estus, why is she stuck scheming behind his back?"

James shrugged. "Estus is beloved. He is a seemingly human figurehead for a race that has become all too human. Our people would never follow a creature like Sivi."

The woodsmoke was beginning to sting my eyes, but I still wasn't ready to lose the warmth of the fire. Instead, I rolled over so that my back was to James and the fire, and squeezed my eyes shut.

"Is Aislin a seemingly human figurehead as well?" I asked, suddenly wishing that I could still see James' expressions as he spoke.

"More or less," he replied. "She's more powerful than Estus, but is struggling to gain control since many of our people were born during less enlightened times, and are unwilling to follow a woman."

The statement had me rolling back over toward the fire so I could give James a look of disgust.

He raised his hands in surrender. "Hey, *I* follow her. Don't shoot the messenger."

With an irritated sigh, I scooted away from the fire to keep an eye on him. The silence stretched out, only to be broken by the hoots of a distant owl, and the chorus of crickets that surrounded us.

"So back to your time spent serving Estus," I began again, still curious about the whole arrangement. "Thirty years seems like a big investment just to find a charm, especially when the charm wasn't even in the Salr to begin with."

James stared into the woods. "It wasn't always about the charm," he admitted.

"What was it about then?" I pressed.

He'd lived with those people for such a long time. It was hard to imagine sacrificing thirty years just to be a spy.

"That's no longer relevant," James answered quickly, almost as if he was nervous about the line of questioning.

He rose to throw a few more logs onto the fire with

more force than was necessary. I had to scoot back to avoid the sparks he created with each new log.

I glared at him. "Suit yourself. Just trying to make conversation."

He returned to his original seat in the dirt. "And why is that? I'm well aware of your . . . distaste for me. Why even attempt conversation at all?"

I shrugged, not entirely sure of my answer. "I'm not going to argue that I think you're a monster, but not everything is black and white. I could throw stones at you for enjoying your work, but . . . " I trailed off, not wanting to complete my thought.

"You enjoy yours too," James finished for me.

I stared into the fire, regretting starting the conversation to begin with, because he was right. I hate what I was, but the actual taking of life, the release, felt like nothing else. I'd been frightened when I'd accidentally killed one of my foster parents, and I'd been devastated when I'd accidentally killed Matthew, but the Vaettir I'd released, and the hearts . . . it felt amazing. I was pretty sure that it made me evil, or a sadist, or . . . something, but I couldn't help it.

I glanced back at James with his icy eyes that practically promised death all on their own and shook my head.

I could avoid thinking about the monster at the door as long as I wanted. The monster in the mirror was another story entirely.

16

I awoke to the sound of fighting. Not huge, battle-style fighting, but the distinct grunts and curses of a one-on-one fight. I opened my eyes to see that the fire had burned down to embers, but I didn't get to look at it long as I was pulled roughly to my feet.

Someone gripped my back tightly against their chest, with their arms wrapped around my shoulders protectively, not quite pinning me. I recognized Alaric's voice immediately beside my ear as he said, "She's coming with me. I don't know what lies you've been telling her, but she won't want to stay with you once things have been set straight."

James came into view with blood dripping from his nose. "She's just about the only person who knows the truth, actually." He looked at me when he said it, though he spoke to Alaric.

I shoved Alaric's arms off me, and took a few steps to give myself some space, putting us all into position for a three-way standoff. If only I had a gun.

Alaric turned his dark gaze to me. His black hair was tied back to leave his face bare, and he wore casual clothes perfectly suited to the woods.

I could sense his anger, but his voice was hurt when he asked, "How could you trust *him*, of all people? I would have gotten you out of the Salr, if you'd only given me time."

I snorted and crossed my arms. "Sorry, I got tired of starving and getting stabbed while I waited."

"But *he* stabbed you." He gestured toward James. "Surely my crimes are not worse than his?"

"He never pretended to be something he's not," I countered, "and when he decided to help me escape, he actually followed through on it."

Alaric's shoulders slumped in defeat. "I've only tried to ensure your survival, Maddy. You must believe me."

"No, I mustn't," I replied haughtily.

James watched our exchange with an annoyed expression. When no one had spoken for a moment, he stepped forward.

"We need to get going. There's no telling who could have followed *him* here," he said with an irritated nod toward Alaric.

I glared at Alaric. "How *did* you find us so quickly?"

"He's Bastet," James answered before Alaric could say anything. "He sniffed us out."

I'd seen the teeth, eyes, and claws, but I'd never considered that Alaric might have a heightened sense of smell too.

Alaric just stood there looking miserable while James snuffed out what remained of the fire. Once he was finished, he walked away through the trees wordlessly. I took one last look at Alaric, then began to follow.

"Maddy, please," he begged.

I stopped, then turned to look over my shoulder at him. "I've got things to do. I'd appreciate it if you would keep this meeting to yourself, but I'm sure you'll run to Estus the moment my back is turned."

I started walking again, hoping that he would go back to where he came from, but he quickly caught up to my side. I was out of luck it seemed. Not that I had any to begin with.

I stopped walking and glared at him. "What are you doing?" I asked sharply.

"I'm coming with you," he answered, looking forward at James' back in the distance instead of at me.

With a huff, I began walking again, and Alaric kept pace wordlessly beside me. As we made our way through the woods, Alaric unbuttoned his navy flannel, then took it off and held it out toward me. Although I was still quite cold in the lightweight dress I was wearing, I ignored the shirt and walked a little faster.

"I don't want you to come with," I pressed. "I think I've proven that I don't want, nor do I *need*, your help. You're lucky I'm too tired and fed up to attack you."

Alaric snorted and let his hand with the shirt fall to his side as he trotted to keep up with me. "Well if you've chosen to trust James, then you *do* need my help. It wouldn't surprise me if this was all some elaborate plan orchestrated by Estus to trick you into to finding the charm."

That stopped me dead in my tracks. I'd trusted James because he was willing to risk his life to help me escape, but what if he wasn't risking his life at all? Estus could have easily assigned James the task of making me believe he was an ally, so that I'd be willing to find the charm. Then once James had the charm, he could just give it to Estus instead of Aislin.

"Didn't think about that, did you?" Alaric asked with a bitter smile.

I started walking again, trying to brush off my reaction. "Of course I thought of that," I replied, "but he's helping me at the moment, and if he *does* turn on me, I'll be prepared."

He caught up to walk at my side. "Well since we're being so logical, I'm sure you can see that your best option lies in having me join you as well."

"On the contrary," I replied, "I'd rather only have to watch my back against one traitor, not two."

Alaric laughed, annoyingly delighting in our repartee. "If one of us is a traitor, then the other one can help you escape. You'll have the odds of two against one either way."

I glared at him, then quickly turned my eyes forward. "Unless you're both on the same side, and Estus sent you *both* to trick me."

Alaric shrugged. "Do you think I'd be Estus' plan A, or plan B?"

"Plan B," I grumbled.

Alaric shifted his gaze quickly to me, then back to the woods ahead of us. "And why is that?"

"Because Estus would have to be an idiot to believe I'd ever trust you again," I answered. "He wouldn't waste Plan A on the underdog."

Alaric was silent after that, though he stayed by my side. When it became clear that I wasn't going to take his shirt, he put it back on. The moment he did, I shivered and wanted the shirt even more, but I refused to ask for it.

We followed James for several hours. The protests from my stomach grew louder as my feet began to drag, and I grudgingly accepted Alaric's help as I stumbled and almost fell several times.

Just when I thought I couldn't go on any further, James stopped. At first I was unsure of why we'd come to a halt, as all I saw were more trees ahead of us, then the air went all shimmery. As the shimmers dissipated, a small cottage came into view.

I balked at the cottage's sudden appearance as James confidently opened the front door, walked through, and shut it behind him.

"Son of a bitch," I grumbled under my breath, hurrying toward the door. I eyed it, wondering what to do. At a loss, I raised my fist and knocked.

No answer.

Feeling irritated because Alaric was watching me with a raised eyebrow, I grabbed the doorknob and turned it, then pushed the door open and went inside. I scanned the interior for any sign of life, but it seemed abandoned. Where was James? Given his absence, I desperately hoped that who or what ever might live in the cottage wouldn't try to eat us, and would possibly offer us food instead. I stepped inside, my too-big hiking boots echoing on the floorboards.

Alaric followed me in, keeping close to my side. I could feel tension radiating off him like tiny ants marching across my skin.

"This should not be possible," he said quietly, peering around at rickety furniture covered in a thick layer of dust.

I stepped out of the way as a mouse scampered past my boots. "What should not be possible?"

"The Vaettir are forbidden to live above ground," he explained. He crept around the room, running his fingers along the wall as if looking for a secret panel.

"I don't think anyone lives here," I whispered, following his progress around the room.

He traveled down a nearby hallway, forcing me to either follow, or stay in the creepy, dusty room by myself. I followed.

"It's an illusion," he explained, "a facade to turn away any who might discover the nature of whoever lives here."

"Forgive me," an elderly female voice said from behind me.

I whipped around to find an old woman standing in the middle of the living room. The room she stood in was the same one we'd just left . . . only different. The dust had all been lifted to reveal spotless furniture, and a few candles were lit to make the place cozy.

"I needed a moment alone with James," the woman explained. "It is not often I receive visitors, especially other Vaettir."

The woman was dressed in a long, pale blue robe that obscured any other clothing she might be wearing underneath. The hood of the robe was pulled up to cover her short, curly, gray hair.

"And where is James now?" I asked suspiciously.

"He's fixing you supper, little mouse," the woman said with a smile. Her eyes were the vibrant green of fresh-leaves, and looked out of place in her pale, deeply lined face.

"I really wish people would stop calling me that," I grumbled.

The woman chuckled to herself, casually removing the hood from her head. "I am Diana," she introduced, "and I offer you refuge for the evening."

"Um, thanks," I replied hesitantly. "I'm Madeline."

James entered the room from the hallway opposite us. He carried a large tray stacked with sandwiches on one side, and several teacups on the other. He set the tray on the low coffee-table that stood in between the couch and two comfy-looking chairs. He sat in one of the chairs, followed by Diana, who sat in the other.

Alaric sauntered past me and took a seat on one side of the couch. The three of them watched me as I considered where to sit. With a final pointed look at Alaric, I sat cross-legged on the floor in front of the coffee table. The position I'd chosen put me closer to Diana than I wanted to be, but it was the spot farthest from both James and Alaric.

"Sit by your man, child," Diana scolded. "There's no need to sit on the floor."

"He's not *my* man," I replied politely. "I much prefer the floor."

Diana huffed. "Just because you're mad at him, doesn't mean he isn't yours."

The woman was obviously senile, but I humored her none-the-less. "I'm not just mad at him," I explained. "He had me put in a cell, and then he watched while *James* stabbed me. Mad doesn't even begin to cover it."

Diana tsked at me. "You will see things differently in time."

James stared at her. "What else do you see?"

Diana turned toward him. "You know better than to ask," she chided. With that, she took a cup of tea into her bony hand and settled more comfortably into her chair.

Confused by the conversation, I turned my attention to the sandwiches lying only a few torturous inches away from me. I smelled peanut butter and jelly. While it was a strange choice for supper, I was just glad there wasn't any meat in them. Noticing my gaze, Diana gestured toward the sandwiches with a smile.

"Now, about this charm," Diana began as I snatched a sandwich and bit into the hearty bread.

My mouth half-full, I interrupted, "James sure told you a lot in that short amount of time, didn't he?"

She set her teacup on the table, then laced her hands in her lap. "He told me very little, though he did mention your current quest. I wanted a moment with him before I met you so that I might scold him for not warning me of his visit."

I narrowed my eyes at her, suddenly feeling very uncomfortable. I had a suspicion that Estus could sometimes read the thoughts of others. Perhaps this woman was the same.

"Then how did you—" I began, wondering how she'd known about me and Alaric.

"I see things," she interrupted. "What has been, some of what will be, but only sometimes what *is*."

Well that explained her observations about Alaric, which I'd have to think more upon later. At that moment I was more concerned with the look in Diana's vibrant green eyes as she stared at me. It was a look that said she was imagining peeling my skin off layer by layer.

"Could you please stop looking at me like you want to eat me?"

"I have offered you sanctuary," she replied. "You are safe from my appetites . . . tonight."

I gulped. I hadn't actually thought she wanted to eat me, but I had seen a similar, predatory look from James.

Diana turned her attention to Alaric. "Now my dear," she said, "I haven't seen you since you were a boy. Where is Sophie? You two were never far from each other as children."

Alaric looked truly surprised. "I'm sorry, do I know you?"

Diana smiled. "I asked my question first."

"Sophie is . . . " Alaric paused, seemingly at a loss for words.

It only occurred to me in that moment that I wasn't the only one Sophie had abandoned. She had never even planned on telling Alaric that she was going to leave with Maya. It had to hurt.

"Sophie is away on business," I answered for him. That was a whole can of worms we didn't need to open.

Diana cocked her head at me. "You're not lying," she began, "but you're also not telling me the truth."

I shrugged and took another bite of my sandwich.

Diana sniffed and turned her attention from me. I glanced up at James, who was sitting stiffly with an unreadable expression. Something told me that we didn't want Diana to know that Sophie had left the Salr, though I wasn't sure why.

"I will help you find the charm," Diana said suddenly,

"but I want to share in the credit when you deliver it to my sister, Aislin."

"Aislin?" Alaric sputtered as he choked on his tea at the same time I asked, "Sister?"

Alaric turned to me for verification. "Why would we give *her* the charm?"

"Because Aislin didn't have me hung from a wall and tortured," I answered sweetly.

Diana chuckled, her glittering eyes on Alaric. "I see someone has yet to choose the correct side."

Realization dawned on Alaric's face as he stared at Diana. "Aislin knows that you're living above ground, doesn't she? And she allows it?"

Diana's smile grew. "Like I said, the *correct* side."

Alaric turned his glare to James. "I wonder which side you *actually* work for," he mused darkly. "In the end, which will you betray?"

Diana snorted. "James would not abandon his own grandmother, and I have no intention of betraying one as powerful as Aislin, sister or no."

I was doing my best to figure everything out while the attention was off me. If Diana was James' grandmother, then that made Aislin his great aunt. Given the family connections, James was probably telling the truth about working for Aislin during his time with Estus. The family ties lent him credibility. Then again, lies might run in his family as well.

I started eating another sandwich as Alaric and Diana continued to bicker. I felt like a little kid, sitting on the ground while the grownups talked about grownup things. I might have even been offended if I wasn't so bone-achingly tired.

James watched me with a small smile on his face throughout the exchange. Eventually he nodded toward the hallway, then stood. Not particularly wanting to remain in Diana's presence, I rose to my feet as he walked past me and down the hall. I followed warily, still expecting some sort of trick.

A moment later the bickering stopped, and Alaric was following close behind me. James pushed open the first door he reached, revealing a small, clean bedroom. He stood to the side of the door while he waited for Alaric and I to walk through.

Once in the room, I turned and looked a question at James. "I hadn't hoped for a private room, but separate beds would have been nice."

James regarded me with an evil smile. "I figured I'd let you two lovebirds have the honeymoon suite. I'll sleep on the couch."

I glared at him. "I knew you would betray me."

James gave me a little salute, then shut the door in my face, leaving me alone in a dark room with a man I once could have loved.

I hugged my arms tightly around my stomach, not wanting to turn around and face Alaric again. Sure, I'd spoken to him in the woods earlier that day, but we hadn't been alone. Being alone made me nervous.

The room was small, and fit with the rest of the cottage-style decor. The single bed stood ominously, lit by the moonlight shining through the room's only small window.

I jumped when a hand landed gently on the side of my arm. Alaric's long fingers gripped my bare skin, turning me to face him. I moved stiffly, not wanting to look at him, but knowing I couldn't avoid it.

"We shouldn't stay here," he whispered. "We need to look for Sophie. She can give us a place to hide and regroup until we decide what to do."

"There is no *we*," I hissed. "There is only *me*, and I'd like to get some rest, if you don't mind." I looked at the lower half of his face while I said it, not wanting to feel the full pressure of his gaze.

He put his fingers underneath my chin and raised my eyes up to him. "You're putting yourself in the middle of a war, Maddy. You don't understand what you're doing."

I took a step back out of his reach. I'd thought my anger was exhausted, but I was wrong. "*You* put me in the middle of a war. I had no choice in the matter."

Alaric's shoulders slumped as his hand fell to his side. "Nothing would have happened to you if it weren't for Maya."

"Maya?" I scoffed. "You mean the woman who was being *tortured* right in front of me?"

Alaric raised his hands in frustration, but seemed to calm as he closed his fists, then dropped them back down. "Maya's problems weren't your fight, Maddy."

"Then whose were they?" I countered.

"You're defending a woman who abandoned you!" he growled. "I didn't see Maya coming back to risk herself when *you* were the one in the cell."

"Well I didn't see you risking yourself either," I snapped. "Just because Maya didn't save me in return, doesn't mean I shouldn't have saved her to begin with. I didn't help her because I thought she deserved it. I helped her because that is the type of person I want to be. I don't want to be the person who leaves others literally hanging from manacles."

"That type of person does not exist among the Vaettir," he replied coldly. "Do not risk yourself for others, because they will never risk themselves for you."

"And yet here you are," I stated blandly, "*risking* yourself for me."

"So you believe me?" he asked, instantly jumping on what I'd just said.

I shook my head. "I don't believe anything anymore. Not without solid, indisputable proof."

Alaric took another step toward me, and this time I didn't back away. "I'll prove it to you in time," he said with an almost smile, "that is, if we live long enough."

"You think Estus will come after us?" I questioned, though I already knew the answer.

"He will. Especially after you released all of his hearts. He put two and two together, and he would rather die than let you hand the charm to Aislin."

"And you would let me give her the charm, even though your Doyen forbids it?" I pressed.

"I left the Salr against his wishes," he answered. "He is no longer my Doyen. The life I had is gone."

"You didn't need to follow me," I stated coldly. I'd be damned if he'd make me feel guilty for his loss.

He shook his head. "I was already planning on leaving once I managed to free you. If we would have been more swift, or if *you* had bothered sharing your plan with me, I would have left with you the night Sophie escaped with Maya."

I shook my head. "I don't believe you. You would have had no reason to make such a sacrifice for me. You barely even know me."

"You keep insisting that I've made some huge sacrifice," he replied, his head tilted slightly to one side.

The movement made his now loose, dark hair fall over his shoulder. I didn't know at what point he'd untied it, but I had the overwhelming urge to reach out and run my fingers through the soft tresses. Repressing the impulse, my hands balled into fists at my sides.

"You left your home," I explained. "Leaving home is always a sacrifice."

He shrugged. "I've had other homes, and I'm sure I'll have more in the future."

It was my turn to tilt my head in confusion. "It was my impression that you and Sophie grew up in the Salr."

He laughed, the abrupt sound startling in the darkness. "Sophie and I grew up in a very different world from the one we know now."

"James informed me that the Vaettir don't always look their age," I said as an idea formed in my mind. "How old are you, exactly?"

He shrugged. "Old enough."

I shook my head. "No. No more lies. I'll need two forms of I.D. before I'll believe anything you say."

He sighed and turned to wander around the room. He ran his fingers along the quilted bedspread, then went to fiddle around with the bedside lamp like it actually interested him.

"I've lost track of the exact time," he said finally, "but I was born around the year 1500, give or take a few years."

"You're trying to tell me that you're over five-hundred years old?" I scoffed.

He flicked the lamp on and off absentmindedly. "Don't believe it, if you wish. I wouldn't have told you if you would have let the subject go."

I went to stand in front of him with my hands on my hips. "And why wouldn't you have told me?"

He smiled. "You don't seem like a woman who'd be interested in a much older man."

I laughed, and it felt strange after the past few days I'd had. "It *is* a little creepy, now that you mention it."

He held a hand to his chest dramatically. "Oh Madeline, you wound me."

I laughed again, and it felt a little more natural. "We should get some rest," I said finally. "I hope you find the floor comfortable."

He let out a dramatic sigh. "I suppose arguing tonight would be a moot point?"

I nodded, "Just in case you're lying, I'd rather not revert to snuggle buddy status."

He cringed. "I suppose I deserve that."

I nodded again, then stood on my tippy-toes to plant a kiss on his cheek.

"And what was that for?" he asked in surprise as I took a step back.

I shrugged and climbed into bed. "For the possibility that you're telling the truth."

"Would another truth earn me a pillow?" he asked hopefully.

I tried to look as disinterested as possible when I said, "It might."

He was standing far enough back that all I could see was his silhouette as he said, "In all of my five-hundred years, letting James stab you was the most difficult thing I've ever done."

Tears started to well up in my eyes, and they were tears that I didn't want to share with anyone. I grabbed the extra pillow off the bed and tossed it to Alaric, then I laid my head on the other pillow with my back turned toward him.

I listened as he lowered himself to the floor. A long while later, his breathing slowed to the even rhythms of sleep. Finally I let a few, silent tears slip out. They weren't tears for Alaric, or for anyone else but me. They were tears for the life I'd lived thus far, and for what might lay ahead. Sometimes you just have to cry for yourself, because no one else will.

Moments later, loud snoring that could only belong to James echoed through the wall, and I wished I had the extra pillow to sandwich my face. Instead I pulled the quilt over my head in a futile effort to muffle the noise. And here I thought there wasn't supposed to be any rest for the wicked.

17

I woke up early to find Alaric already wide awake, sitting at the foot of my bed, watching me with a distant sort of look. He perked up as I struggled my way out of the tangled mess I'd made of the bedding.

"How long have you been sitting there?" I groaned.

He shrugged. "A few hours. I couldn't sleep."

"You know, a normal person would have found a book or something else to occupy their time," I chided.

He shrugged again, then stood and offered me a hand to get up. I ignored his extended hand and stretched my arms over my head. I had to put them back down quickly though, as it dawned on me that I hadn't showered in a while.

"I'm going to find the bathroom," I announced, hoping that Alaric hadn't caught a whiff of me, but knowing that he had.

"Would you care for some company?" he asked with his eyebrows raised.

"Absolutely not," I mumbled, then made a beeline for the door.

The bathroom was just across the hall from the room we'd been given, so I was able to make a quick escape. I locked the bathroom door behind me, thinking that I should have asked Diana before I went to take a shower. Oh well, I wasn't about to go back into the hall in my state of stench, so I found a spare towel rolled in one of those little towel baskets and started the water.

I stripped out of the black dress, immensely displeased that I'd have to put the tattered thing back on after my shower. At least the river had washed away the blood from my stab wounds.

I observed my naked side to find two small scars where the knife had punctured my flesh. In that moment I realized how someone with my particular gifts could abuse such a power. The ability to take lives in order to heal others should never have existed.

Feeling more cold than the temperature of the room could account for, I stepped under the hot stream of water. I used the shampoo and soap that had been left in the shower, but couldn't find any conditioner. I scowled. Long, unruly hair needs conditioner. I'd be a total poofball by noon.

By the time I finished my shower and emerged from the bathroom in my shabby dress, coffee and breakfast had been made. We all sat at a small kitchen table like a nice, dysfunctional little family. James and Alaric sat to either side of me, leaving me to look directly at Diana as I sipped my coffee.

Diana was dressed more normally today, in khaki

slacks and a pale green, floral blouse. The green of the blouse made her leaf-green eyes stand out vibrantly in her pale face. She watched me carefully as I ate my french toast.

I had been mildly surprised the night before when James made sandwiches. When I'd found out that he'd also made the french toast, I was shocked. It was perfectly cooked, the outside crispy, and the inside sog-free. I was also pretty sure that I detected a hint of cinnamon and nutmeg. Maybe torture was just James' day job, and he secretly moonlighted as a chef. Then again, maybe not.

"The place you seek is not on this continent," Diana said suddenly.

It took me a moment to figure out what she was talking about, then I realized that James had probably filled her in on what I'd told him.

"Please tell me you're joking," I replied with my mouth full of french toast. I looked to James for confirmation.

He shrugged, like it didn't really matter. "It looks like we'll be taking a trip. Passports and IDs are all taken care of in case Estus tries to track us by more mundane means. Your new name is Nicole, FYI."

I blinked at him. A sudden international flight? Fake passport? Was I working with spies?

"But we'll need to find Sophie first," Alaric chimed in.

I turned my dimwitted stare over to him. "Why do we need Sophie?"

"Strength in numbers," James replied plainly. "Plus, I already had a passport made for her. I'd hate for it to go to waste."

I sighed, dropping my fork onto my plate. "And you two

just planned this whole thing out while I was in the shower?"

"You should not be so remiss to visit your homeland," Diana interrupted.

"I was born in California," I countered. "I've visited my homeland plenty."

"The Vaettir originated in Scandinavia," Alaric explained. "She's not referring to where you were born."

"Scandinavia?" I asked incredulously. "You expect me to believe my ancestors are Scandinavian?" I gestured to myself. "I might be tall, but blonde I am not."

Diana tsked. "Truly, have you boys taught her nothing?" Addressing me, she continued, "When our race first came into being, Scandinavia is where we originated, but we come from many pantheons of gods with different ethnic origins."

"Okay . . . " I trailed off, wondering what pantheon I'd come from. "So skipping over all that confusing information, if this charm is in another country, why did Estus ever believe it was in Washington?"

"The Salr is not in any one place," Alaric explained. "The entrances are stationary, but the actual structure resides on its own plane of reality. It's not really in Washington, nor is it anywhere else, and there are many more Salr spread out across the world."

"That doesn't make any sense," I replied slowly. I knew that the Salr was a place of magic, but it had to *exist* somewhere real.

Alaric shrugged. "The Salr were created long before my time. I cannot explain any more than I know. All I can tell you is that they are a place of refuge. They came into being where they were needed."

Dianna nodded. "Yes, originally the Salr were meant as places of sanctuary, but clans began moving into them permanently as our numbers dwindled. Those who did not have a clan were left out in the world alone. Leaders stepped forward to rule over those who resided within each Salr. Those rulers became Doyen, like Estus and Aislin."

I shook my head. I understood the theory of what I was being told, but the mechanics didn't make sense at all. "Okay, so Estus became Doyen over a Salr, how, just because he wanted the job? Was there another Doyen before him?"

"Enough chit chat," James interrupted irritably. "We need to get moving."

I tilted my head. This was more information than I'd been given previously by a long shot. I wasn't about to stop questioning now. "So say we hop on a plane, and end up in Finland or wherever. How will we find the charm once we get there, and how can we be sure that it is even there?"

"Because I know the place that you were shown in your vision," Diana replied, "and I will be going with you."

"Couldn't you just draw us a map?" I asked hopefully.

Diana bared her teeth in an unpleasant smile. "Do you not desire my company?"

"It's not that," I corrected quickly, though really it was. "I just don't see the need for everyone to drop what they're doing to fly to Scandinavia."

Diana stared at me until I finally looked down. Strangely, I was much more nervous about the idea of traveling with one little old woman than I was about traveling with my almost sort-of ex-boyfriend and a man who might very well be a psychopath.

I averted my gaze and ate the rest of my french toast in silence, even though it felt like cardboard in my stomach.

"I should find Sophie before we all leave this place," Alaric announced, breaking the silence. "We are well hidden here. It makes no sense to risk Madeline being out in the open until we are ready to depart."

"So we should just let you run off to Estus while we wait here for the ambush?" James countered.

Alaric glared back at James. "If my sister sees us together, she'll hide. I have a better chance of talking to her on my own."

"Sophie won't hide from me," James muttered, looking down at his plate.

I snorted. "Wanna bet?"

"You don't know what you're talking about," he snapped.

I looked back at him, too surprised to be angry. Normally James could take any insult I had to throw at him.

I turned to Alaric. "What exactly am I missing here?"

"James and Sophie were once lovers," Alaric explained, "and he is somehow deluded enough to believe she still cares for him."

"You don't know what you're talking about either," James said to Alaric. "What happened between Sophie and me is our business. Period."

I held up my hands before an argument could begin. "I'm still having trouble grasping the fact that Sophie would ever even look at James to begin with. How recent was this?"

"The breakup occurred roughly one year ago," Alaric answered while still looking at James.

I was beginning to understand all of the tension between James, Alaric, and Sophie. Both siblings had told me not to trust him, but wouldn't give me a reason. My guess was that James had betrayed Sophie's trust, and Alaric had gotten protective of his sister. It was all a moot point as far as I was concerned. I'd never trusted James regardless.

"It doesn't matter," James snapped. "You're still not going alone to find her."

"And I'm not going to let you two run off and kill each other," I added. "Plus, Sophie owes me an apology."

"I'll wait here," Diana said calmly. She rose from the table and walked toward the sink to fill her tea kettle.

"It's settled then," I stated flatly.

"It's not settled," Alaric argued. "We don't need to risk your life any more than we have to, and our best chance of recruiting Sophie is if I go alone."

"First," I replied, holding up a finger dramatically in the air, "I don't think Sophie will run from me. She may have deserted me, but she's no coward. Second," I said as I held up another finger, "you've risked my life plenty. There's no need to start getting squeamish about it now."

"I agree with Madeline," James added.

"I don't care if you agree with me," I snapped. "I'm the only one here that can find the charm, so we're going to start doing things on my terms. I don't know if either of you realize this, but I'm no longer a prisoner."

"Maddy—" Alaric began.

"She's right, you know," James interrupted with an infuriating smile.

"Why is it," I began as I looked at James, "that even when you're on my side, I still want to slap you?"

"Oooh, please do," he taunted.

"Enough," Alaric said, bracing his hands on the table. "If we're all going, we may as well get on with it. If I know Sophie, she'll be hiding in the city. She wouldn't go far until she knew whether or not I'd be following her, and she sure as hell wouldn't hide out in the woods."

"So we go to the city, and what, sniff her out?" I asked.

"Yes," he replied, "but we might run into a problem."

"Which of our myriad of problems are you referring to?" I asked tiredly.

Alaric looked at me like I was being silly. "You're technically a missing person, Maddy. Someone must have noticed that you're gone by now. Walking openly around Spokane is probably not the best idea."

"Well then we should probably get me something more to wear than this stupid dress," I said irritably. I didn't feel the need to point out that I probably wasn't a missing person yet, given that there would have been no one around to miss me.

"We'll be sure to stop at *Nordstrom*," James sniped.

Alaric took a deep breath to say more, but Diana cut him off with a tsking sound. "Enough bickering, children. We have things to do, and time is short. Estus may not know where the charm is, but he'd be a fool to discount the possibility of Madeline finding it. Do what you must, then meet me at the airport."

I had to wonder just how old Diana was to be referring

to Alaric as a child, but I wasn't about to ask her. Instead, I straightened my dress and got to my feet like a good little girl.

Soon we'd be off to somewhere in Scandinavia. Though it was true that I needed a vacation, I would have been happy with a beach in Mexico. Something told me I wouldn't be getting any margaritas with Diana around.

18

Our only choice was to leave on foot, which was fine, except that Spokane was a good five miles away from Diana's hidden home. Normally I'd be fine with a five mile hike, but a five mile hike in boots that were a size too big, with two very grumpy hiking companions was not my idea of a good time.

Also, it was *cold*. Fall had just begun in Spokane when I was snatched out of my bed and taken to the Salr, but it felt like winter had taken over in the relatively short time I'd been gone. I knew winter would get much colder before the year was through, but normally I would be properly attired for the occasion.

I'd grudgingly accepted Alaric's long-sleeved shirt, and he didn't seem fazed as he walked bare-chested in the chilly air beside me. I'd have to remember to give him his shirt back before we made it to civilization. I was pretty sure a bare-chested, 6'2", ethereally gorgeous man walking through town would draw more attention than a woman who may or may not have been reported as a missing person.

I did my best to keep my eyes off of his bare skin as we walked, but I might have lagged behind a few times just to get a good view of his back for a while. Of course, every time I lagged behind, he would turn and wait for me, dashing my plans to bits.

"You two are pathetic," James commented from behind us as Alaric stopped to help me over a fallen log.

"It's a good thing that I don't value your opinion at all," I replied, "or I might have some hurt feelings right now."

"That's all well and nice for you," Alaric said with a smile, "but I think I need to go cry in a dark corner for a little while."

James snorted. "Mock all you like, but *I'm* not the one acting like a teenager with their very first crush."

"I *saw* you as a teenager," Alaric replied without looking back, "I'm not sure I could ever match how ferociously you flirted with Sophie."

"Wait," I said as I stopped walking, "Sophie was an adult while James was a teenager, and she still dated him?"

Alaric laughed. "Well it was much later that they dated, and he was as much of an adult at the time as he is now . . . which is, of course, debatable."

"Oh you guys are just barrels of fun to be around," James muttered, picking up his pace to walk past us.

"You started it!" Alaric called after him.

When James was a good distance ahead of us again, I turned to talk to Alaric as we walked. "It almost seems like you guys are friends."

Alaric shrugged. "Perhaps once, but things change, and some things are unforgivable."

"And those unforgivable things have to do with Sophie?" I pressed, my curiosity getting the better of me, as it often did.

"Sophie and James were together for two years, just after Maya left, and then Sophie lost interest. Sophie was unfazed, but James had taken their relationship very seriously," Alaric explained.

"Why was Sophie so unfazed?" I asked. "Two years is a long time to spend with someone."

He shrugged. "Two years to someone who has only lived a human lifetime can seem like a lot, but when you live long enough, two years seems like a blip on the radar. Sophie tried to explain the concept to James, who is much younger than us, but he wouldn't accept how casually he'd been brushed aside. My sister admittedly could have had more tact, but she has a short attention span, and moved on almost immediately with another man."

I glanced at him with an eyebrow raised, then glanced at James in the distance to make sure he wasn't close enough to hear us. "You know, that's exactly what Sophie said about you when she warned me not to develop any feelings."

"That I moved on immediately with another man?" Alaric joked.

"The short attention span," I replied without mirth, though I was pretty sure he knew what I meant.

He peered at the ground as we walked. "My sister needs to learn when to keep her mouth shut."

"Was she telling the truth?" I prodded, not willing to let the subject drop so easily.

He sighed. "Perhaps, but the past is not always a predictor of the future."

We walked in tense silence for a moment, then Alaric said, "But back to my story."

I blushed, because I'd completely forgotten that we'd originally been talking about Sophie and James. I cleared my throat. "Yes, do go on."

"James couldn't handle seeing Sophie with another man," he continued, "though he never admitted it. Instead he befriended the man, Sammael was his name."

"Well that was big of him, I suppose."

Alaric shook his head. "James spent a good deal of time befriending Sammael. They became quite close really. Sammael would have trusted James with his life. It was at that point that James tortured and killed Sammael. This happened roughly six months before you came to us. James later admitted that he spent the time to gain Sammael's trust in order to make his vengeance more rewarding. He also wanted to allow Sophie enough time to grow attached to Sammael, so that the loss would hurt her more."

"And he was allowed to remain in the Salr?" I asked, shocked.

"That was the day James became Estus' pet torturer," Alaric replied distantly. "Estus claimed that James would prove to be the very best man for the job."

I let out a slow breath. "Well, Estus was right on that count, I suppose."

"Though he was wrong to ever trust him."

"Wasn't he wrong in trusting you as well?" I countered.

"You didn't exactly hold up well on the loyalty meter either."

Alaric glanced over and offered me a small smile. "I suppose you're correct."

I shrugged. "It still seems too simple to me . . . " I trailed off.

"That Estus would put so much faith in any of us?" he questioned, reading my mind.

"Escaping shouldn't have been as simple as it was," I elaborated, "and even after James and I escaped, to let you go as well?"

"I've considered that," he replied.

I rolled my eyes. "I'm going to need a little more feedback than that."

"I've considered the fact that perhaps we are doing exactly what Estus hopes. Perhaps he knew all along that the charm was not in the Salr. He couldn't trust us to go free and find it for him out of loyalty, so instead he set us up to do it out of a need to defeat him," he explained.

"What if that's all true?" I asked. "We could very well be doing exactly what he wants us to do."

Alaric's expression turned somber. "We must continue on regardless, and hope that we can defeat Estus when the time comes."

I let out a huff of breath, fogging the chilly air. "I'm not doing it to defeat Estus. I'm doing it to join Aislin's clan."

"And why would you want that?" Alaric countered quickly, like he'd been wanting to ask for a while. "You're out here, free. You could just move somewhere far away and live your life."

"And have to look over my shoulder forever?"

He shook his head. "That's not why you're doing it."

"What is it that you want me to admit, exactly?" I snapped.

I wasn't sure why I was getting angry, I just knew that I didn't like being pressed on things I didn't want to talk about . . . even if I didn't know why I didn't want to talk about them.

Alaric shrugged. "Nothing at all. I'd only like you to consider the fact that not having a clan does not automatically mean you will be alone."

That was it. He'd hit the nail on the head with the word *alone*. I looked ahead again to see how far James had gone. He was barely visible in the distant trees ahead of us, but I lowered my voice none-the-less. "What exactly are you saying?"

Alaric moved closer to me so that we were walking shoulder to shoulder, except my shoulder was quite a few inches lower than his.

"I propose that we destroy the charm," Alaric whispered. "Our people are not meant to be ruled. Destroy that power, and perhaps we can escape them all."

"Just a few days ago you were all, *Estus is Doyen, he asks and I obey*," I argued, shocked at what Alaric was suggesting.

"He pushed too far," he said simply.

"Really?" I balked. "Was it the assigned kidnapping, the maiming of your sister's girlfriend, or the maiming of your own girlfriend that caused you to finally draw the line?"

"My *girlfriend*?" he asked with a lascivious smile, ignoring everything else I'd said.

I rolled my eyes. "You know what I mean. What finally changed your mind?"

"My mind was changed as soon as you and Sophie decided to leave the Salr, as I no longer had much reason to stay," he began. "The only reason we were there to begin with was because I wanted to protect Sophie. I thought it the safest place. But when James harmed you . . . " he shook his head, as if reliving the moment. "I will not again put myself in the position of obeying one leader blindly."

Now that I understood his reasoning, I couldn't argue with him. He was right to assume that I'd give the charm to Aislin just so I wouldn't have to be alone again, even though I didn't relish the thought of becoming another clan's pet executioner. I didn't trust myself around humans, but any Vaettir I might associate with would be impervious to my gifts. I'd thought joining another clan the only solution. . . but if Alaric would hide with me, if he would be willing to teach me more about my curse . . .

"Please tell me what you're thinking," Alaric said after I'd been silent for a while.

I glanced up toward James again. "I'm thinking that this could very well be the biggest decision of my life, but you're acting like it's an easy choice for you and Sophie."

"You're young," Alaric stated. "My sister and I have been part of many clans, and we have been on our own as well. The centuries change things. Eventually big decisions become inconsequential."

"Well that's depressing."

"It is something you'll learn to deal with, in time," he said with a small smile.

I snorted. "Barring the fact that I'll probably be killed

off any day here, I doubt I'll live anywhere as long as you have."

He blinked at me. "Why would you say that? You are Vaettir, just like the rest of us."

"James explained about the more powerful Vaettir aging slowly," I answered. "I imagine I'll be aging rather quickly."

"It is not as simple as that," he sighed. "My sister and I are long-lived not because of our power level, but because we are more closely linked to our goddess than others. Many no longer even know from which god they descend."

"So you're like, part god?" I asked incredulously.

Alaric shook his head. "I am Vaettir. We come from the earth, just as the gods and goddesses of old. We embody their energy."

"Then where do I come from?" I asked, perplexed.

He shrugged. "A death goddess, I imagine. You inherit your gifts from your mother's side."

"And what about my pesky penchant for empathy?" I asked.

He shrugged again. "Now that, I have no explanation for, and it was clear that Estus did not expect you to come with such interesting gifts."

"Okay," I began, reverting back to our original line of conversation. "If I am a *denizen of death*," I said spookily, "and other Vaettir like Sivi identify with the elements, what exactly do you, as Bastet, embody?"

"War," Alaric replied simply. "I believe Sophie mentioned this to you."

I bit my lip, thinking back. "She said something about

me being attracted to you because war and death go together, but how can you *embody* war?"

"Well, I'm very good at killing."

"Well that's comforting," I mumbled.

He laughed and pushed against my arm playfully. "Since when is death intimidated by a little bit of war?"

My legs were beginning to tire from all of the walking, and my brain was tired enough that I didn't quite know how to answer him. Sure, death was a part of war, but death wasn't supposed to feel the pain and emotions of those who were to be claimed.

I took a deep breath, and gave Alaric the only answer I could think of.

"Since death grew a heart."

19

I felt like my feet were about to fall off by the time I first heard sounds of traffic. The sun was making its slow descent past the trees, robbing us of the last of its warmth. James had eventually fallen back to walk with us, though he'd remained silent by my side.

I unbuttoned Alaric's shirt, not looking forward to baring my arms to the chilly air. He took the shirt absent-mindedly and began putting it on as he sniffed the air, reminding me of a lion, or some other large cat.

"Anything?" James asked as he eyed our surroundings.

Alaric shook his head. "I know a few places she would go. We might have to search for a while."

"We don't have much time," James replied sternly. "That we're yet to see any sign of pursuit from Estus is shocking, to say the least."

"There's probably time for food though, right?" I chimed in.

My stomach was cramping terribly from the lack of

food over the last few days. Alaric and James didn't seem affected by it, but they didn't seem affected by a lot of things. Me, I needed food and a nice warm coat.

Alaric pulled me toward him and wrapped an arm around me. My first instinct was to fight, but I was freezing, tired, and hungry. I simply didn't have any fight left, and his body heat was one small comfort I wasn't willing to refuse.

James gave us an irritated look, but didn't comment. Instead, we all began walking again, following the sounds of traffic.

Soon we started seeing houses here and there, and our footing transitioned from dirt and pine needles to sidewalk and asphalt. I didn't recognize where we were, but Spokane is a large city, and there was no way for me to be familiar with all of the suburbs.

As darkness fully fell, we reached a small strip mall. The smell of cooking food wafted out of a few restaurants, but the few clothing stores had already closed. Maybe it was Sunday. I'd completely lost track of the days.

"Get her something to eat," James instructed, his attention on Alaric. "I'll find her a coat."

I raised a finger in the air. "And some socks . . . if you don't mind."

James sighed loudly, then turned and disappeared into the darkness of the nearby storefronts, presumably to steal me a coat. Alaric ushered me across the street, then toward the nearest restaurant, a small pasta/pizza place.

"It's like we're going on our first date," he intoned happily, his arm still snug around me.

I glared up at him, my feet dragging as he gently urged me toward the restaurant. "The first date usually occurs before the breakup, and it definitely occurs before the . . . " I trailed off, not wanting to say what I had originally intended.

"The sex?" Alaric finished for me. "So we like to do things backwards," he went on, "it's part of our charm."

"There is no *we* or *our*," I corrected, "and this is *not* a date."

"No roses, no wine," Alaric joked. "Got it."

"Wonderful," I grumbled.

Alaric held the door for me as we went inside the small restaurant. Nervous, I pulled my hair forward to cover my face. The chances that someone would recognize me as a missing person were slim, but it was still a possibility that I'd rather avoid.

I received a few odd glances at my tattered dress, though the glances were probably more because of the small amount of fabric I was wearing in the cold weather than the state of my clothing. Grunge was in again, or so I'd heard.

With no sign of a hostess, we slid into a corner booth with our backs to the wall. Even with a full view of the restaurant, I felt like Estus would pop out and nab us at any moment.

I fiddled with my place setting. "Maybe we should have gone with fast food."

Alaric slouched against the backrest like he hadn't a care in the world. "I don't eat fast food. That stuff will kill you."

I snorted. "If five-hundred years of living among the Vaettir doesn't kill you, the fast food surely will."

He smiled and raised an eyebrow at my joke, then

turned as a young waitress came to the table for our drink orders. Her eyes lingered on Alaric for longer than was polite, and she looked a little confused as she took in my disheveled, frizz-haired appearance.

I ordered an iced tea and gave the waitress an uncomfortable amount of eye-contact. Alaric ordered a glass of red wine and gave the waitress a cheerful wink, completely undermining the hopefully intimidating stare I had going on.

"I thought you said no wine," I grumbled as the waitress walked away with a smile on her face.

"I lied," he said simply. "I'm supposed to be a liar, remember?"

"And here I'd thought you'd changed," I sighed.

Alaric feigned a hurt expression. "Well at least you're talking to me now."

I opened my mouth to argue that I was only talking to him since he was the only company present, but the waitress came back and placed our drinks in front of us. I hadn't had time to look at the menu, but it would have been a moot point as Alaric started ordering for us: fettuccine, spinach lasagna, mozzarella sticks, fried mushrooms, a pizza, and three different deserts.

I looked at him in astonishment as the waitress walked away. "Are we expecting guests?"

He winked one dark brown eye at me. "Who knows when our next meal will be? We should enjoy ourselves, for tomorrow we might be dead."

I stared dejectedly at my iced tea, unsettled by Alaric's way of thinking. Suddenly I wished that I'd gotten something more extravagant like a strawberry daiquiri or a milkshake. If I was going to die soon, I really didn't want to waste my time with bland iced tea.

Alaric used his index finger to slowly scoot his glass of red wine in front of me. Not needing any more of an invitation, I wrapped my fingers around the stem of the glass. He smiled as I took a long sip, then offered the glass back to him.

He reached out for the glass, brushing his fingertips across mine as he took it. His expression had lost its playfulness. The look in his eyes made me gulp, and I quickly turned my gaze back to my iced tea.

Movement caught my eye, and I let out a sigh of relief as James entered the restaurant. I didn't know how to deal with the heat in Alaric's eyes, and James was a welcome distraction. He approached our table and handed me a knee-length black coat with a fur-lined hood that I sincerely hoped was faux.

"Put it on and keep your face covered," he said quickly. "We need to go."

Alaric stood immediately, taking James' mood seriously. I stood and wrapped the coat around me, wanting to cry at the fact that I was going to miss another meal.

"Socks are in the pocket," James said to me, "but you'll have to put them on later. Now move."

He grabbed my arm and pulled me forward so that I was walking in front of him. Our waitress watched us leave with what looked like our appetizers in her hands. In fact, the whole restaurant watched us leave. Hopefully we'd be long gone before they noticed we hadn't paid for the wine.

So much for not making a scene.

"We were tracked," James said as we spilled out into the

parking lot. "Marcus confronted me. He's dead, but there will be more."

My eyes darted around the half-full parking lot as we walked, but everything in the night was still. Who the hell was Marcus?

"If Marcus was here, then Siobhan won't be far behind," Alaric said.

Since I didn't know who they were talking about, I kept my mouth shut and allowed myself to be led down the dark sidewalk and past more closed or closing businesses. We crossed the street, then went into the parking lot of a large, abandoned warehouse. The yard was strewn with refuse, and didn't look like it had been used in many years. Whatever suburb we were in, the place had definitely seen better days to leave such a space right in the middle of town.

"Give up the girl," a female voice said from behind us.

The three of us turned in unison.

A man and a woman stood under the illumination of a streetlight. The woman's long, white coat made her strawberry blonde hair stand out vibrantly in the light. The man looked out of place beside her in his casual street clothes and knit winter cap.

"I don't want to hurt you, Siobhan," Alaric replied, "but the girl you cannot have."

As the girl in question, I didn't like being talked about like I wasn't there, but I'd complain later. The mismatched pair left the sidewalk and approached us warily, sizing up the odds, then everything exploded into chaos.

James shoved me out of the way as the man rushed us, and Alaric had already collided with Siobhan.

I stumbled aside, then turned to see James' grappling

with the man. Within seconds he had him pinned, then I smelled burning. James' hands seemed to melt through his attacker's chest. I clutched at my own chest as searing agony hit my skin. Lesser pains I could block out, but this was too much. My vision blurred. I couldn't quite make sense of what James was doing to the man, then the smell increased. I was pretty sure I'd just figured out how James had started the fire in the woods.

Miraculously still alive, the man bucked his legs, throwing James off him. He staggered to his feet, then lunged at James as if he didn't have two palm-shaped, scorched craters in his chest. I panted against the pain as the pair tumbled to the ground again, then James lifted the man up by his neck. I didn't have much time to contemplate James' apparently super-human strength as his hands burned through the man's neck, cutting off the sound just as he tried to scream. I was glad that it was a quick death, because the moment of pain I'd felt in my throat was almost unbearable. His hands now gripping a charred mass of flesh, James cast him aside like a rag doll.

"You burned him," I croaked in astonishment.

"How else did you think I cauterized my victims wounds?" he replied, brushing his hands together to remove the man's charred flesh.

I didn't have time to answer, as Alaric drew my attention with a loud bang against a large, metal dumpster. The woman, Siobhan, had him pinned against it with fingernails that had grown to be as long as daggers at his throat. They seemed sharper too, more like claws than nails.

I opened my mouth to speak, hoping to draw her attention, then someone with a black curtain of hair moved behind them. Siobhan's pain echoed through me as a blade sliced into her flesh, pushing up through her abdomen into her heart. I made a grunt of pain, then Siobhan slumped to the ground, dead. Sophie stood before her brother, bloody blade in hand.

"I never liked her," Sophie commented, peering down at Siobhan's body.

"I was *trying* not to kill her," Alaric answered hotly.

I personally was stunned to see Sophie, but judging by Alaric's expression he was not at all surprised that she'd found us first.

Sophie rolled her eyes at him as James and I approached. "Don't be so sentimental," Sophie chided, "the two of you dated, what, two-hundred years ago?"

Ignoring Sophie and Alaric's bickering, I kneeled down and released the spirit from Siobhan's body, averting my gaze from her bloody wound. She was pretty, and I felt like maybe I should be jealous that Alaric had dated her, but really I just appreciated the fact that he didn't want to kill her. Maybe he could be sentimental after all. With that task done, I went to the man, once again not looking too closely at his wounds, lest I lose the meager food in my stomach. I stood and flicked my hands, hoping to cast away the little thrill the fresh energy sent through me.

"Do I not even get a hello?" Sophie said in irritation at my back.

I turned to glare over my shoulder at her. "Do I not even get an *I'm sorry*?"

Sophie had the grace to look abashed. "I did what I had to do, and Maya left me anyway." I stood and stepped away from the now lifeless corpse, feeling much better with the new burst of energy in spite of myself. "Seriously?"

"She was working for Aislin all along," she explained. She didn't let her pain show in her expression, but I knew that she felt it none-the-less.

"Sorry to break it to you sweetheart," James interrupted, "but so are we."

Sophie glared at James for a moment, then turned to her brother. "Is this true?"

Alaric shrugged. "I couldn't really argue with the decision."

Sophie snorted at his answer, but seemed to accept it as well. "We need to move," she instructed. "I could smell you from a mile away, and there will be more where these two came from." She gestured to the two corpses on the asphalt.

"Plus," I added, "we might want to run away from the corpses before someone calls the cops. We're not in the Salr anymore."

For once everyone listened to me, and we made our way past the abandoned warehouse and into the alleyway behind it, but something still nagged at me. If Maya was working for Aislin, why didn't James know the information she'd held, and why had he tortured her? Unless . . . unless James *wasn't* actually working for Aislin. I eyed him askance as we walked, but his deadpan expression gave nothing away.

Sophie and Alaric began whispering in a language I didn't recognize. I knew it was probably just so they could talk freely around James, but I didn't appreciate the exclusion. For all I knew, they were talking about running off and leaving James and I to find the charm on our own. *Or*, they had reached the same conclusion I had.

I caught Alaric's gaze, attempting to convey my worry.

I wasn't sure if he understood, but he lagged behind to take my hand. "It will be alright," he whispered. "I promise."

I knew I shouldn't trust him, but my shoulders relaxed at his words. It hit me then that I'd been expecting Alaric to leave since he'd first found us. I'd expected at some point he'd decide that I simply wasn't worth the trouble, and he'd abandon me.

Yet, when we reached a busy street and hailed a cab, Sophie took the front seat, and James and Alaric each slid in on either side of me. When we reached the airport and boarded a plane with Diana, who met us there as planned, Alaric was still by my side. When I fell asleep on his shoulder during the long flight, I vaguely sensed him as he craned his neck to give me a kiss on the top of my head.

It was strange, because in that moment, while we were flying to another land, with danger at our backs, and plenty of more danger to face, for the first time in quite some time, I felt like I was going home.

LATER, I woke up groggy, sometime mid-flight, and glanced back at Diana and James. They whispered to each other conspiratorially. I knew with surety in that moment that they were both playing us. Neither was working for Aislin. Only Maya was her actual spy.

I settled back into my seat, glancing at Alaric, who was

dead asleep. I'd share my fears with him later, or maybe I wouldn't. Not just yet. We needed Diana's help to find the charm. Once it was found I'd be damned if Diana, Estus, or maybe even Aislin got a hold of it. Something that caused so many lies had to be protected. If it was as powerful as Maya said, even the fate of humanity might be at stake. A protector was needed.

Unfortunately for humanity, all they had was me.

NOTE FROM THE AUTHOR

I hope you enjoyed the first installment of the Bitter Ashes series! For news and updates, please sign up for my mailing list by visiting:

www.saracroethle.com

SNEAK PEEK AT BOOK TWO

COLLIDE AND SEEK

The sensation of the plane bouncing on the tarmac woke me. It had been a trying few days, and the extra sleep on the plane was a welcome reprieve. I didn't mind lying on Alaric's shoulder either.

I still wasn't quite sure how to feel about him. Okay, I knew exactly how I *felt*. I just wasn't sure what to do about it. As much as I wanted to ignore the fact that he'd misled me about many things, and had allowed my torture, those two facts still ate at me.

Forgiveness is one thing. I'm great at forgiveness. Being an empath means I'm a seasoned pro at putting myself in the shoes of others. At some point I had relented to *mostly* forgive Alaric, but I couldn't forget what had happened, and I sure as hell couldn't trust him.

Betrayal is a funny thing. The sting of it often sticks with us longer than the thrill of love, the fire of hatred, or the emptiness of loss. Betrayal eats at us when we know we should be happy, and it overwhelms us when we're already sad.

I raised my head up from Alaric's shoulder as the plane came to a slow stop. He smiled down at me, unaware of my thoughts, and I couldn't help but smile in return. Despite everything, it felt good having him by my side. It would have felt even better if we were on a plane to some romantic destination, but we weren't.

Although, I suppose Norway *could* be romantic, given the right circumstances. The pictures I'd seen were gorgeous and fairytale-esque, and I was traveling there with a handsome man, but I'm pretty sure romantic vacations aren't supposed to include being hunted by supernatural beings while looking for a charm that's guarded by the dead. Running for your life is a major mood killer.

We waited while the rows of people ahead of us stood and un-stowed their luggage. I shifted uncomfortably, feeling trapped. Once there was enough room, I stood and glanced back toward James and Diana, wondering why each of them *really* wanted the charm, and to what lengths they would go to get it.

James pulled Diana's luggage down from the storage compartment. He had none of his own. In fact, he was still wearing the white tee-shirt he'd worn while he tortured me, just as I was still wearing a black dress with holes in it where he'd stabbed me. Luckily James had stolen me a long, black winter coat with faux fur trim around the hood. It hid my dress, but looked slightly out of place with my too-large hiking boots and thick winter socks.

Sophie waited in her seat across the aisle for James and Diana to get out of the way, pushing them closer toward me. Her original seat had been next to the unwelcome pair, but she'd managed to flirt her way into a seat trade, leaving James to sit next to a man who could have easily taken up two seats on his own. The man in question was still asleep in his seat by the window.

Squeezing past me, Alaric woke the man with a gentle shake of his shoulder, then signaled for him to move, much to the chagrin of the people behind us who would now have to wait even longer.

The line ahead of me moved and I scurried forward, eventually exiting the plane. It was a surreal feeling leaving the West Coast a few hours after dark to arrive in another country where evening had already come again. I'd never traveled such a long distance. Heck, I'd never traveled much at all. Living as a recluse with meager monetary means had prevented me from seeing much of the world.

My next shock came after we went through security and emerged into the cold night air. My coat was warm by West Coast standards, but it could not contend with the icy temperature of Oslo in late October. I clutched the meager protection closer to my body, but my bare legs still erupted in almost painful goosebumps.

James and Sophie stepped ahead of the rest of us, scanning the busy street like a pair of vengeful angels, dark and light, illuminated by the halo of a streetlamp. I could sense their nerves. We all knew Estus wouldn't let us escape so easily.

Alaric, seeming unaffected, smiled and put an arm around me.

Diana tsked at us like we were all being silly children and went to the curb to hail a cab. She clutched a modern black cape around her small form, the fabric swirling around her legs in the cold breeze like it had a life of its own. Though she was small and elderly, with perfect gray, granny-styled hair, I would never mistake her for anything less dangerous than she was.

She was the sister of Aislin, ruler of several clans, which made her old, and we're talking centuries, not decades. Though I was yet to see her do anything out-rightly scary, the threat was always there. She was twenty times scarier than James, and he'd stabbed me and tormented me for fun.

A cab pulled up, and it became readily apparent there were five of us, and only four available seats.

"We'll wait for the next one," Alaric announced, clearly referring to him, myself, and Sophie.

James smirked. "I don't think so. Madeline will come with *us*."

My heart sped at the idea of being left alone in a cab with James and Diana, but Alaric stepped forward before I could move. "*I'll* go with you, and Maddy and Sophie will catch the next cab. You can kill me if they don't show up."

My eyes widened, but I wasn't about to argue.

With a curt nod, Diana climbed into the front seat of the cab while James put her suitcase in the trunk. Alaric gave me a quick kiss on the cheek, then slid into the back-seat after James. I touched my cheek where he'd kissed me, feeling a mixture of annoyance and apprehension.

Diana rolled down her window and relayed the address of the hotel, then suddenly we were left to wait for another cab by ourselves. It was the first time Sophie and I had been alone since she'd rejoined our party after leaving me to be tortured in her place. I crossed my arms and turned away from her, half-wishing I would have just gone with the others, leaving her to catch a cab on her own. It wouldn't compare to her leaving me in the Salr to face punishment for her crimes, but it was a start.

She sighed dramatically at my back. "How long are you going to ignore me? Maya left me. I think I've paid for my actions."

I looked over my shoulder at her. "So because someone betrayed your trust, it makes it okay that you betrayed mine?"

"I said I'm sorry," she snapped, quickly losing patience.

I turned away from her again and mumbled, "Barely."

Another cab pulled up to the curb. I turned and followed Sophie as she opened the back door and climbed in. The heat inside was almost stifling, but felt good after standing on the chilly curb.

I would have been tempted to take my own cab, but one, I had already forgotten the address, and two, I had no money to pay the cab driver, so I was stuck with Sophie.

The driver barely even looked at us as Sophie told him where to go. I crossed my arms again and stayed silent as he drove the cab through a few roundabouts leading out of the airport, then onto the highway. I had no idea how far away the hotel was, but I hoped it was close. Sophie was staring at me intently, her face a pale oval in the darkness of the cab, and I wasn't sure how long I'd be able to maintain the silent treatment.

"You would have done the same," she said eventually.

I looked into her dark eyes, so similar to her brother's, and could see she really believed what she'd said.

I shook my head. "Not everyone is like you."

"Look," she sighed. "I said I was *sorry*. It's not something I say often, and I wouldn't have said it if I didn't mean it. What else do you want from me?"

Her emotions were intense enough at that moment that I could sense her frustration, and underneath it, guilt. She really did feel remorse over leaving me. It might not make up for the original act, but it was a start.

"Okay," I replied.

She narrowed her eyes at me. "Just . . . okay? Why don't you seem angry suddenly?"

I shrugged. "I know you regret leaving me. I'll get over it . . . eventually."

Sophie's eyes widened. "You empathed me! That's not fair."

I rolled my eyes. "You know I can't help it. Strong emotions leak through whether I want them to or not."

She harrumphed, then glanced at the driver as he swerved to the right and cut several people off so he could exit.

She turned back to me. "So you've forgiven my brother?"

I shook my head. "Not quite. Maybe with time."

She shook her head in return. "I don't know how you do that."

"Do what?"

"Forgive so easily," she explained. "If I were you, I'd have already tried to kill me, and Alaric would have been dead the moment I saw his face. Not that I'm not grateful that you're not attacking me . . . "

I shrugged again. "It's the empath thing. Trust me, I did

want to kill Alaric, but guilt is a very strong emotion. So is fear. It's hard to blindly judge someone's actions when you can literally *feel* what they are feeling."

It was Sophie's turn to cross her arms. "I am *not* afraid."

I laughed. "Oh please, you're terrified, and you're sad."

She glared at me as the cab pulled into the parking lot of a large, well-lit, resort-style hotel. "I don't think I like you very much."

I grinned. "And here you were just begging for my forgiveness."

The cab halted, and I quickly opened the door and climbed out, leaving Sophie to pick up the tab.

"I was not begging!" she shouted after me.

I laughed as I walked across the asphalt toward the hotel. Torturing calm, cool, and collected Sophie with my empathic abilities was far more rewarding than snubbing her.

Alaric and James, who had been waiting outside the hotel lobby for us, came striding forward to meet me. The warmth I'd collected in the cab was quickly fading, and the expanses of surrounding near-darkness made me nervous. Anyone could be out there watching us, and we wouldn't even know. I gazed at the hotel longingly as the men reached me.

"Ms. Moneybags has us staying at the most expensive hotel in the country," Alaric explained. He was still just dressed in his navy flannel and black jeans, unfazed by the cold.

"I wouldn't let Diana hear you calling her that," James chided.

Sophie reached us, then breezed on by without a word, like a tall, dark, angry cloud.

Alaric watched his sister's back, then whispered, "You *must* tell me what you did to make her so angry."

I wrapped my arms tightly around myself, fighting shivers. "You wouldn't be able to pull it off. Now can we please go inside before I freeze to death?"

Alaric placed a hand at the small of my back and guided me forward. The building rose up in front of us as we neared. I counted ten stories, the exterior done in a crisp white that matched the surrounding patches of snow on the ground.

James strode past us toward Sophie.

Alaric smiled down at me. "We have our own room," he said with a waggle of his eyebrows.

I stopped walking, though my bare legs were burning with cold. "Why?"

He shrugged, placing his hand against my back again to keep me walking. "If I didn't know any better, I'd say Diana is trying to play matchmaker, but I think she has much more nefarious plans in mind."

My stomach lurched, but I kept walking. She *was* planning something, I knew it. But why the room? "If she's manipulating us, shouldn't we, I don't know, *not* go along with it?"

"Why would I argue with plans that benefit me?" he said happily as the automatic glass doors slid open in front of us.

Some of the tension seeped out of my body once the doors slid shut behind us. The bellhop waiting inside gave us a strange look, probably due to our lack of luggage. The young man shrugged his narrow shoulders and sighed, then led us to a row of elevators. James and Sophie had already gone up, leaving us to ride up with the bellhop alone.

Alaric put an arm around my shoulders as the elevator lurched into motion.

I dutifully removed it, then took a step away, thinking that it was a really bad idea for us to share a room. Not only was Diana up to something, but I didn't fully trust myself. It had been impulsive to fall into bed with Alaric the first time, and I didn't want to be that stupid again. Of course, we still might die tomorrow. Normally it was wise to err on the side of caution, but was it really wise to make good life-choices when my life might not last much longer? Shouldn't I just enjoy being alive while I could?

Alaric could act like we weren't in danger all he liked, but I knew better. If Sophie was scared, it meant we were up a very smelly creek with no paddles, with plenty of holes in our boat. I'd seen first hand how Estus dealt with those who opposed him. If he found us and sent more of the Vaettir to capture us, we would all suffer very ugly ends.

The elevator came to a stop and the doors slid open. Without a glance in our direction, the silent bellhop led us down an extravagantly decorated hall to our room. He used a key card on the door, then handed it to Alaric as we entered. The room was bigger than my old house, with a full sitting area, king-sized bed, and a kitchenette partially obscured from view by bar-style seating, all done in delicate gold and pale blues.

My eyes scanned the room, then came back to rest on

the bed. They lingered there, then went back to the couch. It looked comfortable enough.

Alaric tipped the bellhop, then urged him out of the room. Once we were alone, Alaric walked past me to flop down on the bed. He laid on his back with his arms behind his head, watching me as I took a closer look around the room.

"So what do you want to *do*?" he asked eventually, putting emphasis on the word *do*, to make it seem dirty.

I walked past one of the cushy chairs on either side of the couch to peek into the bathroom. "I *think* we're here to find the charm, so that's what I want to do."

"Diana claims the location is very near, but she doesn't know exactly how near," he explained, "she needs time to pinpoint it, which means we have some time to *kill*."

I glared at him. "Stop emphasizing random words to make them seem sexy."

He grinned. "Is it working? Are my words . . . *sexy*?"

I shook my head and turned away from him.

In an instant he was up off the bed and at my side, moving a lock of my dark brown hair behind my shoulder to bare the side of my neck, grazing his fingers across my skin as he went. It might have been a sexual gesture if he wasn't watching me with such a concerned look on his face.

"I take it your attitude means I'll be sleeping on the floor again," he said softly.

I glanced at him, but didn't pull away. I had to audibly gulp before I could answer, "I'll take the couch this time. It's only fair since I had the bed at Diana's."

He let my hair fall from his grasp, then took my hand

into his grip instead. He kissed my knuckles one by one, then answered, "As you wish."

I slowly pulled my hand away. "Why are you being so agreeable?"

He glanced into the large bathroom that boasted a full-size jacuzzi tub as well as a glass-walled shower. "I think I'll take a bath."

I crossed my arms. "You didn't answer me."

"I don't suppose you'd like to join me?" he asked, still not answering me.

"We don't have any clean clothes," I commented. If he wasn't going to answer me, I wasn't going to answer him either.

Alaric shrugged and walked into the bathroom. "It's late. We'll buy you a whole new wardrobe in the morning."

I stayed where I was standing and glared at his back. "Some jeans and a sweater would suffice."

He began to unbutton his shirt with his back still to me. As the fabric fell to the floor, I blushed and turned away, marching dutifully over to the couch to turn on the TV. The screen came to life. The commercial that came on was in Norwegian, obviously, but it didn't matter because I was so distracted by the sound of Alaric filling up the bathtub that I wouldn't have been able to concentrate on it regardless.

"Maddy?" Alaric called out.

"Yes?" I asked hesitantly.

"Come keep me company."

My mouth suddenly went dry. I cleared my throat. "I don't think so."

"Do you really find it entertaining to watch a show in a language you don't speak?" he pressed.

I glanced at the TV screen again, then back to the open bathroom door.

"I'll be a perfect gentleman," he added. "Scout's honor."

Silently cursing myself, I stood and made my way to the bathroom. Keeping my eyes dutifully averted from the bathtub, I entered the steamy room and took a seat on the closed lid of the toilet.

I could feel Alaric's eyes on me, but refused to look. "There are plenty of bubbles," he assured. "You won't see a thing."

With another sigh, I rolled my eyes as I turned my head to look at him. There were indeed plenty of bubbles, but I could still see the top of his chest, slick with water. He'd wet his dark hair, pushing it away from his face to make him look even more ethereal than usual.

I did my best to maintain eye-contact as Alaric slipped a little further down into the bubbles. "You know, it seems like a waste of water to fill this gigantic bathtub just for one person," he commented.

I smirked. "Well you're the one that did it, that's on your conscience." Desperately wanting to change the subject, I added, "I thought Diana said she knew of the place the hearts showed me. Why does she need time to find it now?"

"Norway has changed a great deal since she was last here," he explained, "and this is not a place you can see, it's a place you have to *feel*. She's using her connections to at least get an idea of the general area so we can go there and search."

"So what do we do until then?" I questioned.

A small smile curved across his lips. "You could get in the bath with me."

I stared at him for several heartbeats, then sighed, "Fine."

His eyes widened. "Fine? I was expecting a lot of things, but *fine* wasn't one of them."

I shrugged and tried to act like my heart wasn't racing. "We're stuck in a hotel in a foreign country," I explained, "waiting for a very scary old woman to lead us to a place that you can only *feel* and not *see*. Meanwhile, we have an angry, sociopathic Doyen thirsty for our blood. Normally, I would be appalled by your offer, and I would snub you to the fullest extent, but I'm scared, and I'm cold, and I have no idea what tomorrow will bring, so I say *fine*."

Alaric raised his eyebrows in surprise. "You are a very strange woman, Madeline."

I smirked as I stood and began undressing. "Says the guy with cat fangs."

He grinned to show his dainty, pointed canines, then watched my every move as I took off the holey dress, bra, and panties. I quickly slipped into the tub on the side opposite him, inhaling sharply at the heat of the water. I let out my breath slowly as my skin adjusted to the temperature change, then settled down until the bubbles nearly reached my chin.

Alaric's smile turned mischievous, and I eyed him warily. Before I could react, he reached through the water and grabbed my arm, then spun me around in one fast movement so that my back was pressed against his. A little wave of water splashed out of the tub a moment later to soak his towel where he had set it on the tiled floor.

"I said I'd take a bath," I replied coolly, "I didn't say I was going to snuggle with you."

"Shh," he breathed as he lowered his lips to the side of my neck.

He laid gentle kisses all the way up to the base of my ear, making my chest and upper arms erupt in goosebumps, despite the warmth of the water.

"I—" I began, but he cut me off by turning my face to the side with one damp hand so he could kiss me.

My thoughts were a jumble of emotions, ranging from nervous excitement to guilt. The guilt was all for me, like I was letting myself down somehow, but it was drowned out by the feel of Alaric's free hand making its way down my ribcage.

I pulled away from the kiss and looked up into Alaric's eyes, which looked even darker surrounded by his wet hair. "Desperate times call for desperate measures?" I questioned weakly, looking for an excuse for my actions.

He chuckled. "Something like that."

He pulled my face back up for another kiss and I gave in. I would probably regret everything tomorrow, but that was tomorrow. This was tonight, and Alaric's soapy body felt far too good against mine to just go to bed.

Some time later we ended up on the king-sized bed with the covers pulled partially up. Alaric was lying on my lower body with his head cradled on my stomach while I stroked his drying hair. My original plan of sleeping on the couch seemed pretty silly now, and seemed even sillier as Alaric's hand slowly slid up from my hip to the side of my waist.

His fingers found the little scars where James had

stabbed me. His entire body seemed to tense. When I didn't react, he relaxed, and began running his fingers back and forth across the scars.

I could sense he wanted to say something, but was probably afraid of opening up a can of worms since the scars were kind of his fault.

"What is it?" I prompted.

"How did you know I wanted to say something?" he asked with a hint of laughter in his voice.

"I'm an empath, remember?" I reminded him, though really I was just going off intuition.

He chuckled and ran his fingers over the scars again. "How did you heal them so quickly?"

It was a good question. In theory I knew how I'd done it, but I wasn't sure if I could replicate it, or even explain it. "I used the energy from the hearts, just like I did when I healed Sophie after the battle."

He moved his arms underneath my lower back and squeezed me tightly. "You know executioners aren't supposed to be able to heal, right?"

I smirked, but he couldn't see it. "Actually, I don't know much about executioners at all."

He lifted his head to meet my gaze. "And you know nothing of your parents?"

"N-no," I stammered, taken aback by the question. "Do you?"

He shook his head. "No. There's a chance I may have met them at some point, but I don't know who they are. Estus probably knows."

I shifted to put another pillow behind me so I could see him better. "Would they be executioners too?"

I'd gone so long without thinking about who my parents might be, I hadn't considered that they might be still be among the Vaettir. The thought was both intriguing and terrifying.

Alaric lifted one shoulder in a half shrug. "We inherit the traits of our mothers, but some lines are more specific than others."

Confused, I nodded my head for him to go on.

"Since Sophie and I are descended from a goddess of a major pantheon, we have similar gifts to our mother. Other smaller deities are simply embodiments of nature, and the gifts inherited may vary. Your mother could have been descended from a major death goddess, in which case your gifts would be similar to hers, or she could have come from a lesser nature deity. Death is a part of all things, and can be inherited at random."

"So what about my empathy?" I questioned.

He laid his head back down on my stomach, rubbing his hair across my skin to cause a delightful shiver. "I do not know," he answered finally. "It should not be, just as your ability to heal should not be. Few among the Vaettir are true healers, and they usually descend from major deities."

I sighed. He spoke like all of these gods and goddesses actually existed. I would never have believed it before, but I'd had a rough few weeks. I was willing to believe most anything now. I thought about my next question, then asked, "What would other executioners do with the leftover energy of releasing someone's life force?"

He kissed my stomach, sending another shiver up my spine. "They would keep it, or use it as a weapon."

I took a shaky breath, then decided to ask a question I'd

been wanting to ask ever since I found out what I was. Really, I'd been wanting to know the answer since the first time I'd killed. "Do you think I'm evil?"

Alaric lifted his head and looked up at me again, surprised. "How long have you been holding onto *that* one?"

I stared back at him. "Just answer it, please."

He eyed me seriously. "You're not evil, Maddy." I felt a moment of relief, but it was short lived as he added, "but you're not entirely good either."

At my horrified expression, he rolled off me so he could sit by my side and pull me close.

"I don't mean that how you think I do," he explained. "In nature there must be polarity. A forest fire may kill many trees and creatures, but it also brings new life and fertility to the land. Death is neither good nor bad, just as you are neither good nor bad. You simply *are*."

"But I'm a person with emotions and a moral compass," I argued. "I'm not simply *death*."

"Ah," he said with a coy smile, "but you were not asking me about your moral compass. You were asking if you are innately evil, because of your gifts."

I took a moment to think about what he'd said. "I guess I understand, but what about you? How could war ever be viewed as a good thing?"

He pulled me in a little closer, nestling me in the curve of his arm. "You are thinking of war in terms of bloody battles and rotting corpses. While that is part of what I am, that is not what war is in its purest form."

"Okay," I commented, "you've lost me again."

"It goes back to polarity," he explained. "Without one

side, the other does not exist. Without conflict and chaos, there can be no victory nor peace."

"I suppose that makes sense. Without darkness, there's no light, and so on and so forth."

He gave my shoulders a squeeze. "Precisely. Now we should probably get some rest. Come morning we will likely have work to do."

I turned, my expression utterly serious. "Well then it's probably time for you to move to the couch."

His eyes widened in surprise, and he opened his mouth to say something, but no words came out.

I snickered.

Realizing my joke, he lifted me off him and pinned me to the bed with a wicked gleam in his eyes.

"I thought we were going to bed!" I exclaimed, still laughing.

He smiled wide enough to flash fang. "Not quite yet."

My laughter died down as I gazed into his now serious eyes. He leaned down and kissed me, and as he pulled away, I smiled. I'd already made one bad decision that night, so I might as well make another.

As he kissed down my chest, I glanced over at the heavy curtains covering the window. It likely wouldn't be long until the first light of dawn edged along the corners. Early rising Diana was going to be *pissed* if we weren't up and ready when she was.

Pissing people off seemed to be fast becoming a hobby of mine, but it was better than a lot of the alternatives.

Printed in Great
Britain
by Amazon